A beautiful and enthralling story of obedienc
love. From the very first line to the final pag
every moment of this novel too!

—Danielle Macaulay
Author of *Table Talk: Family Dinner Devos* and *Why Can't We All Just Get Along?!*, blogger at www.frommilktomeat.com, and marriage TV show personality on *A Better Us*

The themes of love, loss, forgiveness, and redemption are beautifully woven throughout *One More Tomorrow*. Melanie does a masterful job intertwining the lives of Katie, Rachael, Aidan, Zack, and Justin with great honesty and courage.

Life is messy. Life is hard. But as Melanie writes, with an authentic relationship with Jesus, you can find grace in everything.

—Melinda Estabrooks
International speaker, TV and podcast host of *See Hear Love*

One More Tomorrow is a perfectly refreshing read for today! Katie, the heroine, meets struggles with honesty in a moving portrayal of loss, trust, and renewal. Melanie Stevenson takes us on a journey through the twists and turns of life and love, showing us beautifully how God's grace is indeed sufficient.

—Dr. Carolyn Weber
Award-winning author, speaker, and associate professor at Heritage College & Seminary

Melanie Stevenson

One More Tomorrow

a novel

ISBN: 978-1-4866-1537-7
eBook ISBN: 978-1-4866-1538-4

Word Alive Press
119 De Baets Street Winnipeg, MB R2J 3R9
www.wordalivepress.ca

MIX
Paper from
responsible sources
FSC® C103567

Cataloguing in Publication information can be obtained from Library and Archives Canada.

For my husband and children,
who never let me give up on my dreams.

ACKNOWLEDGEMENTS

I WOULD LIKE TO THANK MY HUSBAND OF TWENTY-SEVEN years, Ralph, who is my biggest fan. Thanks for dreaming with me and believing in me more than I do myself. I'm continually amazed at your tenacity, strength, and faith to overcome. We've been through enough crazy things in this life to fill two, but I'd still pick you. I'm so thankful for your optimism in all things. I love you dearly.

I originally wrote this book at age thirty-one when our children were little. Tuesdays were my writing night. Ralph would take the kids out to dinner and a movie, or bowling or another activity, so I could write. I would go downtown, get a giant latte and sandwich at a local coffee shop, then steal away into my office for hours. The kids would only disturb me to say goodnight, and Ralph would do the whole putting-to-bed routine. On more than one occasion, my early-riser, middle son Konnor, awoke to find me writing the next morning after having pulled an all-nighter. I'm grateful they understood the need to give me time and space to write.

Many years have passed since then. Those same kids have grown up and, amazingly, God has blessed us with another child and a daughter-in-law too. We homeschooled for eighteen years, and, knowing I couldn't do it all, I set aside publishing until I could focus full-time on my writing. Throughout those years, my kids would occasionally ask me, "When are you going to publish your book?" They never forgot and wouldn't let me either. Kurtis, Konnor, Elanna, and Keira, I'm so thankful for your priceless lives and love, the years we've spent together, your generous encouragement, and the immense joy you bring to my life. I love you forever. You mean the absolute world to me.

Mom and Dad, thank you for letting me be that kid who spent hours in her room reading, writing, drawing, painting, and manufacturing Barbie soap-operas. Those hours of unbridled creativity formed the foundation of my writing today. I'm so grateful for your unconditional love and quiet championing. Mom, you're an amazing role model and your kindness makes the world a better place. Dad, your generous, soft heart impacts everyone around you. I love you both so very much. Heather, my sister, on whose birthday I arrived in this world. Although I always find new ways to annoy you, I adore you. We couldn't be more different, but oh how I appreciate you! Thanks for celebrating those differences and cheering me on in my journey.

I'm thankful to my dear family and friends who read early copies of my manuscript, offering suggestions when something wasn't clear. Thank you to all of you who continue to ask about my book, and those who read my weekly devotionals on my blog and send me encouraging messages. Nancy White, my "spiritual mom", how you inspire me! Your walk with God is rich and beautiful, your heart and life are a bright light in this world. Thank you for your constant love, support, and encouragement. My sweet mom-by-marriage, Doris, who has delighted in my creative pursuits from day one. Thank you for your love and care.

My editor, Sara Davison, grateful thanks for your insight and thoroughness in every aspect. Among other things, my book has many fewer exclamations points now, thanks to you! Shannon Earnshaw, I'm so grateful for your notes and eagle-eye edits. Thanks to Marina Reis at Word Alive Press, for your support and patient help through this first-time process. Thank you, John Elliot, for the cover design.

I thank my God, who gives me more ideas and words than I naturally have. Without you there would be no book, no writing, and only scraps of hope. Thank you for answering my prayer at the critical age of eighteen and giving me a greater life than I could have asked for or imagined. Your love is life.

And thanks to you, the reader, into whose hands I could have only ever hoped my book would fall. I'm incredibly grateful for the privilege of serving you in this way. It's my sincere desire that by reading it you would not only be entertained but would find hope and be encouraged in your faith journey. Thank you for reading.

PART

One

CHAPTER
One

"DADDY, NO!"

Her fists scrunched the front of her father's shirt.

"Please, Daddy! Don't go!"

He sat on the edge of her bed. Katie clung to him, sobbing and pressing her face into his chest. She wouldn't let him go. She would hold on to him so he couldn't. How could he talk about leaving? He was her daddy.

His confusing words tumbled over her like an avalanche. His body shook. When she looked up, tears were sliding down his cheeks. The expression in his eyes made the pain in her chest hurt worse. *He's lying. He doesn't mean it. Why won't he say the right things? Why won't he take off his coat and say everything's going to be okay?*

"You can't go, Daddy. Please…" Her eyes filled to overflowing with questions and tears.

He opened his mouth then shut it again without making a sound. The creases between his eyes grew deeper. Over his shoulder she could see suitcases waiting in the hall. He pulled his hands from hers and lifted them to the sides of her face, his rough thumbs wiping the tears from her cheeks. Then he let her go and stood up. She watched him walk down the hall and pick up his bags. *What did I do wrong?*

"Kat? Katie? You okay?"

Katie Banks looked up from peeling her orange. Across the cafeteria table, her best friend Rachael stared at her, head tilted.

"So? What do you think?"

Katie's forehead wrinkled. "About what?"

Rachael planted her palms on the table and leaned in. "About Zack? Did you even hear what I said?"

"Sorry. I guess I didn't."

Rachael inhaled and began again. "Zack smiled at me in the lunch line on Monday."

"He did? That's great." Katie studied her best friend. *It's weird to see her behaving like a giddy sixth grader.* "What did you do?"

"I smiled back, but I couldn't bring myself to talk to him. I wish I could get up my nerve."

"You should."

"I know. I'm afraid I'll say something stupid and wreck everything."

"Everything? What everything? You haven't even met him yet."

"True. But he's in fourth year."

"So? You have nothing to lose." Katie pulled apart her orange. A spray of juice shot into the air, releasing a pungent citrusy cloud.

"I guess you're right."

"At least say hi, maybe ask him what he's doing in a first-year class."

"If only I were you." Rachael let out a sigh.

"Oh, come on."

"No really. You always seem to know what to say. Plus, it's a fact that most guys would think they'd died and gone to heaven if Katie Banks spoke to them."

"Very funny." Katie reached across the table and swatted Rachael on the arm.

"Admit it. You know it's true."

Katie shrugged and pretended to be busy repacking the contents of her lunch bag.

"You know," Rachael leaned back in her chair, "I always thought I was shy, but you're the one who can't take a compliment." She popped the last bite of her chocolate chip cookie in her mouth and brushed the crumbs from her fingers. "It wouldn't hurt to say thanks from time to time instead of simply brushing it off."

"I would if you weren't being so ridiculous."

"I'm actually speaking the truth. And pointing out an opportunity for improvement." Rachael pointed a finger at Katie, cookie crumbs flying out of her mouth.

"In that case, thank you so much."

"There you go. That wasn't so hard, was it?" Rachael smirked at her.

Katie rolled her eyes.

Rachael tugged an apple out of her lunch bag. "Seriously though, you're great at making everyone else feel good, why do you get so embarrassed when the attention's on you?"

"I don't know. It makes me feel uncomfortable, I guess."

"I don't get that," Rachael said, "when you make everyone else feel so comfortable. I wish I could do that."

"Well, here comes your chance."

Katie nodded across the room. Rachael's gaze shifted in that direction as Zack strolled across the crowded dining hall. Katie pursed her lips. She could see why Rachael was so enamoured by him. He was striking. His tall, lean frame was relaxed and he had a calm confidence to his demeanor. He scanned the room as he made his way from the lunch line to their table.

Rachael bent down to rummage through her shoulder bag on the floor. When she popped up a moment later, her cheeks were flushed. "I think he saw me looking." She chewed on her thumbnail.

Katie scooped up the orange peels and dropped them into her bag. "Calm down. I've never seen you this way."

"It's crazy, isn't it? Any quick advice?"

"Take a deep breath, or five. Here he comes."

"You've got to be kidding." Rachael snatched her sandwich from the bag and busied herself unwrapping it.

"Is this seat taken?" Zack's voice was friendly and self-assured.

Katie said nothing, forcing Rachael to speak up. "Uh… no. Go ahead."

"Awesome. Thanks." He sat down next to Rachael. "Hey, I'm Zack Wilson."

"Rachael Myers. Nice to meet you."

Katie grinned at the faint look of panic that crossed Rachael's face.

"And you are?" He looked across the table at Katie.

"Oh, sorry, this is Katie Banks."

"Nice to meet you, Zack." Katie started to hold out her hand, but he'd already shifted his attention back to Rachael.

Zack poked a straw into his smoothie. "You're in Dr. Robert's philosophy class, right?"

"Uh huh."

"I thought so. What do you think of his class so far?" He took a sip of his drink.

"It's not really my thing. I have trouble keeping all the names straight—you know, between Bertrand Russell, Descartes, Spitzoa, uh Spinoza... Ugh, see? I can't even remember them now."

"Yeah? Me neither."

Katie was content to sit back and watch the exchange. Rachael babbled on and Katie hid a grin behind her sandwich. When had her friend ever had trouble remembering names?

An awkward silence descended over the table. Katie pressed her lips together—Rachael really needed to figure this out on her own.

"What are you doing in this course?" Rachael finally asked, tucking a strand of brown hair behind her ear.

"What?" A frown creased his brow.

"I mean... you seem older than first year."

"Oh, well, I was short an arts credit to graduate and put off taking it until now. I thought it would be easy, but I'm finding out philosophy is not my forte."

"What are you majoring in?" Rachael swept crumbs off the table with the side of her hand.

"Business. I figure I can't really go wrong with that. What about you guys?"

Although he addressed them both, his eyes were firmly on Rachael, so Katie kept her mouth shut.

"I'm taking business too."

"Really? I'm surprised I haven't seen you around before."

"I'm actually *in* first year."

"Ah. That explains why you're not in any of my other classes."

The flush on Rachael's cheeks deepened. So many times over the years Katie had spoken up for her, covering for her in awkward moments. It took a great deal of effort to hold back now and risk leaving her friend to sink when she most needed her help. "What about you, Katie?" Zack shifted to face her.

"I'm taking Fine Arts with a minor in English."

"An artist, huh? What's your specialty?"

"We have to try pretty much everything, but so far my favourite is oil painting." She twisted the lid onto her water bottle and pushed back her chair. "On that note, I need to head to the studio to finish up some stuff. Nice to meet you, Zack."

Standing, Katie tossed the rest of her lunch in her backpack and slung it over her shoulder. She turned to Rachael. "See you back at the dorm later?"

Rachael looked up at her with a stiff smile. "Yeah... sure. Let's grab a bite before my night class."

"Great. See you then." Katie waved and headed for the door, sidestepping a group of students gathered between two of the tables. She could feel Rachael's heated gaze on her all the way to the exit but didn't look back. She wouldn't always be around to bail out her friend. It was time Rachael learned to stand on her own two feet.

CHAPTER *Two*

IT WASN'T UNTIL HER STOMACH GROWLED THAT KATIE PUT down her paintbrush and looked at her watch. She hadn't finished her lunch, the result of waiting for an opportune moment to leave Rachael alone with Zack. A twinge of guilt worked its way through her. Should she have done that? Katie had noticed Zack around campus and he always seemed to be in the company of a different female. It wouldn't have mattered to Katie except for the fact that her friend was so smitten with him. Rachael's dangerous habit of using guys to fill the lonely hole in her life made her vulnerable. Maybe Katie shouldn't have encouraged her to speak with him at lunch.

She had worked all afternoon in the luxury and solitude of an empty studio. Her thoughts flowed with her brush and blended with the colours on the canvas. Always deliberate and serious about every line or stroke, when she created, she slipped into a different world, a place where anything was possible and she could control the outcome.

Her thoughts drifted to the past. Her five-year-old self had begged her father to stay, thinking that if she held on tight enough, or long enough, he might not leave. For a long time after he had gone, she tried to think of how she could have been a better daughter. If she had been good enough, maybe then he would have stayed. Maybe then she would still know him. Maybe then she could have shared her years with him. That night, and many after, she had soaked her pillow in salty tears, wondering if she would ever see him again. She was still wondering.

Rachael had caught Katie doing just that at lunch when she should have been listening to her friend. It didn't happen as often as it used to, those remembrances of her father, but as it had today, an ordinary event or word might ignite a distant memory.

After he left, Katie frequently escaped into an imaginative world of drawing, colouring, and painting. For her, creating became as necessary as breathing, filling the empty place her father's absence had left. Her life had stopped mid-breath while continuing for everyone else around her. To fight back the pain, the loneliness, and the helplessness, she created, and, for a while, her heart didn't hurt so much.

"Hey, nice work."

Startled by the voice, Katie dropped her brush and whirled around.

The stranger bent and picked it up for her, a dark curl falling into his face. When he straightened, an amused smile animated his features. "Sorry. I didn't mean to scare you."

"Do you always sneak up on people like that?" Katie smoothed her painting apron with both palms, attempting to regain her composure.

"Actually, I wasn't sneaking. I was observing."

She hated that she suddenly felt self-conscious.

He handed her the brush, smiling. "You have a very unique style."

"Thanks." She shifted back to her work and began to mix colours on her palette to distract herself from his warm brown eyes.

"I just came in to clean my brushes. The sink is plugged across the hall." He jerked his thumb over his shoulder, looking apologetic.

"You paint?" She dabbed at her palette.

"Yeah. I'm in Engineering, but I've been taking some art courses as electives."

"That's an unusual mix."

"I guess, but it's great stress relief. I'd take more if I could."

"I've heard Engineering's pretty demanding."

"First year was the worst, but it's a lot better now. Is Fine Arts your major?"

She nodded, wiping her brush on a rag.

"Hey, want to see what I'm working on? I could use a critical eye."

Katie studied him a moment. His strong jaw and two-day's growth of beard made him look more like a movie star than a university student. "Sure, why not?"

The dorm was quiet. Glad for some peace, Rachael opened the door to the room she shared with Katie. Her best friend's side was a disaster with rumpled sheets on the bed and books and papers scattered across the desk. Stepping over a pile of Katie's clothes, Rachael positioned her headphones on her ears and selected a playlist. She settled onto her bed, tucked her arms behind her head, and gazed up at the ceiling, smiling.

When Katie had left her in the cafeteria with Zack, Rachael was mortified. The thought of making up an excuse and leaving herself crossed her mind. She felt tongue-tied and struggled to think straight. Her heart felt as though it could be seen beating through her T-shirt, she was sweating, and she couldn't find a natural place to put her hands. She was certain that would be the first and last time she'd ever talk to Zack Wilson. But by the end of their lunchtime conversation, Rachael had found herself more at ease with him. Feeling proud of herself for having taken a risk, she played over their conversation in her mind.

"My buddy and I are having a party Saturday night. A few B. Comm's will be there. I could introduce you to some people in the program if you wanted to come and hang out for a bit." He wrote his address on a napkin and slid it towards her. "I'll watch out for you. Bring Katie if you want."

She took the napkin and scanned the information, more to give herself a place to focus her eyes than out of interest.

"I've got a macro-economics class to get too. You'll love that one." He smiled as he stood. "Nice to meet you. See you Saturday then?"

Rachael nodded, her heart pounding in response to the smile that reached his light green eyes. As he walked away, her insides danced with nervous excitement. *I hope I didn't sound too eager.* Had she been smiling idiotically the entire time? She couldn't recall. When he disappeared into the hall, she sagged against the back of her chair. Had that really happened? Had Zack Wilson really eaten lunch with her and asked her to a party?

She certainly hoped so, because for the moment she felt truly happy, and the empty hole in her life disappeared.

———

"You look comfortable." Katie tossed her backpack on the floor, surprised to see her friend, who was usually working at her desk or studying at the library, horizontal on her bed. She pulled off her boots and tossed them into their shared closet.

Rachael bolted upright. "You'll never guess what happened after you left."

"What?" Katie sank onto the twin bed opposite Rachael's.

"Zack asked me to a party at his place on Saturday night."

Katie's eyes widened. "He did?"

"Yeah, can you believe it? I was shocked. I can't stop thinking about it. Will you come with me?"

"Uh, no, sorry I can't." Katie reached for her backpack, shuddering at the idea of some wild university party. She had spent most of high school avoiding parties. Letting down her guard in senior year had been a costly mistake.

"Why not?" Rachael's brow furrowed. "Zack invited you. You have to come. I couldn't go alone. Oh my goodness, being alone with him at lunch was bad enough—I hardly knew what to say. And speaking of which, how could you leave me like that?"

"Sorry."

"Sorry? That's it?"

Katie shrugged, trying to conceal a grin.

"I knew it. You left me alone with him on purpose, didn't you?"

She shrugged and dumped her books on her bed. "You know how much I love parties, but I have plans Saturday night. A few of us from Cru are meeting at the coffee pub."

"Is that your Jesusy thing? Can't you get out of it?"

Katie took her time piling the books on her bed in random order.

"Please? You know how much this means to me, don't you?" Rachael swung her legs over the side of the bed, bumping into Katie and sending the books toppling.

Katie glanced up at Rachael's puppy-dog expression and sighed. "Yeah, okay. I'll go with you."

"You will? Thanks so much!" Rachael launched herself across the space between their beds and hugged Katie. "I couldn't go alone."

Katie extricated herself from her friend's embrace and stood up. "You're welcome, but yes, you could."

She carried the books over to her desk and set them down before bending to open the door to their half fridge. She frowned at its lack of appealing contents, closed the door, and headed across the room to feed her pet goldfish.

"Hi, Dumpling." She picked up the container of fish food from the windowsill and peered into the bowl.

"How'd the painting go?" Rachael tugged her laptop from her backpack and set it on her bed.

"Not bad. I managed to get a fair amount done, which is good because we have a critique on Friday." Katie tapped at the tin of food, sprinkling in enough flakes to satisfy the orange, fan-tailed fish. Dumpling darted around the little glass bowl, his mouth sucking up both water and food.

"How can you stand everyone talking about your stuff?" Leaning back against the headboard, Rachael adjusted a pillow behind her back and opened her laptop.

"It's a little nerve-wracking, but I'm getting used to it. It's amazing how attached you can get to your work, so an objective view can really help to see a weak area."

"So, you've toughened up?"

"Haven't we all?"

They laughed, shared experiences filling in for words.

"Rach, about Zack." Katie set down the can of fish food and faced her friend.

"I know what you're thinking, but don't worry, I'm okay."

"Are you sure?"

"Yes. I'm pretty crazy about him, but I can handle myself."

"Do you know anything about him? I mean, I don't want you to get hurt."

"Kat, we're not getting married." She tapped the cover of her laptop. "I just met the guy."

"I know. That's why I wanted to talk to you about—"

"Stop worrying. It'll be fine, okay?" Rachael fitted her ear buds into her ears and focused on her screen.

Katie attempted to brush off the uneasy feeling that clung to her insides.

———

Justin Burke strolled back to his house near campus, filled with thoughts of the girl he had finally met. The serious look on her face when she examined his painting flashed through his mind. She hadn't spoken until he finally asked her opinion. He wished he could have memorized her expression when she gave him her critique and would have given anything to paint the playful smile that danced on her lips and warmed her eyes when she laughed at his jokes.

He had first encountered Katie Banks during Frosh Week when he and his senior classmates led the welcome celebrations for the first-year students, introducing them to the university and leading games to muster comradeship and school spirit.

"Wow, check her out," his roommate Chris had commented in passing as they stood on the sidelines watching the volleyball game.

Justin had already noticed Katie but didn't let on. He watched her as she played. She appeared completely at ease with herself, not self-consciousness or displaying an attitude like so many other girls he knew. He found himself smiling when she laughed, willing her to make the tough shots and getting upset at unfair calls. Since that day, she had been lodged in his mind. The few times they had passed in the halls of the Fine Arts building he had attempted to smile at her, but she seemed either in a rush or distracted.

Standing beside her an hour ago as they looked at his painting, every one of his senses tingled. *No way I have a chance with someone like that.* Her blue eyes captured him, so beautiful, open, and light. Their colour, like a cloudless, midsummer's day sky, drew him in. He had to fight to pay attention, to keep the conversation natural and his voice cool and controlled. *Get it together, Burke. She's not interested in you.*

Katie shifted her backpack on her shoulder. "I should get going."

A tight knot formed in Justin's stomach. If she walked away now, he might never have another chance to talk to her. "My friend's having a party on Saturday night. Are you busy?"

"Yeah, sorry. I already have plans."

Was that an excuse or did she really have something else to do? *I blew it. Should have asked her out before now.* "Maybe another time."

"Yeah, maybe." She'd tossed him another of her million-watt smiles before walking out of the art room.

Justin reached his student house and pulled the key from his pocket. *Maybe she already has a boyfriend.* That thought sent a pang through him.

"Hey," his roommate called from the living room.

"Hey, Chris." Justin hung his coat on a hook by the door and joined his friend who was eating in front of the television.

"There's a hot dog left if you want it," Chris offered, his mouth full.

"No thanks. I'll grab something later." Justin reached for the mail that was spread across the coffee table and partly covered by Chris's elevated feet.

"There's not much to grab."

"Yeah, I know. We need groceries again."

Chris wiped a blob of ketchup off his shirt with his finger while chuckling at something on the television.

Justin waited for the commercial before tossing the flyers he'd been going through back down on the coffee table. "Remember that girl?"

"What girl?"

"The one we saw during Frosh Week. You know, at the volleyball game?"

"Sorry man, you'll have to do better than that."

"The pretty blonde. First year?"

"Yeah, I think so." Chris's attention remained on the TV. "Why do you ask?"

"I met her today."

"Cool. Hey, are you watching this?"

"Nope." Justin tore open a card from his mom.

Chris stood, turned off the TV, and tossed the remote on the worn sofa. "I'm going to the pub. Wanna come?"

"No thanks. I've got work to do."

"Good, 'cause I'm meeting Sarah there."

"Three's a crowd." Justin scanned the note.

"Hey, Zack and Tom are having a party on Saturday night." Chris shoved his feet into his permanently untied shoes. "You goin'?"

"Yeah, I was planning on it."

Chris thrust his arms into the sleeve of his coat and repositioned a worn baseball cap over his disheveled hair. "Gotta run. I'm meeting her at seven."

"It's seven."

"I know. I'm gonna be late and she hates that."

"See ya later." Justin shook his head. Chris never seemed to worry about anything and incessantly teased Justin about his copious planning and goal-setting.

"Relax man," Chris would tell him. "Stop being so serious about life. You gotta live a little, ya know."

Chris was probably right. Justin could stand to lighten up a little. Growing up in a high-pressure home had a way of making you perform. From as young as he could recall, the report card was the main event. He had always tried to please his parents, working for that, "I'm proud of you, Son" moment that never came. When he was twelve, his parents' tumultuous marriage ended when his dad left for a younger woman. On few and far between visits, Justin watched his dad live the high-life, wielding the power of his money and making a hobby out of dating a long string of women. Part of Justin hated him, but worse, an obscure fragment revered him and longed to be loved and accepted by him. It was that piece that tormented Justin with the frightening idea he might turn out like his father, even though he vowed he would never let that happen. He had determined, a long time ago, to be a better man than the man who had given him life.

Smiling at the words of encouragement from his mom, Justin folded the card and stuck it in his shirt pocket before reaching for an apple and heading to his room, prepared for a night of studying. An hour later, he was still staring at the same page, trying to get Katie Banks out of his mind. He couldn't stop thinking about her smile, and the way her eyes lit up when she spoke. *How can I work it out to see her again?* Justin flipped the page of his textbook so hard he nearly ripped it.

"Concentrate!" In spite of the admonition, he found himself reading the next sentence five times. He slumped in his seat and reached for his phone. If he was going to be up all night, he might as well order himself a pizza.

CHAPTER
Three

MUSIC AND PEOPLE SPILLED OUT OF ZACK'S FRONT DOOR. Katie's heart sank. *Can I go back to my quiet dorm room now?* She turned to Rachael, ready to make her excuses, but the anticipation written across her friend's make-up clad face stopped her. Katie took a deep breath to bolster her resolve. Rachael pushed her bangs to one side and pressed her lips together to ensure her lipstick was even. She grinned at Katie. "Here we go."

Inside, every square inch of the house was packed with bodies and noise, a cacophony of music and voices competing to be heard. Katie's mind reeled as she stumbled through the crowd behind Rachael.

From the corner of her eye, she caught a movement. Someone was waving at them. Through the veil of smoke and people, Katie saw Zack working his way through the crowd toward them.

"Hey there!" he shouted above the noise, a broad smile crossing his face. "Glad you could make it. Come on, I'll introduce you to some of my friends."

Katie clung to Rachael's arm to keep from losing her friend. They weaved through the mass of people, heading for the kitchen where several students stood in a loose circle, engaged in conversation. A petite brunette stood in the middle of the group, telling a story to a captivated audience. She momentarily shifted her attention in their direction, or at least to Zack. She grinned and waved at him, but Katie didn't miss the look that flickered across her face as she took inventory of his new guests.

Zack shouted introductions. A stocky, grinning fellow Zack introduced as Tom-Cat jumped down from the counter and roughly squeezed Katie's hand. He held on several seconds too long, and when Katie made eye contact, she caught the sneer on his face. She yanked her hand free and ran it along the side of her jeans to wipe off the wetness from beer or sweat.

Zack introduced the brunette as Melissa. Still speaking to her friends, she glanced in Rachael and Katie's direction and waved a blanket hello.

"Would you like a drink?" Tom-Cat held out a bottle. Rachael took the offered beer. "What about you?" A smirk curled the corners of Tom-Cat's ample mouth as he studied Katie.

"Just some juice, thanks."

He chuckled, poured the juice then paused, "Want some vodka in that?"

"No thanks. On the rocks."

"This is the biggest party you guys have ever had." Melissa swooped in and commandeered the conversation.

"You're right. It's nuts." Tom-Cat surveyed the room, his chest puffing out a little, then handed Katie her drink. "Here. Go easy on it—it's pure O.J."

Katie forced a smile, accustomed to the jests at her abstaining. She reached to take the glass from Tom-Cat, who held onto it a few seconds before releasing it, his fingers brushing against hers as he did. Her insides tightened.

Zack led Rachael off for more introductions. Katie swirled the juice in her cup and took a sip as she scanned the room. *Really wish I was anywhere but here.* Melissa stood a few feet away talking with a girl sporting a short skirt, tall boots, and a loud laugh.

"That must be the latest." Melissa's voice rose above the melee as Rachael and Zack walked through the crowd. "Wonder how long she'll last?"

"I don't know. She's definitely not as pretty as the last one."

"He must be getting a bit bored. Changing it up a little."

"Yeah, moving on to first years now. Shame on him." Laughing, they brushed past Katie and wove into the crowd.

Katie pressed a hand to her hot cheek. They'd obviously intended for her to hear their words. How could they be so callous? *I need some air.* She pushed through the crowd to the exit and found a place on the deck. Gripping the railing, she stared up at the clear, star-injected sky. The cool air calmed her burning cheeks, but not her insides. Should have gone to the coffee pub for her

Jesusy thing. Katie grimaced at the thought of Rachael's dismissive words. Would her friend ever realize how much she needed God in her life?

"You look like you could use some company." The voice came from behind her, gentle and friendly. Katie turned to look into chestnut-brown eyes framed by dark curls. The guy who'd startled her when she was painting. "I tried not to sneak up on you this time."

Justin leaned against the railing beside her. The scent of his cologne mingled with the outdoors, clean and fresh after the stale air inside.

"Thanks, I appreciate that." She grinned.

He pointed to the house next door. "My place is right there. I usually come through the yard and use the patio door."

"Oh, I see." A set of stairs she hadn't noticed led from the side of the deck down into a dimly-lit yard.

"So, these were your other plans?" he asked.

"Actually, no. I was supposed to go to another meeting, but I ended up coming to this party to keep a friend company."

"Looks like it."

Katie smiled and looked down at her glass.

"Where is she… or he?"

"*She's* with your neighbour."

Something washed over his features. *Is that relief?* An unexpected warmth rushed through her chest.

"Tom-Cat?"

She shook her head, "No, Zack. Do you know him?"

"Yeah, I met him first year through a mutual friend. We're in the same year, except he's in the Business program. He's actually the reason I ended up here this year. He helped me get the place. A couple friends of his graduated and Zack knew the landlord pretty well, so my friend and I got in."

So, Zack has a kind side. That's encouraging. She gazed into the dark sky, contemplating that thought. Brushing away a stray piece of hair the breeze had caught, she met his eyes again. "How's your painting coming along?"

"Actually, I haven't worked on it since you saw it."

"You haven't? When is your critique?"

"Friday. I guess I'll be at the studio a lot next week." He shoved his hands into the pockets of his jeans, his grin boyishly adorable.

"Same here. I'm almost done my painting, but I have a sculpture to finish as well."

"Almost? It looked done when I saw it."

"Yeah, but I'm picky."

"You must be. It was great."

"Thanks. It's always a relief when you're happy with the finished product."

"For sure. I've had some real failures."

"Same."

"I have the classic story of a pet wrecking my homework." He chuckled and turned to face her, leaning a hip against the railing. "It was during mid-terms last year. I was pushing a deadline on my first oil painting, so I decided to bring it home to work on between studying. I had no clue how long oil takes to dry, so starting the day before was a bad choice."

"No kidding."

"I finish it up the early hours of the morning and crash for a couple of hours. When I wake up, the cat is using it as his bed."

"Oh no. That's awful. What did you do?"

"I tried to salvage it, but the cat hair was fairly prolific."

Katie enjoyed the sound of his deep laughter.

"How about you? Any disasters?"

"Artwork disasters?"

"Or life ones."

"Enough of each."

Justin raised his eyebrows. "Any good stories?"

"Not as good as yours."

"Tell me."

"Let's just say even a Ziplock bag can't save your pen and ink drawing from a full water bottle leaking inside your backpack."

"Ouch. Note taken. And what about life?"

"Well, you know what they say, art imitates life." Katie gazed out over the darkened yard. She wasn't about to share a single heartache with a complete stranger, however cute. Someone opened the patio door and noise, like a rush of warm air, spilled onto the deck. Katie's phone vibrated. She tugged it out of her pocket, grateful for a distraction from Justin's questions. A text from Rachael. The digital clock at the top of the screen caught her attention. Had she really been outside for over an hour? She read Rachael's message and slipped the device back into the pocket of her sweater. "My friend is looking for me."

"Oh, okay." Justin took his hands out of his pockets and stepped back. "Hey, do you want—"

"Justin, you came!" Melissa wrapped an arm around his neck and hung out over the railing to face him. She kissed his cheek as her eyes met Katie's. The smug smile of a predator about to swallow her prey crossed her face.

"Hi, Melissa." Justin nodded at Katie. "Do you know Katie Banks?"

"We met. She's the friend of Zack's new hopeful." She pressed against Justin's side. "Hey, a few of us are starting a card game. Come join us." Melissa tugged at his hands while backing up toward the patio door.

He shot a feeble glance at Katie, as if asking her to join them.

"Come on, Justin, don't be a party-pooper," Melissa droned over the din spilling from the house as she dragged him along.

"I'll talk to you later." Katie lifted a hand, excusing him.

"Come with us…" he said as he was pulled through the door.

Melissa tossed Katie a scornful look over Justin's shoulder.

"No thanks. I need to go look for my friend."

"You sure?"

She nodded. As she watched the silhouetted couple disappear into the throng, her thoughts shifted to Rachael, who wasn't known for making good choices. Katie shivered in the cooling air and rubbed her arms, as though the action could wipe off past memories. She shook her head. *It's crazy how the past can either drive or destroy a person.* For Rachael it seemed to do both.

Though she had little desire to return to the party, Katie pushed away from the wooden railing, took a deep breath, and stepped through the patio doors. The living room area appeared to be a solid mass of bodies held together by the haze of smoke that permeated the air.

"Katie!" Lisa, a friend she had met the first day of school, called to her from across the room. Katie waved as Lisa came to meet her. "Quite the party, huh? Are you having a good time?"

Katie shrugged. "Not too bad."

"Do you know many people here?" Lisa surveyed the room.

"Not really. My roommate wanted to come and asked me along."

"Come on. I'll introduce you to some of my friends."

Although Lisa's friends were welcoming, Katie couldn't help checking her phone or scanning the room every few minutes, hoping to find Rachael. When the group of people around Lisa moved on to a discussion about the Student Campus Hall under renovation, Katie excused herself and made her way through the crowd.

A few people were dancing, others stood around yelling to each other above the music. Bodies lined the hall and the staircase, overflowing out the front door and onto the lawn. Katie glanced into the kitchen. When she reached the front hall, a swaying figure stepped off the bottom stair in front of her. She attempted to step around him, but he blocked her. She tried to go the other way and he did likewise. She looked up to see Tom-Cat staring down at her, a roguish smile spread across his wide mouth.

"Going somewhere?" He leaned down a little too close, and the smell of beer crowded the space between them.

"I'm looking for Rachael."

"I'm pretty sure she can take care of herself."

"Have you seen her?"

"Yeah. She's with Zack."

"Where?"

He hesitated. "Upstairs. I'll take you."

Torn between her desire to get away from Tom-Cat and her need to keep Rachael from doing something she'd regret, Katie followed him up the stairs to the upper hall. At the top, he turned and pushed her against a closed door, placing one hand on the wall beside her head to block her passage. Katie's insides tightened, but she stared at him coolly. He leaned close to her cheek, his warm, alcohol-saturated breath searing her ear.

"You know Katie, I have a feeling you don't like parties," he whispered, running the cold bottle in his hand up her arm. "But you're a really pretty girl. We could have a good time together."

A sickening disgust grew in her stomach as his cunning eyes moved from her face and down her body. She moved to escape, but he grabbed her by her wrist. Returning his gaze with challenging eyes, she willed herself to bury the rising panic, even though she could feel the heat from his chest pressing against hers.

"I'll show you how to have fun." He leaned in to kiss her.

A thudding noise stopped him. A couple was climbing the stairs. With the interruption, Katie pulled free and ducked under his arm. She darted down the stairs and through the hallway. In a blur, she swept through the swelling crowd, searching for Rachael in case Tom-Cat had lied to her about her friend being upstairs.

A loud cheer rose from another room. Katie turned and caught a glimpse of Rachael at the far corner of the den sitting beside Zack. Justin sat in a chair by the wall with Melissa draped over him. Everyone in the room raised their glasses in a toast. Katie forced herself through the maze of people, forging a path to her roommate.

Slow recognition crossed Rachael's flushed face and she lowered her glass.

"Kat, come join us," she slurred. The others turned their attention to the newcomer, lifting their shot glasses in her direction before throwing them back. Liquid spilled out the sides of Rachael's mouth, and she carelessly wiped the excess from her chin with the back of her hand. Her head came to rest on Zack's shoulder, and sweaty, stray strands of brown hair pressed into the side of her face.

"Look everyone, it's Katie," Rachael said, working to push herself off the couch. After a few seconds, she gave up and sank back down beside Zack.

"Come join us, Katie." Zack patted the seat on the other side of him.

Katie ignored him and leaned down close to her friend. "Let's go home."

"Not yet. Aren't you having fun?" Not giving her a chance to answer, Rachael waved a hand toward Katie. "Everyone! This is my very best friend in the whole wide world." She held up her empty shot glass for a refill. After someone poured vodka into it, she tipped it in Katie's direction, sloshing some of the clear liquid over the edge. "To Katie."

"Katie, come sit down." Justin tried to get up and offer her a seat, but Melissa adjusted her position to prevent his escape.

Katie shook her head and stayed rooted beside her friend. "Come on, Rach. Let's go."

"I'll be okay. You go ahead."

"I'd rather not go without you."

Justin managed to extricate himself from Melissa and came over to stand beside Katie. "Katie, this is my roommate Chris and his girlfriend Sarah." He motioned to a couple holding hands and sitting on the floor close to where he had been sitting.

"Nice to meet you." Katie forced a polite smile.

"You too." Chris nodded, and Sarah smiled and waved.

Justin touched Katie's elbow. "Can I get you something to drink?"

"No thanks, we're about to leave."

"Your friend isn't ready to go. Just one?"

"No thanks. I don't drink."

"I didn't say it had to be alcohol." He tipped his beer bottle toward her in a salute.

"I can see that." Katie tamped down her annoyance. *He's just trying to be nice.*

"Hey, are you okay?" His face grew serious as he contemplated her.

"I'm fine." Her voice shook and she pressed her lips together. *I need to get out of here. Now.*

"I met your friend. She's really nice."

"Yes, she is." Katie gestured for Rachael to come with her.

"She said you've known each other since you were kids."

"Since grade three," she confirmed. Was it necessary for them to have this conversation right now?

"That long? Wow."

Justin grinned and swayed beside her, closer than he would have likely stood had he been sober. There was nothing threatening in his demeanor, no hint of the behaviour she had encountered moments before from Tom-Cat. Justin's dark hair hung in loose and dishevelled curls that framed slightly-reddened cheeks. He hugged his beer bottle to his chest and leaned back against the wall.

Katie pushed back her shoulders. "I'll see you later, okay?"

"What? You're leaving?"

She nodded, pausing to look back at her friend whose head still rested on Zack's shoulder. Katie made one more vain attempt to motion for Rachael to come with her.

Rachael shook her head and mouthed *I'm fine* in an exaggerated fashion.

Katie clenched her fists to keep from yanking her up from the couch.

Justin pushed away from the wall. "How are you getting home?"

"I'll text Campus-walk."

"I can take you."

She eyed the bottle in his hand. "That's okay." Melissa giggled behind her.

"I mean I'll *walk* you." He set down his beer.

Katie's attention returned to Rachael.

"She'll be fine. Zack is harmless. Come on." He slid a hand through the crook of her elbow.

Not sure I believe that. The gossip in the kitchen hadn't been exactly favourable, and Zack's roommate was a definite threat. "No, stay and enjoy the party. I'll be fine." She tried to pull her arm away, but he maintained his grip.

"Let me take you." He led her out of the den. Katie sent a final glance back at Rachael, who was sipping on another drink, before following Justin through the crowd.

The noise of the party faded as they pushed through the door and made their way down the front walk to the dimly-lit sidewalk. Katie filled her lungs with late-autumn air and slowly exhaled. A crowd of students passed by laughing, leaves whisking up in their wake.

"Not much of a party-goer, huh?" Justin shot her a sideways look.

"How'd you guess?"

"It didn't take much."

"I guess I'm a bit of a homebody."

"You don't drink, that's why."

"Why I don't like parties?"

"Probably. It's one good reason anyway."

That's true. Drinking is a waste, I don't like what too much of it does to people, and I don't care what you or anyone else thinks. She kept the thoughts to herself.

"Plus, you're worried about your friend."

"I have good reason to be."

"She can take care of herself."

"That's the second time I've heard that tonight. Besides, I don't need to drink to have a good time."

"No problem, Mary Poppins."

He let go of her arm and elbowed her lightly in the side, the words teasing. Some of the tension left Katie's shoulders and she chuckled.

The two of them strolled in comfortable silence. Between streetlights, darkness pressed in, and she found herself grateful for his company. The night air had cooled, and Katie rubbed her arms.

"Here." Justin stopped, pulled off his leather jacket with the word *Engineering* emblazoned across the back, and slung it over her shoulders. She felt strangely safe as the heavy coat, emitting the faint smell of leather mixed with cologne, wrapped around her. She struggled to free her hair from under the weight of the collar. The sudden feel of his warm hands briefly touching the back of her neck as he helped remove the strands sent a tingling warmth down her spine.

Katie met Justin's gaze. Attempting to contain the feeling bubbling up in her chest, she pulled the front of the coat tighter.

"It suits you."

"Thanks. I've always admired them."

"You don't have one?"

"No, arts doesn't carry quite the same swag, does it? Besides, they're pricey."

"True, but I wouldn't mind wearing an arts jacket."

"You always want what you don't have, right?"

"I guess that's true." His gaze lingered on her face for a few seconds.

At the entrance to her dorm, Katie turned and faced him. "Thank you for your company earlier, on the deck. It was nice talking with you. And thanks for walking me home."

"No problem. Sorry you didn't have a good time tonight." Concern creased his forehead from behind the curl she had the sudden urge to touch.

"It doesn't matter."

"And what I said about drinking. I didn't mean to…"

"It's okay." She shrugged. "It's just not my scene."

"It was nice of you to go for Rachael though."

"I guess. Hey, if you're going back to the party, could you look out for her for me?" She slid his jacket off and handed it to him.

"Yeah, sure." The reassuring warmth in his eyes comforted her. Although she couldn't force Rachael to come home, she could make sure she was okay. At least, she could try.

———

When Justin returned to the party twenty minutes later, his thoughts were full of Katie. He paused at the front door. *What if Melissa grabs on to me again?* He gritted his teeth. It would have suited him to stay outside with Katie the whole evening. When he had come out onto the deck and seen her, a thrill had coursed through him. Her hair, spilling down her back and illuminated by the light of the moon, struck him as strangely angelic. And later, when he took his jacket from her outstretched hand, her fingers lightly brushing his sent a rush of warmth through him more intoxicating than the beer. He'd watched as she slipped through the door and out of sight. For a few moments he'd stood there, staring at the space where she had been, before finally turning to leave.

A sweet innocence surrounded her that was entirely captivating. She was breathtaking but didn't seem aware of it. Her smile both unnerved and set him at ease. He had struggled to keep his composure, to act natural and ignore the heat rising up his neck. He couldn't remember ever having such feelings, but Katie brought something alive in him.

A darkening awareness swept over him, bringing the realization that, from what little interaction he'd had with her, they might be complete opposites. *It doesn't matter.* All he knew for sure was that he had to figure out a way to see her again.

He went in to the kitchen and grabbed a fresh beer. After drinking deeply to repress the sudden stirring anxiety in his chest, he joined Chris and Sarah who were just beginning a game of poker.

Light streamed around the sides of the blind. Katie rubbed her eyes and reached for her phone on her bedside table. 9 am. She squinted across the room to Rachael's bed and her heart sank. It was empty and looked untouched. Dread filled her stomach. Rachael hadn't come home last night. She sent a text checking on her and stared at the screen a few moments before returning it to the bedside table.

Katie groaned and threw off her covers. After swinging her legs over the side of the bed, she stood and stretched then headed for the bathroom. The warm water of the shower washed over her and she hoped it would remove some of the tension she could feel lodged in her neck. *I shouldn't have gone to that stupid party. When will I stop feeling responsible for Rachael's choices?* Sometimes it was better not to know everything that was going on.

From behind the shower curtain, Katie heard the bathroom door swing open, followed by the sound of heaving. She poked her head from behind the curtain; Rachael knelt in front of the toilet. After vomiting, she flushed. Katie's warm water was replaced with an icy cold stream and she let out a small gasp as she rushed to turn off the taps.

"Hey… you okay?" She reached around the curtain to grab a towel.

Rachael groaned. She remained crouched in front of the toilet, her elbow propped on the seat and her head resting on her hand.

Katie dried herself and draped the towel around her body. Stepping out of the shower, she tried to gather sympathy for her roommate. *How can anyone find getting drunk fun?* Apart from the drips from the shower and Rachael's laboured breathing, the room was silent. Full of conflicting emotions, Katie was lost for words. She bent to peel away the stringy strands of hair glued to the side of Rachael's cheek. Sudden tears pooled in Katie's eyes, blurring the view of her friend. She dabbed them away with the corner of her towel.

"Do you need anything?"

"No, I'm okay." Rachael's voice was weak, as if even the act of speaking was too much.

"Did you stay over at Zack's?"

"Yeah. A bunch of us passed out in the living room. Zack, me, Chris and his girlfriend, Tom-Cat…"

At the mention of Zack's roommate, Katie's stomach lurched, and a sudden shiver scaled her back. Deep concern and regret mingled with the guilt she felt over leaving without Rachael. Tom-Cat's smirking face flashed in her mind and sent a second shudder up her spine. *I should have insisted she come home with me.*

She helped Rachael into bed then went to get ready for church.

———————

Her friend was still there, a miserable heap huddled under the covers, when Katie returned. She crept across the dark room and placed her purse on the desk. Rachael stirred and turned over. "I'm awake. What time is it?"

"Noon. How are you doing?"

"Not so good."

"Do you need anything?"

"No, I'm okay." She reached for the laptop at the end of her bed. "I've got to get my philosophy essay done. It's due at midnight."

Katie shrugged out of her coat and tossed it on her bed. She bent to remove her boots and was nearly knocked over as Rachael rushed past her to the bathroom. More vomiting. Katie kicked her boots under her bed then made her way to the desk. She slumped into the chair and sighed. It was going to be a long afternoon.

Rachael crawled back into bed, her laptop open and discarded on the floor beside her. She yanked the covers over her head and groaned. Soon she was snoring. There was no way she could complete that essay in her condition. Katie drew in a long breath and reached for her friend's laptop. *Jesus, you healed a man on the Sabbath; surely it's okay to help a friend in a bind?* But tending to a sick friend was one thing. Finishing an essay *for* her was somewhat questionable. Why did doing the right thing have to be so hard? She wanted to show love, to be patient and kind, but the grey areas in life were frustratingly unclear.

CHAPTER
Four

KATIE HALF-WALKED, HALF-RAN ACROSS CAMPUS TO HER art history class. The air was still and crisp and she drew in a satisfied breath. Brittle, brilliant-coloured leaves crunched beneath her feet and made a path of their own, crowding the sidewalk and collecting in blazing mounds near the grassy edges. Early-morning frost decorated the trees, and blades of grass jutted out of the ground, silvery and stiff. Squirrels scurried about burying nuts or hunting for secret caches. The sun exaggerated the pristine blue sky and brightened the pigment of everything alive.

The desire to capture the morning scene on a canvas nearly overwhelmed Katie. Too bad she had to go to class in a dark lecture hall to look at art slides. She sighed. Already five minutes late, she decided to take a shortcut through the math building, giving herself a pep talk along the way. *Studying the masters, however dry it seems, builds a knowledge base for my own work.* She vowed she would gather her easel after the tutorial and head back outside to paint.

Still tired from the weekend, Katie had hoped to have enough time to buy a coffee before the lecture, but it had taken her too long to gather the strength to get out of bed after being up until midnight helping Rachael with her essay. Thankfully, her friend had managed to crawl out of bed at dinnertime and complete most of the work herself, which eased Katie's guilty conscience.

Once inside the Fine Arts building, she retrieved her notebook from her cubicle, threw her coat and knapsack into the small space, and leaned her portfolio against the plywood wall. When she entered the darkened lecture room, the open door emitted a beam of light that cut across the projected image and onto the professor, already several slides into her talk. *So much for being inconspicuous.* Katie bumped past knees and chair backs as she made her way to an empty seat.

The prof was explaining the work of Gustav Klimt. The slide projected on the screen was *Death and Life.* Katie pulled down the folding seat and settled onto the chair to study the group of figures. The picture depicted the life cycle, so beautiful, even juxtaposed with the lurking form of Death.

Before the next slide flashed onto the screen, thoughts of the past weekend crowded in and Katie's concentration waned as paintings of other artists in "The Vienna Secession" were introduced. When she had pressed her roommate for more information about Saturday night, Rachael had been able to offer few details. It frightened Katie that Rachael couldn't recall everything that had happened the night of the party. It frightened her even more that her friend didn't appear concerned about that. Katie couldn't imagine not having full control over her body, especially with the threat of guys like Tom-Cat nearby.

The professor moved onto Franz Marc, one of Katie's favourite artists. She glanced at the image displayed on the screen. *The Large Blue Horses*, she thought, before the title was spoken. Katie fought to focus on the explanation of the style, atmosphere, and message the painter intended to relay. She gazed at the image of the horses in a seemingly idyllic place, far removed from reality and appearing to move in a dance of their own. In spite of her best efforts, however, her thoughts returned to Zack's party.

The unsettled feeling grew inside her at the memory of Tom-Cat. *His nickname is more than appropriate.* Rattled by the idea of what could have happened, she tightened the grip on her pen. She feared for Rachael's safety, knowing she and her friend weren't on the same page when it came to alcohol. Rachael would think Katie was overreacting if she commented on her level of consumption. Most people, including Rachael, thought this was fair game for university life. Even before they reached high school, Rachael had begun to change. By grade nine, Katie had stepped away from their friendship when her friend started taking drugs. She had made it out of that alive, somehow coming to her senses, but Katie still worried. It was impossible not to—they had been friends their whole lives. Katie swallowed hard. However difficult it was to remain silent, it wasn't her job to save her friend.

Fifty minutes later, when the lights in the lecture hall rose and the students filed out of the aisle, Katie was still wrapped up in her concern for Rachael. She stood, letting the padded seat flip closed behind her and, with it, the unfortunate memories of the weekend. She would go and paint something beautiful to forget.

Katie stood on a hill overlooking the campus. The frost had faded, but she remembered its appearance and planned to recreate it. She was halfway through covering the canvas with an initial wash of paint when Justin came to mind. *It was nice of him to walk me home.* She hadn't asked him how long he had been dating Melissa or what she may have thought about him walking her home. Perhaps they had an "open" relationship. That would certainly suit Melissa.

Katie stabbed at a dab of paint with the tip of her brush, feeling slightly guilty in her meanness. But only slightly.

———

Justin filed out of the math tutorial, ushered along by a crowd of exiting students. He blinked in the brightness of the perfect autumn day as he turned the corner toward the coffee pub. He saw her right away. A lone figure perched on top of the hill, leaning over an easel, her unmistakable blonde hair breathtaking in the sunlight. His pulse quickened and he moistened his dry lips.

He forced his feet to move in her direction, ignoring the fact that he would be late for his photography club meeting. As he drew closer, Katie repeatedly lifted her head, her eyes moving between the canvas and the scene before her. One outstretched arm moved in fluid, graceful sweeps, periodically dabbing the palette cradled in her other arm.

Justin stopped, drinking in the sight of her. An overwhelming desire to capture her this way filled him. He tugged the camera out of his backpack. Peering through the viewfinder, he framed the shot, marvelling at her beauty. He worked to keep his hands still as he focused the lens. After taking several shots, he replaced the lens cap.

Part of him loathed disrupting her, she appeared so content, but he suddenly had to be near her. Justin had spent his Sunday struggling through an assignment, feeling the effects of both the alcohol and the time he'd enjoyed with Katie. He had hoped he would see her again, but hadn't expected to get an opportunity this soon. Yet there she was, like a sudden apparition.

Doubt assaulted him. Why was he torturing himself? What would a girl like her ever see in him? He pushed the thoughts away as he walked toward her, silently rehearsing what he might say.

Seemingly unaware of his presence, Katie wiped her brush on a rag and stood back from her work to study it.

"Can I see it when you're done?"

She looked up with eyes as clear and bright as a summer sky. Recognition swept over her features, bringing the very smile already etched in his mind.

"Justin. Hi." Her eyes moved to the camera hanging around his neck. "Great day for pictures."

"There's some beautiful scenery around here," he ventured. His voice sounded as though it came from some faraway place and he cleared his throat.

"You're right." She scanned the campus before turning back to him. "I see you're still in the habit of sneaking up on people."

Heat crept up his neck. "I wasn't sneaking. I was observing." Thankfully, the words came out sounding more confident than he felt.

A knowing grin lit her features.

He moved beside her to contemplate her painting. "That looks great. How long have you been out here?"

"I don't know." She pulled a phone from her pocket and glanced at the screen. "Long enough to miss lunch."

"Well, I really like it. Are you done?"

"The proverbial question." She sighed. "What do you think?"

"Just a few touch-ups left," he mimicked, using her words from their first meeting.

She laughed. "I guess I deserved that."

The sound made him want more. "I was thinking of grabbing a coffee. Do you want to join me and warm up?"

"Sorry, I can't." She returned the phone to her back pocket. "I actually have a class in twenty minutes. Good thing you interrupted me, or I might have missed it."

"Can I help you bring this stuff back?"

She slid her brushes into their holder. He reached to pick up her backpack and held it out while she unzipped the front pocket to put the brushes away.

"I'll let you take that." He inclined his head toward the painting. He wouldn't risk carrying her work, especially when it was still wet.

She smiled and picked it up by its crosspiece. Justin folded the easel.

Fifteen minutes with Katie was better than none, but the walk across campus had never seemed so short. Too soon he dropped her off and waited until she scaled the steps and disappeared into the Humanities building. Although their encounter hadn't lasted nearly long enough, a satisfied smile animated his features and stride as he started back to make the last half hour of his meeting.

————

Late Friday afternoon, Katie was putting the finishing touches on a painting due the following Wednesday when the sound of footsteps broke into Tchaikovsky's Violin Concerto in D Major. Her prof walked through the door of the first-year studio, and Katie reached to pull out her ear buds.

"Hi Katie. Working late, I see."

"Oh hi, Professor Hodges."

"Very nice." He stood in front of her painting. "Looks like it's finished."

"You think? It's so hard to say—I could keep tweaking it forever."

He smiled. "I know. That's the angst of the artist, never knowing when to put the brush down. Our work never does feel finished, does it?"

"No, it doesn't." Katie enjoyed the smile lines around the corners of the professor's eyes.

"I wanted to talk with you about something. Do you have a minute?"

"Sure." She wiped off her brush and propped it on the edge of the palette.

"Every year we offer a scholarship of sorts to one of our students who shows real skill and determination in a certain area of art study. With it they have the choice to study at one of several universities around the globe. Have you heard about this program?"

"Yes." Her pulse quickened. Why was he talking to her about this?

"It's called the Ally Peters Foundation." Professor Hodges leaned back against a table. "Ally was a student here and has gone on to become a well-known artist. She set up this fund for selected students to study abroad for a year. The faculty has asked me to give them a list of people I would recommend. Is it all right with you if I include your name?"

Blood pounded in Katie's ears. "I thought you had to be in at least second year to qualify."

"Normally, but that's only a guideline. From what I've seen so far, I feel confident in submitting your work to the faculty for consideration. If you're chosen, it would certainly be to your benefit to go. What do you think? Are you game?"

Katie's mind reeled. "Of course! How could I not be?" She rubbed sweating palms over her jeans. "But I'm shocked to be considered."

"I think you give yourself too little credit."

How could he know so soon? It was only mid-October. Wasn't it too early in the year to figure out which students would be suitable for such a thing? As if reading her thoughts, he held up a hand. "I know you haven't been a student of mine long, but your acceptance portfolio was exceptional, and your in-class work is above par."

Katie drew in a deep breath. "Thank you. What do I need to do?"

"I'll give you an information package on Monday. It will tell you everything you need to know. In the meantime, start thinking about what pieces you would like to enter. Even though you don't have to submit a portfolio for another few weeks, it's obviously worth being well prepared. Look over the package and, if you have any questions, let me know."

"I will. Thank you."

"My pleasure." He pushed away from the table and exited the room.

Katie pressed a hand over the heart thudding in her chest. What an exciting opportunity. Where would she pick to study if chosen? She couldn't wait to tell Rachael. She gathered her brushes, cleaned them, and lugged her easel and painting into her partition. After grabbing her coat and backpack, she hurried out into the late afternoon sun.

As she raced across campus, her mind reeled with the prospect of being selected. *Stop getting ahead of yourself, Katie.* She attempted to halt the flow of building excitement and anticipation, but the idea of studying overseas at a school of her choice was irresistible.

A memory slammed into her mind, banishing her excitement. Katie stopped in her tracks and pressed a hand to her stomach.

———————

That summer had been a beautiful mistake.

From the moment they had met, she had made it clear they couldn't get serious. At summer's end, she and her mom were moving to England. In spite of that assertion, Katie and Aiden began to spend every moment they could together. Katie convinced herself that she was in control, that she would be able to let Aiden go, that she wasn't in over her head. After all, she was moving far away. But this was something altogether different, like uncharted, dangerous territory into which her seventeen-year-old heart tumbled blindly, unprotected.

Aiden was the first to say the words aloud. Katie didn't offer a reply. It wouldn't be fair. He had surprised himself—and all his friends—by dating a "good" girl who preferred to stay home and paint than go to parties. He stayed home with her, taking a temporary leave of absence from partying. Now, he was telling her he loved her, and it was all she could do to avoid expressing the sentiment that threatened to complicate both their lives.

In the growing darkness of those intoxicatingly warm summer nights, they walked hand in hand, sharing their hopes and dreams for the future. They rested on their park bench, Katie's head in his lap, without the need for words. They lay in the grass behind fir trees or under the open timber roofs of half-constructed houses and sampled young love without making love. Katie had made it clear she was going to remain a virgin until she was married.

Too soon, the beauty of midsummer faded and the crickets chirped their warning of approaching autumn as the couple reclined under the dark, star-strung sky, trying to prolong time and hide from the inevitable.

Katie's mother used to tell her, "All good things must come to an end." Never had her words held such truth as the day Aiden loaded her suitcases into the trunk of his car. They drove to the airport in silence, knowing there were no words to fabricate a safety net. Instead, tears of helpless sorrow streamed down Katie's cheeks.

She loved him.

Leaving seemed perfectly insane. There was no reason in it. No control.

At the airport, they held each other and cried. The ache Katie felt inside was unbearable, the moments before her, unthinkable.

Then, she climbed on a plane and flew away from love.

———

Katie forced the bittersweet memories, perpetually close to the surface, away as she pushed open the door to her room.

"Oh good, you're just in time." Rachael stood in front of the full-length mirror. "Which one?" She held two blouses up in front of herself.

Katie peered at Rachael's reflection. "The blue one."

"Really? I was leaning towards the green."

"That's nice, too." Katie kicked her shoes off into the closet.

"You think so?"

"They're both lovely." She sat on the edge of her bed, still trying to push away the lingering memories of Aiden.

Rachael slid the green blouse onto a hanger and carried her makeup bag into the washroom. "What are you doing tonight?"

"Not much. I have some Psych reading."

"I'm going to the pub with Zack. Why don't you come?"

"No thanks." Katie flopped back on the bed and let out a long sigh.

Rachael popped her head around the frame. "If I can meet people and have fun, you should too. You were always the more social one."

Katie rolled onto her stomach and reached for a textbook.

Rachael returned to her makeup. "Honestly Kat, I hope you don't get boring on me. You've changed since high school."

"I'll take that as a compliment. I'm fine. Go on and have a good time."

"Okay, Mom," Rachael called from the bathroom. "But if you change your mind…"

"Don't worry, I won't." Katie opened the book and scanned the first page.

"What are you doing tomorrow?"

"Studying."

"Big surprise. Wanna go for a coffee?"

"Sure. What time?"

"Not too early, Miss Morning Person. When I wake up."

"See you at noon then."

Rachael laughed. "Touché." She came out of the bathroom, dressed in the blue blouse. "Don't wait up for me!" she called, closing the door behind her and leaving a draft of perfume in her wake.

Katie rolled off the bed, put on her pyjamas, and pulled her hair up into a bun. She tugged open the door to their mini-fridge, the top of which housed a kettle and a few snacks, and reached for a leftover sandwich. After plugging in the kettle, she shuffled to the windowsill and picked up the small container of fish food.

"Hi, my little Dumpling." She sprinkled fish flakes into the water and watched the overfed fish wiggle to the top of the bowl and greedily suck up the floating food. "You're pretty hungry tonight, huh?"

After returning the container to the ledge, she peered out the window into the dark. A curving row of lights lit a pathway that led to a small concrete bridge over a narrow stream that flowed beside the ring road that looped around the main campus. The far-off lights from the Dana Porter Library rose above the other buildings and lit the campus sky. Several students from the dorm passed by the window and waved. A fleeting sense of loneliness passed over her as she returned their friendly gestures.

The kettle whistled. Katie turned away from the window, found a mug, and poured hot water over a tea bag. She set the mug on her nightstand and propped up her pillow before climbing into bed and re-opening her textbook. She'd finish the section on Sigmund Freud and get a head start on studying by reviewing her class notes. Two pages in, thoughts of Aiden returned, uninvited.

After she had left, they'd kept in touch through daily calls, marathon Skype conversations, and countless text messages that spanned the thousands of miles that separated them. She was desperate to find a way to get back to Canada to be with Aiden again.

Katie had alternated between bouts of despair, determination, and longing. Time crawled by like a slow, stubborn reptile. The three thousand miles and three months between them clouded her brain like dense English fog, leaving a residue so thick she could hardly remember the sound of his voice or the features of his face. Finally, unable to see the point, she dropped out of school and worked as much as she could, saving every penny with the goal of returning to Aiden.

Their one hundred and fifty days of separation ended as the plane attached itself to the skyway, like an umbilical cord linking her life to Aiden's once again. Katie saw Aiden as soon as the frosted glass doors slid open and she passed through the final physical barrier to him. His arms received her and held her tightly as the hardship of the previous months spilled out of her insides, down her cheeks and onto the shoulder of his coat.

He lowered her to the ground and kissed her trembling mouth. Their lips parted and he straightened, smoothing her silky hair from her wet cheeks and brushing the tears away with his thumbs. He smiled and kissed her again, ending the embrace with a final squeeze when the airport worker ushered them along.

Katie closed her eyes in an attempt to blink away the persistent memories and bring the words on the page in front of her back into focus. She took a sip of tea then rearranged the pillow behind her back in a vain effort to settle herself. But she was restless and struggled to think of something, anything, but Aiden.

God, please help these memories to go away. Why are they are always so close to the surface? I know that, after being determined not to, I ended up making the mistake of giving myself away to him, maybe that's part of the reason why. But I asked for your forgiveness then did what you told me to do and let him go. You know how hard that was for me. Please help me to forget him.

Desperate for a distraction, she closed the textbook and unwrapped the sandwich. The bread was soggy. Groaning, she climbed off the bed and opened the refrigerator door. As she reached for the last apple, her phone vibrated and she leaned across the bed to answer it.

"Hi Katie. It's Justin. I hope you don't mind. I got your number from Rachael."

"No, that's fine." She pressed a hand to her abdomen to still a sudden fluttering.

"I hear there's a great old foreign movie playing at the Humanities Theatre tonight. Are you busy?"

"Um…" Katie glanced down at the apple in her hand. "Sort of."

"I know it's last minute, but is what you're doing that important?"

She rubbed her hand over the discarded textbook. "I guess not."

"So you'll come?"

She looked down at her pyjamas and fought the urge to say no. Then, remembering Rachael's earlier words, she pushed back her shoulders. "Sure. What time?"

"The movie starts at eight. I'll pick you up around seven-thirty."

"Sounds good. I'll meet you in front of my dorm."

"Perfect. See you then."

Katie checked the time before tossing her phone on the bed. Yanking out her hair elastic, she strode into the bathroom and stopped in front of the mirror. Was she about to go out with another girl's boyfriend? *Relax. It's just a night out. Nothing serious, just a movie with a fellow student.*

She pulled on a pair of worn jeans and a comfortable sweater, applied a light touch of makeup, then sprayed perfume into the air and walked through it. After scribbling a note for Rachael on their message board, she shoved her feet into boots and locked the door behind her. She walked down the dormitory hall, relieved to have a solid distraction from the relentless memories of Aiden.

Justin's call just might be an answer to my prayer.

CHAPTER
Five

KATIE STEPPED OUTSIDE INTO THE CRISP AIR AND PULLED her scarf around her face. The temperature had plummeted the last few days, the cold bringing with it an early snowfall that blanketed the ground. It likely wouldn't last long, but Katie loved seeing the world looking so fresh and clean, like a blank canvas. Justin was waiting and climbed out of his car as soon as she passed through the glass doors.

"Let me get that." He smiled and rushed around to open the car door. He held it open until she climbed inside. She reached for her seatbelt, aware of the smell of his cologne, the same scent from the night of the party.

"I was surprised to find you home," he said as he climbed in on the other side. "Thought I might have to track you down at the studio. Hope I didn't pull you away from anything too important."

"Not according to Rachael. She's worried I'm getting boring."

"Really?" He glanced at her sideways. "And are you?"

"We have different ideas of what's fun."

"What's your idea?" he asked, manoeuvring the car out of the parking lot.

She shrugged. "I don't know."

His eyebrows rose. "You don't know? Well, I know it's not parties. So what does Katie enjoy doing on a Friday night?"

"Um... it might not sound all that exciting."

"Try me."

"I actually like staying home."

"Oh yeah?"

"Yeah. I don't mind being alone. I like peace and quiet. A lot of times I read or write poems."

His eyebrows notched even higher. "Wow."

"I told you it wouldn't seem very exciting."

"No, it's cool. I'm glad I rescued you from having too much fun tonight though."

She cocked her head. "Hey." Was he making fun of her?

He grinned. "Of course, the pressure is on now. Maybe I won't be able to compete with one of your books."

"Don't worry, the movie might."

The sound of his laughter put her at ease; she liked that he felt confident enough to joke with her.

When they arrived at the campus theatre, they found a line-up already wrapped around the side of the building. They said hello to a few familiar faces and stopped for casual conversation before taking their place in line.

"Where's Melissa tonight?" Katie tried to sound casual.

"I don't know, why?"

"It's Friday night. Wouldn't you two normally go out together?"

He frowned. "No, why would we?"

"Isn't that what couples do when they're dating?"

His mouth dropped open. "Dating? Melissa and I? What made you think that?"

She shot him a "do-I-have-to-ask" look and his face registered understanding.

"Oh, I get it. The party. No, she's just like that. I guess you got the wrong idea."

"I guess so." Heat crept up her neck and she adjusted her scarf a little higher.

He faced her. "Does it matter?"

"Well, yeah. I wouldn't want anyone to get the idea that I'm on a date with another person's boyfriend."

"A date? Is that what you'd call this?"

She shot him a warning glance but couldn't force a straight face when she saw his teasing smile. Then there was that ridiculous curl hanging just above one of his playful eyes.

"Don't worry. You'll be happy to know you aren't stealing anyone's boyfriend." As though he'd caught her looking at it, he brushed the curl away.

"I'm not worried."

"Good. Glad we have that settled." The playful grin hadn't left his lips.

A minute later the line began to move, and his hand slid to the small of her back to gently guide her forward. A flutter rose in her stomach. It had been a long time since she had felt the touch of a masculine hand, even if it was just a polite gesture. She remembered the night he had walked her home and the way she had felt when he slid his coat over her shoulders. *He's so considerate.*

Maybe tonight would be fun after all.

———

Justin tried to concentrate on the movie but was keenly aware of Katie seated next to him. Her laugh made him laugh. Her perfume drew him in, like flowers in some idyllic, exotic garden. Just being next to her sent ripples of nervous excitement running through him, as though he'd ingested too much caffeine. The feeling grew even stronger when he started to reach for her hand, changed his mind, and grabbed for some popcorn instead. She'd slid her hand into the bag at the same time, and her skin brushed against his. The spot felt as if it had been pierced by electricity. *Get it together.* But that would take more control than he had. She was closer to him than she had ever been and the movie faded into insignificance.

———

They stepped out of the theatre and onto the sidewalk. The snow illuminated their path and fell in fat flakes all around them, and Katie felt as though they were walking through another world. She lagged behind and discretely gathered up a snowball. It hit her intended target, delivering a cold shot to of the centre of Justin's back. He hardly missed a beat, just stooped down, grabbed a handful of snow, and retaliated. Katie clutched her arm, pretending to be hurt by its delivery, and bent to scoop up another mound of snow.

"Are you okay?" A concerned look on his face, Justin trotted toward her, directly into her trap. For his trouble, he ended up with a handful of snow in the face.

He lifted her up and playfully swung her around before lowering her, screaming and kicking, to a soft landing on the snow-covered ground. She struggled to her feet but slipped and fell back down onto her bottom. Justin dropped to her side, dangling a snowball inches from her face.

"Truce?"

"Truce," she tried, but the unrestrained giggling prevented the word coming out clearly.

He studied her briefly, then, in a clear act of faith, tossed away the snowball and reached for her hand to help her up. She sank her other hand into the snow, pretending to push herself off the ground but subjecting him instead to another dousing.

Katie shot off running down the street, her half-crazed laughter trailing after her. She could hear his quick steps and laughter behind her and the final grunt before he took her down. They tumbled, laughing and gasping, into the soft snow. When they came to a stop, he was on top of her, their misty breath meeting in the air between them. He stared down at her face. Katie could barely draw in a breath. *Is he going to kiss me?* Then he was on his feet and pulling her up. His smile was full of boyish charm as he brushed the flakes out of her hair. "It looks like you know how to have fun after all."

"I have my moments."

"I can see that." He swiped at the clumps on the back of his neck and his coat.

They crossed the street toward the car in silence. *He's taking me home.* The thought made her feel oddly deflated. Her forehead wrinkled. Hadn't she been ready to stay home alone just a couple of hours earlier?

Justin spoke into the silence. "Hey, it's not that late. Do you want to grab a hot chocolate or something?"

The thrill that shot through her scared her. "Sure." *Slow down, Katie. It's just one date, not the rest of your life.* Even so, as they wandered down the sidewalk side by side, she no longer noticed the chill in the air. For all she knew, it could be a balmy evening in June.

———

They wandered down the street to the coffee pub. Warm air greeted them when Justin pulled the door open. The café was unusually quiet and soft music played in the background. Katie settled at a table next to the fireplace while he ordered. As he waited at the counter, he watched her from the corner of his eye. She blew on her hands and pressed them to her face to warm her cheeks. She was intoxicating, and he drank in the sight of her.

He carried their mugs to the table and set one in front of Katie.

"Thanks," she said, wrapping her hands around the mug. "How did you know I like whipped cream?"

"Doesn't everyone?" He settled on the chair across from her.

"It's not the same without it."

He resisted the urge to reach across the table to touch her flushed cheek and ran a hand over his wet hair instead. "You're a good shot."

"Thank you." She looked very proud of herself.

"And a good actress. So, how do I measure up?"

"I have a much better shot."

He laughed. "I meant to your poetry and books."

A thoughtful expression crossed her face. "A close second."

"They must be extremely good books."

She lifted her shoulders and blew on her drink.

"So where is home for you?"

"Not far. I live in Cambridge." She spooned off some whipped cream.

"Have you always lived there?"

"No. We emigrated from England when I was five. We lived in Kitchener for a few months, and then my mom and I moved to Cambridge when my parents split up. How about you?"

"My mom lives in London. That's where I grew up."

"Not too far either. Do you go home often?"

"I went at Thanksgiving. I'll go at Christmas break for a few days then go visit my dad in New York City."

"How often do you see him?"

"Maybe two times a year. He travels a lot. We usually plan a windsurfing trip and meet somewhere." He grew distracted by a spot of whipped cream on her lip. Without thinking, he reached over and wiped it with his napkin. She reached for her own napkin. The glow on her cheeks grew a shade deeper and he repressed a grin. It was the first time he had seen her look uncomfortable.

"What?" She cocked her head.

"I was just thinking how beautiful you are."

She dropped her gaze to the table and busied herself fingering the handle of her mug. *Too soon, Justin.* He mentally kicked himself. The last thing he wanted to do was scare her away by being too forward.

Because he wanted to spend a whole lot of time with Katie Banks in the future.

CHAPTER

Six

KATIE LAY IN BED THINKING ABOUT JUSTIN AND THE evening they had enjoyed together. He was easy to be with, had a good sense of humour, and seemed an absolute gentleman. She'd enjoyed his jokes and the snowball fight. She flopped onto her side. *I'm glad I went—I think I've made a good friend.* Katie pursed her lips. *Friend.* She pushed away the feelings that came when she thought about the way his smile made her feel, or the warmth from the slightest touch of his hand.

But an uncomfortable thought crept in, one that she preferred not to entertain.

Justin reminded her of Aiden.

They looked nothing alike, but for some reason, being with Justin rekindled thoughts of the months she had spent with Aiden. Already having enough trouble dealing with ever-present memories, she was unnerved at meeting someone so similar. Her thoughts drifted to the painful way their relationship had ended.

Aiden hadn't seen it coming.

"We need to break up." The words were not hers, although she heard herself saying them.

Then tears. Tears from a boy almost a man. Tears she had never seen him cry before.

She fought her own and lost.

She tried to explain, but there were no words. Tried to make sense of something that seemed senseless. Tried to force herself to believe she wasn't making a terrible mistake.

"Let's give it two more weeks," he said, trying to recover something that had been lost but clearly not knowing how.

"Okay, two more weeks," she agreed, unable to bear the pain in his eyes but knowing it was over.

It had to be. She couldn't find a way to make him understand how, three months earlier, she had prayed to an invisible God and for the first time learned the truth. She couldn't explain enough for him to grasp how she had opened her heart to Jesus and was filled with joy that couldn't be contained, unlimited love, and a deep contentment that flooded the ever-present hole in her life. She couldn't make him believe in something he was unwilling to accept.

All her explanations had fallen into the widening chasm between them. There weren't enough words to make him understand. She'd given up when he had stood, a sudden stranger with cold, expressionless eyes, telling her she'd been brainwashed.

In the three months that followed, she cried herself to sleep night after night. She prayed Aiden would understand, begged God to make him see the truth, to make him believe. But all she heard was a still, soft voice asking her to let Aiden go. The soundless words whispered to her despairing heart were as distinct and certain as invisible wind. Even though she forced her own words and will to silence them, each night when she tried to pray, the persistent request echoed in her spirit: *I want you to let him go.*

The days passed and with each one waves of certainty washed over Katie, affirming what God was asking her to do. She had to obey. And so, even though the bitter ache refused to leave, her prayer changed: *Help him to agree with me. Please, Lord, help him to agree,* she whispered late at night into the dark... until time ran out.

They sat on their bench as they had so many times before, the same one on which they had discussed their dreams, shared their first kiss, and studied the stars while talking about all they would someday become. Only now, they wouldn't become that together.

"You're right, it's not working."

Katie's eyes widened. When had he come to that realization? Was that God, answering her prayer?

There was nothing more to say. The rift had become as large and insurmountable as the ocean that had divided them just months before. They held each other one last time and said goodbye.

But Katie's love for Aiden hadn't ended; she had simply obeyed.

One painful day followed the next in numbing loneliness. She had done what God asked her to do. So why did she feel so awful? Why was there so much pain? She had wrestled with God over giving Aiden up, now she wrestled with her heart to do the same. She longed to see him but prayed for help instead. Wanted to call him but read her Bible into the night, the pages wrinkling from tears shed while mourning the death of their relationship.

During those grievous nights, when Katie felt alone, she learned to trust, to give the fragments of her broken heart to God, to let him fuse the fragile parts back together and allow it to beat in time with his. Although she didn't know it then, she would come to learn that God loved her more than any man ever could, more even than a father can love his child, and had plans and dreams for his daughter greater than she knew or could dream for herself.

And so, Katie stepped out of her old life and began a new one. It was an uncertain and unlikely place to be. She felt as though she now lived with a freedom not recognized until the bondage was broken, as though formerly a blind woman who could suddenly see. The world, and the people in it, she viewed as if for the first time.

Only occasionally did she wonder if she would ever fully understand why God had asked her to let Aiden go. She found herself wondering that again now, her last thought before she slipped into a restless sleep.

———————

Katie woke in the middle of the night and sat up, gasping for air. Her heart raced. She could make out the dim shadow of the closet in her dorm room and the slit of light from the hallway shining under the door.

It's just a dream... a bad dream.

Forcing a deep breath to calm herself, she lowered her head back onto the pillow, but her mind insisted on replaying the dream.

She was a referee at a hockey game, but each time she blew the whistle the players ignored her. Suddenly masked players were shooting slap shots at her. The team captain skated toward her, and from behind the helmet she made out Aiden's face. He lifted his stick and the puck flew toward her. The black disc struck her in the stomach, knocking the wind out of her. She fell hard on the ice. Another player knelt over her, asking if she was okay, but she couldn't breathe or speak. When he pulled his helmet off to give her CPR, it was Justin. Then she woke up.

She drew in another long breath. Strange that she would dream of both Aiden and Justin. Why, after all this time, did Aiden seem to invade her thoughts when she least expected it? Unbidden, the words came. Words she thought she had put away. Words that came too late, months after she and Aiden broke up. "He had sex with Darcy while you were in England."

At the time, the words had washed over her like a tsunami, stealing her breath, knocking her down with a deadly blast of words. They crashed through her mind, seared into her heart, and left scorching shrapnel in their wake. She reeled in the aftershocks of anguish they brought, like deep puncture wounds that caused a slow leak in her heart.

Now, only scars remained, the cruel reminder of a weak moment.

So many times, she wished she had known sooner. Everything would have been so different. She would never have returned to Canada. Would never have seen Aiden again. Never have given her heart and eventually her body to an undeserving eighteen year old. And she would never have been tied with bonds to a boy who hadn't loved her enough to be faithful.

What does it matter now? What's done is done. Katie struggled to push the past far away from her. But even now, it made her insides ache. She had no one to blame but herself. Perhaps her past couldn't be adjusted, but there was a little respite in the knowledge and certainty that she could definitely control her future.

Lord, show me the way, she spoke into the night.

Some time later, she fell back into an uneasy sleep.

———

Katie looked up from her painting. Justin stood in the doorway to the first-year studio, leaning on the doorframe. At the sight of him, warmth rushed through her chest. She smiled.

"Finally. I've been standing here for ten minutes," he said, moving toward her.

"You have not."

"Okay, only ten seconds, but seriously, didn't you notice?"

"Sorry, but no." She dropped her brush into the jar of water.

"You looked like you were a thousand miles away. What were you thinking about?"

Her stomach tightened. *How can I avoid answering that question?* Should she tell him she was thinking about her painting, even though that wouldn't be fully true? Katie gazed at the canvas, avoiding eye contact. "Just about some good news I received last week."

"Oh yeah?" He dragged over a nearby stool. "Are you going to make me guess?"

She picked up a palette knife, scooped up two blobs of paint, and began mixing. He sat down on the stool and crossed his arms, waiting with an expectant look on his face as she began applying colour with a flat brush.

"So... are you going to tell me?"

"Nope."

"Why so mysterious?"

"Maybe because I hardly know you." She dabbed the colour onto the canvas.

"I feel like I've known you a lot longer than a couple of weeks."

She studied her painting. His words hung in the space she was attempting to keep between them.

"Have you had lunch?"

Her muscles relaxed slightly. "Not yet."

"Do you want to go to The Grill?"

"The Grill?"

He leaned in toward her. "Apart from Friday night, when a certain very charming guy took you to a movie, do you ever go out, Miss Banks?"

"Very funny."

"I get the impression you need to live a little."

"Really? What makes you think that?" She looked at him before she caught herself and turned away, but it had been long enough to see the creases at the corners of his eyes and the teasing smile that fueled a warm feeling inside her. *Why does he have to be so handsome?*

"Every time I see you, you have a paint brush in your hand or a serious look on your face. You don't like parties and you... you..."

"I what?"

"You don't even know about The Grill."

She frowned. "What's wrong with that?"

"Tons. It's only the cheapest and greasiest greasy spoon in town."

A laugh escaped her. "Okay," she surprised herself by saying. "You've convinced me. Let's go."

———

The male server, dressed casually in jeans and a black Star Wars T-shirt, filled Justin's cup for the fourth time. Coffee steam rose near his face as he chewed on his last bite of bacon. His leg, jiggling under the table, shook Katie's coffee mug. She wiped her lips with a paper napkin and returned it to her lap. Only after she lifted her mug did she notice he was staring at her. When their eyes met, he grinned and brushed the persistent curl off his forehead. "What's up?"

"Still trying to find out my news?"

"No, you'll tell me that when you're ready. I meant, what's bothering you?"

Surprised by his insight into her feelings, she weighed her words before speaking. Should she tell him what was on her mind? *I have to.* She took a deep breath. "I can't see you anymore."

Something flashed across his face, but he managed a small smile. "Why, are you going blind?"

"I need to concentrate on school."

"So concentrate with me."

"I… can't."

"Why not?"

"I can't really explain it."

"Try." His head jerked. "Wait. Is there someone else?"

"No." Katie clasped her hands on the table. "Look, I don't really expect you to understand this, but I'm a Christian."

"Okay…" His eyes widened slightly, but he appeared to want her to continue.

"And, I don't want to get serious."

"We only had one date and you think we're serious?"

"No, not yet, but I want to stop it here."

"Why?"

She chewed on her bottom lip. "I can't get serious with someone who doesn't understand or share my beliefs."

He surprised her by letting out a laugh. Katie frowned. Didn't he understand how hard it was for her to tell him that?

"That's pretty narrow-minded and slightly absurd, don't you think?"

Her jaw tightened. "It might sound close-minded to you, but it's for the best."

"How do you know that?"

"Experience."

"Oh yeah?"

She nodded.

"How do you know whether or not I share your beliefs?"

"Do you?"

Justin lifted his shoulders. "I do believe in God; I just don't believe in letting him dictate my life." He reached across the table for her hand.

Pull away. Don't let him take it. She didn't move.

"I don't want it to end here," he said.

"I know, but it has to." The words sounded surer than she felt. It took every ounce of strength she had to slide her hand out from under his and back to her mug.

"We haven't even had time to get to know each other properly. At least give it a chance. People change, you know."

"I know, but I can't."

"Can't change or can't give it a chance?"

"Both."

"You are a mystery, Katie Banks... a beautiful mystery." His voice and smile were soaked in disappointment.

A long, thick silence passed between them.

He slowly brightened. "Can I still take you out for breakfast sometimes?"

"I don't think so."

"Can we still be friends?"

She slowly inhaled, hoping a clearing breath would purge the pain. "Just friends."

"Don't friends have breakfast together sometimes?" He lifted a hand, palm up, his eyes twinkling.

She had walked straight into it and struggled to keep focused and remain strong. "An occasional hot chocolate with whipped cream couldn't hurt."

"Great. Do friends discuss their paintings?"

She threw him a warning glance. "Maybe. From time to time."

"Do they give back rubs when they've been working too hard?"

She nudged his arm, nearly spilling his coffee. "Friends, Justin, okay? No strings attached. No expectations. Deal?"

He stuck out his hand. Katie hesitated before she pressed hers into his. He brought it to his lips, meeting her gaze over her hand with playful, challenging eyes as he murmured, "Deal."

She tugged her hand away again and straightened.

"If I may not kiss thee, I prithee I may knoweth the kiss of thine hand, mine lady," he said, using a melodramatic Shakespearean accent.

"Should I slap thee now or later?"

"O, that there 'twere a 'morrow wherefore thou mayest, my love."

She rolled her eyes as a laugh escaped her.

He walked her back to the dorm. When she stopped at her door, he stood several steps away with his hands stuffed into his jean pockets, looking annoyingly adorable.

"I just want to make sure I have it all straight. No dates, no back rubs, no more kisses… is that correct?"

She whirled around. "We haven't kissed."

"I know, but you have no idea how much I've wanted to."

She swatted him lightly.

Chuckling, he rubbed his elbow, pretending to be injured. "Friends then?" He held out his arms.

"Friends," she agreed and accepted his hug. The strength and warmth of his hold beat back her reserves. She slid her arms out from behind his back and he released her. "I go to Cru once a week. It's a group of students who meet to have a Bible study and pray together, in case you're ever interested. I read the Bible every day, but lots of people who come don't, and everyone is welcome."

It was a long shot, but, at the very least, it put the ball in his court.

———

Katie sighed and leaned against the closed door, watching Justin walk down the sidewalk until he disappeared around the corner. As she pushed herself away from the door and went inside, she thought about that boyish grin that reached his eyes and the appealing, though infuriating, way he had of being funny and making her laugh even when she was struggling to be serious.

Why did he have to make it so difficult? She'd tried to make a clean break. *Did we just end up back where we started?* Maybe not. Maybe he would think about what she had said and realize she was right. Maybe he would never call her again.

Suddenly, she wanted to cry, to feel his arms around her, and stop feeling alone. Her hand went to the knob, but instead of flinging the door open and running after him, she forced herself to wait until reason returned. She had learned the hard way that feelings were often miserably unreliable. *I did the right thing.* Katie let go of the knob.

Now all I have to do is make good on my word…

CHAPTER
Seven

SOMEHOW SHE WAS MORE INTRIGUING TO HIM THAN EVER.
Justin had always liked a challenge, and Katie was definitely that. She was courteous yet controlled, kind but closed. She was not only breathtaking but genuinely unavailable. Even so, he commended himself for his perfectly-timed comic relief throughout their difficult conversation and held on to the feeling that he had salvaged a would-be wreckage. *I'm sure I can change her mind.* It wouldn't take long. And, with any luck, he just might be able to persuade her to fall in love with him.

She might be a complete contrast to him, on the opposite side of the colour wheel, but that would make them complementary, wouldn't it? If placed side by side in a painting, they would work to set off one another. The same could ring true for real life. *I'll have to use that argument next time we talk.*

He lay in bed, his arms folded behind his head, his thoughts full of her. She would probably be at church this morning. Growing up, he had been expected to go to church every Sunday. In his early years, he sang in the choir and was an altar boy. In high school, if his mom was away on the weekend, he took the liberty of skipping church in favour of going out with friends. If asked, he would produce the church bulletin one of his more committed friends had procured for him as evidence he had attended Mass.

He had long since stopped feeling guilty about his lack of attendance. These days, he only ever went to Mass if he was home for the holidays. Why was Katie so keen? Not that it bothered him, he just didn't see the point of it.

Last night, before he'd said goodnight, she had invited him to some Christian meeting. What had she called it? Cru? And did she really read her Bible every day? It baffled him that she actually studied a Bible as though it was required university reading. Who had time for that? And she'd called herself a Christian, like it was something exclusive. As far as he was concerned, he was a Christian too. Always had been. After all, he had been christened as an infant, had Holy Communion at age five, and sat through all the required religious training. But she had said it like it was some elite club he hadn't managed to gain a membership to.

He flopped onto his side. *If that Bible stuff makes her happy, who cares? All that really matters is how I feel about her.* He wasn't prepared to let an insignificant thing like religion get in the way of their relationship.

––––––––

Katie's Sunday routine never wavered. She slept until eight, went for a forty-five minute run, ate breakfast, then attended the ten-thirty service. After church, she visited with friends or helped set up for the Sunday night Bible study. Sunday was a day of rest, and she disciplined herself to take a day off from studying. No matter how many deadlines crowded in, she forced herself to put all work aside for those twenty-four hours.

Her runs were a source of stress management, each step measuring out her thoughts and providing a vehicle to sift them through. She often prayed as she ran, silently pouring out her heart to God. Today was no exception.

Lord, give me strength to stay strong. And wisdom—I need wisdom. Thank you for how good you are to me. Please let your will be done in my life with the scholarship, school, and Justin.

Rachael was a constant on her prayer list, and now she added Justin and Zack. Passages she had memorized about forgiveness drifted through her thoughts: *Love your enemies, do good to those who hate you, bless those who curse you, pray for those who mistreat you.* She grudgingly added Tom-Cat and Melissa to her prayers. Finally, she stopped sending up petitions and just listened. She ran beneath heaven, smiling in his presence, and felt the love of God resting on her.

––––––––

"You forgot your phone. Your mom called, so I answered it." Rachael passed Katie the device as she walked in from her run.

"It's about your grandmother. She didn't give me any details, just said she'd text you later and that she was about to get on a plane. I'm on my way out. Be back around five." Rachael disappeared through the still-open door.

Katie set the phone on the desk beside a framed photo of her standing between her mom and grandmother in her grandmother's garden. It had been taken two years ago, the last time she had travelled to England to see her grandma. She picked up the frame and ran a finger over the gentle, lined face. The last time she had spoken to her, her grandma was struggling with complications due to her diabetes. Her mother had just booked a month's trip in order to look after her. So what was this update about? Katie's stomach tightened. *Lord, keep her in your perfect care.*

CHAPTER
Eight

A WEEK BEFORE CHRISTMAS, KATIE HAD COMPLETED HER term papers and was returning to the dorm after handing in her last painting. She had enjoyed the break over Thanksgiving and being spoiled by her mom, who'd flown home just in time for the holiday. During the past month, Katie had worked non-stop to prepare her portfolio for submission. When she was satisfied it was in order, she gave it to Professor Hodges to present to the board.

Justin had made a point of learning her schedule. She never reminded him of their "just friends" conversation, but at times feared their closeness. Often, he would join her for a run, and almost every day he stopped by the studio with a coffee or hot chocolate in hand or a joke to make Katie laugh. He frequently stayed late, sitting on a chair and leaning against the makeshift wall of her cubicle studying while she worked on a painting. They talked and laughed and grew comfortable in shared silence.

Almost every doorway in her dorm was adorned with various tacky decorations, and Christmas music filtered out from more than one of the rooms. She loved this time of year and enjoyed the preparations that led up to the main event, but this year she was struggling to remain upbeat. Her grandmother's health had declined further, and her mom had returned to England to take care of her shortly after Thanksgiving. Katie had decided she wouldn't bother going home to an empty house.

Rachael had gone home to spend the holidays with her family. Katie was about to spend her first Christmas by herself. *Did anyone ever spend Christmas alone in a dormitory?* She entered her room and left the door open to escape the threatening loneliness.

As a reward for all her hard work, she planned to have a long soak in the bathtub. She turned on the faucet, dumped some lavender bath salts into the water, and pulled her hair up into a bun. *I'll just do some work, get ahead on a few assignments, and try to make the best of it.* Leaving the tub to fill, she headed back out into her room.

She fed Dumpling then sighed. *Might as well brighten up the place.* She dragged a mini, pre-lit tree out of the closet, pulled it from the box, and set it on her desk. A tacky wreath, acquired from their dorm gift exchange, already hung on the door, and she taped lights and tinsel around it.

"Voila. Instant Christmas." She stood back to appraise her work.

"Not bad." Katie spun around. Justin leaned against the wall, his hands in his pockets.

Her cheeks grew warm. "What are you doing here?"

"The question is, what are you doing here?" He followed her into the room. "Aren't you going home for the holidays?"

"No, I'm staying here."

"Until when?"

"The New Year. I'm spending Christmas here." It sounded miserable when said aloud.

"Are you nuts?"

She shrugged, too proud to acknowledge that not having anyone to share this time of year with mattered a lot more than she cared to admit. "How did you know I'd still be here?"

"I had a feeling. I saw Rachael this morning at the coffee shop and she told me about your grandma. You okay?"

"I've been better," she admitted, adjusting a still-squashed branch on the fake tree. She bent to plug in the lights. "What do you think?"

"I think you are carrying this enjoying your own company a little too far. You can't spend Christmas here alone."

"I don't really have a choice." She turned to the window ledge to pluck some wilted leaves from an ailing plant.

"Not okay."

Katie tossed the dried leaves in the garbage, sat on the edge of her bed, and sighed. "I know. I wish I could have gone with my mom."

Pushing some clothes aside, Justin sat down beside her. He reached for her hand and gave it a gentle squeeze. The familiar longing returned, and she struggled to keep her emotions in check, as she had so many times over the last few weeks.

He had been obstinate, to the point of annoying at times. But if she was honest with herself, it wasn't his propensity to be near her that bothered her, it was the constant struggle his presence presented. She had to keep checking her heart, her distance, and even the amount of time she dared look at him. Too much of any of the above and she was treading on dangerous ground.

Even now, just the feel of his warm, gentle hand and the touch of his shoulder next to hers sent tingles through her body. One look into his kind, dark eyes was likely to quash any remaining reserves of discipline. They were like the draw of a strong magnet, ever attracting her and pulling her closer. She didn't dare turn her head now, not when they sat so close, not when she knew the soft look of concern she'd find in his face would dissolve all her self-control. Instead, she kept her eyes down, focusing on her ridiculous Christmas socks.

"What's that sound?"

"Oh!" She leaped up. "My bath water."

As soon as she ran into the bathroom, her socks became saturated. Water lapped at the top of the tub, and what couldn't be contained spilled over the edge. *Idiot.* Katie quickly turned off the taps and grabbed a handful of towels. Then Justin was at her side, chuckling and reaching for any remaining towels. Side by side on their knees, they mopped up the water that had soaked the entire floor and threatened to reach the carpet.

"It's all your fault!" Katie flicked her fingers, spraying him in the face with a few drops of water.

"My fault? Since when is your forgetfulness my fault?"

"You interrupted me." She clambered to her feet.

"Oh, okay. In that case, I take full responsibility."

"Good." She flicked him with her wet towel.

"Hey." Before she realized what he was about to do, he bent down, scooped her up in his arms, and swung her over the tub.

She tried to free herself but was weak with laughter.

He lowered her closer to the water.

"You wouldn't dare." Katie struggled in his arms. "You're too much of a gentleman."

"Nice one. But it won't work. Recant."

She shook her head.

"Oh, a stubborn young lady. You leave me no choice." He bent down until she was inches above the water. Then his running shoe slipped on the damp floor and he lost his balance. They both tumbled into the tub. Water flooded the floor as they lay in each other's arms, both laughing hysterically. As soon as he stopped, he struggled to his feet and held out a hand. "Are you okay?"

"I think so." She grasped it and allowed him to pull her to her feet and help her out of the tub.

Breathless and dripping, clothes clinging to their bodies, they stood close in the confining space. Katie's eyes met his, and her breath caught in her throat. He bent to kiss her. His wet lips were warm and soft, his hands strong and gentle as he cupped the sides of her face. Then he pulled back and searched her eyes. She willed herself to look away, but her eyes defied her. He leaned in again, his lips desperate and searching hers. This time she reciprocated. He kissed her fully, intensely, and she did nothing to prevent it.

It took every ounce of her will to finally step back. Breathless and shivering, she searched for a dry towel. Justin reached into the cupboard, retrieved the last dry one, and wrapped it around her shoulders. Katie clutched it to her chest, feeling suddenly exposed, and faced the mirror. Pulling out the hair elastic, she ran her fingers through her hair, sweeping away the saturated strands that clung to the sides of her face. She tried wiping off the black line of mascara that ran beneath her eyes. It was no use. She flushed as she caught a glimpse of Justin studying her reflection. "Wow, I'm a mess."

He didn't take his eyes off her. "You're beautiful."

She let out a nervous laugh, still feeling off-balance from their kiss.

"You are beautiful, Katie Banks." He cupped her shoulders and turned her around. "Spend Christmas with me," he whispered.

———

On Christmas Eve the dorm was silent. Katie tried reminding herself how much she enjoyed peacefulness, but it didn't help. Tonight it seemed out of place and discomforting. Apart from Chi, an overseas student from China, the dorm was empty.

The silence reminded Katie of the first Christmas after her father had left, so quiet and joyless. She had spent every Christmas since then trying to make up for it. This year, her preparations weren't doing the trick as sadness settled in and found a place in her fragile spirit.

She was beginning to regret not taking Justin up on his offer. She turned up her Christmas music and tried to hum along, but her heart wasn't in it. Adjusting the Christmas cards on her windowsill, she saw large snowflakes accumulating on the path outside and felt more closed off from the world than ever. Sighing, she changed into her pyjamas and climbed into bed much too early.

Just as she was dozing off, she was startled awake by a knock at her door. *Must be Chi wanting some company.* She swung her legs over the side of the bed, got up, and opened the door.

"Ho, ho, ho, Merry Christmas!"

It took a moment to discern who was underneath the Santa costume, holding out a bouquet of red and white roses. But the smiling brown eyes gave him away.

"What are you doing here, Santa?" she demanded, forcing back a smile.

"You're my last stop. Have you been a good girl?"

"Go home, you fool."

"I just drove an hour and forty-five minutes through a snowstorm, my reindeer are exhausted, and you want me to turn around and go home? Not quite the reception I was expecting."

"What are you doing?" Katie shook her head. "You're crazy." Still, he *had* gone to a lot of trouble for her.

"You really know how to make Santa feel good. Aren't you even going to invite me in and offer me cookies and milk?"

"Of course, come in."

He handed her the flowers as he entered the room then pulled a box of chocolates from behind his back.

Katie gave up. "Thank you." She hugged him. "I can't believe you're here."

He stepped back and held up a hand to stop her from approaching before disappearing out the door and returning with a garbage bag slung over his shoulder. He set it on the floor, pulled out a large, flat, poorly-wrapped present, and handed it to her. "For you."

"Wow, Santa, did you wrap this all by yourself, or did your elves help you?"

Justin laughed, a dark curl escaping from underneath the fur hat and falling over his forehead. "That bad, huh? Just open it."

"Now? It's not Christmas yet."

Katie tore at the wrapping paper and gasped when she uncovered it. Her mouth dropped open. "How did you take this without me knowing?" She searched his face.

"It wasn't difficult. You're in your own world when you paint. I couldn't help myself."

"It was such a perfect day. You captured it beautifully. The sky... the trees..."

"... you, Katie."

She waved the compliment away.

He grasped her arms lightly. "*You* were beautiful."

"And the photographer wasn't half bad." She pulled him in for a hug. "Thank you," she murmured into his ear. "I love it."

He kissed her forehead. "You're welcome."

She moved back and climbed onto her bed. From her knees, she reached up and removed a faded Renoir print from the wall. She motioned for him to pass the framed photo and hung it on the existing nail. After making sure it was straight, she jumped off the bed and stepped back to look.

"A man of many talents."

"There's one more thing."

"How could there be?"

"Close your eyes."

Katie heard him rustling about the room. *What is he doing now?*

"Wait. Don't open your eyes yet."

After what felt like several minutes, just as she was becoming too restless to wait any longer, he flicked off the light, reached for her hand, and led her forward.

"Okay, you can open them."

Justin had spread a tablecloth out in the middle of the floor and covered it with an entire Christmas dinner. He'd brought a bottle of wine, two glasses, and plates with napkins folded neatly beside cutlery. Tea lights, set on her nightstand, windowsill, desk, shelf, and the tablecloth, illuminated the room.

"This is amazing!" She pressed a hand to her mouth.

He held out his hand. "Please, sit." When she obliged, he spread a napkin over her lap and proceeded to serve her. After filling her plate, he poured wine into her glass.

"I propose a toast." He tugged off his white beard and smiled at her. "To Katie, the most amazing girl I've ever met. Merry Christmas!"

"Merry Christmas, Santa."

They touched glasses.

"Don't worry. You can drink as much as you want. It's non-alcoholic. Which does make it extremely difficult to find an excellent year."

She giggled. He hadn't missed a detail.

"By the way, nice PJs," he said, glancing at her between spooning cranberry sauce on his turkey.

She looked down. Oh yeah, she'd been in bed when he arrived. "I should really change. After all, this is Christmas dinner."

"You're fine. Stay and enjoy it before it gets cold." His warm expression assured her he didn't care one bit, and though she tried to look away, his brown eyes gently pried at the seal of her heart.

―――――

Christmas Eve was tolerable. At least her parents weren't arguing. Rachael's father lit his fifth cigarette since arriving home an hour earlier. Between the smoke and dull mood clinging to the air, it might have been better spending Christmas with Katie back at school. Rachael glanced at her dad reclining in his chair watching television. Her mom was busy with the turkey and didn't want help. She sighed. *Maybe a little fresh air will help.*

Rachael pulled on her coat and stepped outside into the snowy night, the door closing behind her mercifully muting the TV. Snowflakes swirled in the wind, like the ones in the Christmas snow globe her grandmother had given her as a child. How she had wished to be one of those rosy-cheeked children playing in the snow beneath the protective glass. If only she could have joined their play, escaped to that miniature world where their mothers would have warm hot chocolate and hugs for them when they returned home.

Lowering herself to sit on the porch steps, she positioned the cigarette she'd taken from her dad's pack between her lips and fumbled with the lighter in the hungry wind. Inhaling deeply, she dragged her knees up to her chest and wrapped her free arm around them. How was Zack enjoying his Christmas Eve? Was he missing her as much as she was missing him?

From inside, she could hear her mother shouting—probably blaming her father for something she had forgotten to pick up at the grocery store. Rachael exhaled a last lungful of smoke and stamped the cigarette butt beneath her boot. Home was a strange mixture of distant security and partial insanity.

―――――

The tea lights had extinguished themselves, and Justin had packed up the remains of the Christmas dinner and cleared everything away. He and Katie remained on the floor, their backs against the beds as they swapped funny stories about their lives. When the talk turned to their parents, Justin's face grew serious.

"My dad left when I was two. One woman wasn't enough for him. Still isn't. Last time we met up he was dating a model from New York."

He studied the fingers he had clasped on his knees, afraid to meet her eyes. Had he said too much? With her religious background, she might push him away for his less-than-ideal upbringing. When she touched his leg, he forced himself to look up and the tension left his muscles. Her face had softened. Was that sympathy in her eyes?

Even so, he'd play it safe. Time to switch topics. He took a deep breath. "I don't know about you, but there's an unspoken expectation that I'll grow up to be *successful*, whatever that means, but it sure doesn't include being an artist."

"Is that why you chose Engineering?"

"Yeah. I figured there had to be some creativity in that, right?"

"I don't know much about it, but there are all types of creativity. And you can always keep doing art as a hobby."

"I definitely plan on it. What about you? You said your parents weren't together either."

"That's right; my dad left when I was five." Her brow briefly creased as though she was flinching in pain.

"I guess we have something in common. Do you still see him?"

"No, not since he left."

"Wow, that must be hard."

"Kind of. I've gotten over blaming myself for it though."

"Ouch—you blamed yourself?"

"Yeah. It was pretty rough. He never said why he was leaving, and my mom wouldn't talk about it." She bit her lip as though fending off unwanted emotion.

His fists clenched on top of his knees. He imagined five-year-old Katie wondering where her daddy went and a longing to protect her swelled in him.

During the silence that followed, Katie picked at a few stray crumbs on the blanket.

Should he push it? "I know how you feel," he blurted out.

She tilted her head and contemplated him, as if trying to decipher whether or not he could know. After a few seconds, she took in a breath as if to say something. Instead, her lips closed firmly and she lowered her gaze to the blanket. He reached for the hand plucking at the wool balls on the duvet and covered it with his. She let out a small laugh.

"I just... I just don't understand why he has never contacted me all these years. Not a single letter, a card, a call. Nothing. I don't know a thing about him."

She shrugged, but the tears shimmering in her eyes told the truth. She brushed them away with her free hand.

"Hey, what about your art?" Justin decided to help her by changing the topic. "At least no one's stopping you from pursuing that, are they?"

She brightened. "No, thankfully."

"So what are your future goals?"

"Well, I have this crazy dream to become an artist and live like a hermit in a thatched cottage somewhere in England. And maybe one day my paintings will go for millions, like Picasso's."

"In that case, I better get your autograph now." He handed her a Christmas napkin and reached for a pen from her nightstand.

"What do you want it to say?"

"To my one true love Justin."

"Seriously." She shot him a deprecating look.

"You asked. I'm a big fan, you know."

"Okay, you got it." Katie scribbled on the napkin then handed it to him, her lips pursed. "Happy?"

"You have no idea."

She leaned her head on his shoulder, yawned, and whispered, "Thank you for a beautiful Christmas."

Her soft cheek pressed against his neck and he drew in the sweet scent of her hair. Her eyes blinked and closed, and her breathing slowed.

Desire lapped at the shore of his body. He fought to contain it, but its continual waves were relentless until he feared his own lack of control. It took all the strength he had not to pick her up and carry her to the bed.

He'd fallen hard. There wasn't a place he would rather be, or a person he would rather be with, for Christmas. Or any other day of the year, for that matter. His thoughts returned to the week before, when they'd fallen into the tub. He remembered how Katie had looked into his eyes after they kissed, and how in them he had found something strangely different and wildly beautiful, more than the blue itself. The hue was piercing enough, but their brightness shone, probing his with a deep kindness and gentle strength. He thought about her body beneath the wet, clinging clothes and his quenched desire when she quickly covered herself with the towel. She had nothing to be ashamed of. She was perfect.

A deep longing filled him. Afraid he would be unable to contain his passion, he gently shifted away from her and got up. After tugging the blanket from the bed and draping it over her, he pulled on his coat, silently stuffed his feet in his boots, and left.

———————

Some time before dawn, Katie woke to an empty room. Stiff from sitting on the carpet for hours, she groaned as she struggled to her feet. Yawning, she made her way to the bathroom; it too was empty. She frowned. When did Justin leave? It was strange that he hadn't woken her. She climbed into her bed and tried to fall back asleep, but as tired as her body felt, her mind was wide awake.

She pressed her eyes tightly closed. What had she done? Over and over she had reminded herself that she and Justin were just good friends. She liked his company—a lot. Was there anything wrong with spending time together as friends? She couldn't argue with him on that, but somewhere between the coffee and the conversations, she had opened the door and let him in.

During quiet moments like these, when she allowed her mind to ponder it all, she became keenly aware of the effect her decisions were having. The magnitude of many small choices, strung together. Without meaning to, she had started something she couldn't finish and feared she was once again heading for heartache.

CHAPTER
Nine

"KATIE, I'VE GOT SOMETHING FOR YOU."

The secretary of the Fine Arts Department motioned her into the office. She handed Katie an envelope with the U of W logo at the top left corner.

Katie fought the desire to tear open the envelope right then and there. Whatever it said inside would determine where she would spend next term. Instead, she tucked the letter inside her portfolio case. "Thanks, Anne." She zipped up her coat and pulled on her mitts, preparing to face the February cold. "See you tomorrow."

Though she jogged most of the way, it seemed to take twice as long as usual to reach her dorm. As soon as she pushed open the door to her room, she threw off her mitts and retrieved the envelope. For a moment, she gazed at the front then she drew in a deep breath and began ripping. She scanned the letter and joy exploded inside her like fireworks. She had been granted the Ally Peters award. *I'm going to study in Paris!* She danced around the room.

———

The library was getting busier—everyone must be preparing for midterms or researching papers. Katie settled onto a vacant chair and opened her laptop. She checked her calendar to remind herself of pending deadlines. The term was passing so quickly—she could hardly believe it was February already. If all went according to plan, in a little over two months she might very well be in France, sitting at adorable sidewalk cafés and studying at the American University of Paris.

Seven days had passed since she'd received the news of her acceptance, and she hadn't told anyone, despite the fact that her plans were now fully underway. She was about to burst. She had already submitted her scholarship for the program and letter of intent to attend AUP. Now, all that remained was the final nod from the university itself.

Amid all her plans, she and Rachael hadn't had time to connect. Rachael seemed busier than ever and was spending every waking moment with Zack. She hadn't slept in her bed again last night. When Rachael came in that afternoon, she slipped straight into the bathroom and closed the door.

Katie frowned. *Strange. Tonight I'll check to make sure she's okay.*

Thoughts of Justin replaced the nagging concern over Rachael. When she had read the acceptance letter, her thoughts instantly clarified. She couldn't let herself make the same mistake twice and get involved with the wrong guy. Even if he *was* the right one, what kind of fool would knowingly start a relationship only to have to live apart for months?

She couldn't let herself get hurt or place herself in a situation where she must once again let love go. She didn't want to have to survive a broken heart again.

In the quiet of the library, she made the decision to stop the relationship before it was too late. It would be for the best. Justin didn't share her beliefs, and she wasn't willing to surrender hers. Better to put a stop to it now before anyone got hurt. *Tomorrow. I'll tell him tomorrow that it's over.*

Katie pushed away the heavy thoughts and settled in for a few hours of study before dinner.

After entering their room, Katie flung her backpack on the bed and moved to the radiator to warm her frozen fingers. Her phone vibrated in her pocket. She unzipped her coat while reading the text message.

It was from Justin: Be ready for five. I'm coming to pick you up.

She glanced at the time just as the knock sounded on the door. When she opened it, Justin stood in the hallway, strikingly handsome, his dark eyes shining with excitement.

Katie grinned. "I could set my watch by you."

"Pretty good, huh? Come on, I see you already have your coat on."

"But I…"

"But nothing, let's go." He quashed her meagre attempts at protest.

"Where?"

"If I told you, I'd have to kiss you."

Katie planted both hands on her hips. "What's that for?" She nodded at his backpack.

Quiet mischief tugged at the sides of his lips and creased the corners of his eyes.

"Let me guess, we're going to study on a Friday night." She strained to do up the zipper on her coat, but it was stuck.

"You'd probably enjoy that, wouldn't you?"

"Did I ever tell you I don't like surprises?" She struggled to dislodge the caught material, along with the heavy feeling in her stomach.

He moved her hands and took over. "Everyone likes surprises. They just don't like waiting for them," he said, effortlessly pulling the zipper up to her neck and giving her scarf a playful tug. "After you." He held the door open and they walked into the hall.

Katie locked up and returned the key to her purse. Justin reached for her hand and led her out of the building. His fingers felt warm folded around hers and protecting them from the cold, and though she knew she should, she didn't pull away.

Snow crunched beneath their boots as they walked. Katie tried to shove aside the nagging feeling and the resulting nervousness about the news she needed to deliver to Justin. *It can wait.* This didn't seem the right time to break the news to him. Not when he looked so excited.

They reached the Fine Arts building and he ushered her in. A few lights were on, and Katie heard distant music from a classroom; a student must be working late.

"Come on." He gripped her hand and led her down the hall.

"You're strange, Justin Burke."

"I love you, too."

"I didn't say I loved you."

"But you know you do."

Her heart rate sped up. Even though she tried to convince herself it was his surprise, not his words, that brought that on, she knew the truth. She hated that he sounded so confident.

"Close your eyes." Justin reached over and gently covered her eyes with his hand.

Walking behind her, he steered her into a room. She could feel his warm breath on her neck, smell his familiar cologne, and hear the music clearly now. He stopped and removed his hand. "Now open them."

In front of her stood a small table with art stools positioned on either side. The table was set with a white paper tablecloth, a candle, and a single red rose. The scene was so beautiful that tears filled her eyes.

"Happy Valentine's Day," he murmured into her ear.

Her heart dropped, heavy with aching.

"Allow me." He took her coat, pulled out one of the stools for her, and, once she was seated, reached into his pocket and brought out a box of matches. He leaned in and lit the candle, then looked down at Katie's face. His broad smile increased the sick feeling hammering at her insides.

Opening his backpack, he lifted out a Thermos, a box, and a can of whipped cream. He poured hot chocolate into two cups, squirted each with a generous mound of cream, and opened the lid of the box.

Justin turned it toward her to display its contents. The words on the cake had smeared slightly from travelling in the backpack, the "you" almost unrecognizable, but the message made its impact. She bit her lip and closed her eyes to block the words and the threatening tears.

"Katie?"

His voice met closed eyes that spilled hot tears.

"Katie?" He tried again, his voice firmer.

She drew in a settling breath and forced her eyes open. The expression of boyish delight had vanished from his face. "Justin, this is really nice. You are really nice, but I…" Her voice shook and her heart fumbled as her tears wet the tablecloth. "I… I'm so sorry."

He got up and knelt beside her. "What is it, Katie?"

"It's us. You and me."

"You're not trying to push me away again, are you? Why won't you let me in? There's this wall you never quite let down."

"What are you talking about?"

"Come on, Katie. I care about you. And I was pretty sure the feeling was mutual. But you're so careful to stay in control of yourself; you never let go."

"That's not true." She stared at the tablecloth, willing her voice not to betray her as another drop soaked through the paper.

"Isn't it?" He cupped her face in his hands, his eyes demanding her attention. "I mean it, what it says on the cake. You can hide from it if you want, but I do. I love you."

"What do you expect me to say, Justin?"

"Be real—let go for once. Admit you love me too."

She opened her mouth but closed it again without speaking. What was there to say? She'd already said it, over and over and over.

"Really, Katie?" He stood and raked his fingers through the mass of curls over his forehead.

"You don't understand. And I obviously can't make you."

Without knowing it, she had built a wall, a fortress even, using the hardened bricks of past hurts. Somehow Justin had scaled that wall, and now he stood brazenly before her, inviting her to love him, and all she wanted to do was run for reinforcements. She could never explain it to him, and even if she could, he wouldn't understand. It was a dreadfully familiar place to be. Hadn't she tried to explain before, with Aiden? That had been agonizing enough. If Justin was supposed to be her soul mate, God would have to figure it out.

He dragged his stool around beside hers. "What are you afraid of?"

Katie hated that he was so persistent. How could he read her so easily? She *was* afraid, masking a past that she dreaded to repeat, still burying the bruises. She had attempted to keep him at arms' length, tried desperately not to get too close. At least she had been up front from the beginning about her beliefs, and that they could only be friends. He knew about her faith, knew she went to church and attended Cru, but none of that mattered to him. And that was the problem. She was all that mattered to him, not God, and that would never be enough.

He had to want a relationship with Jesus for himself. He would have to be the one to choose.

She couldn't do it for him.

He wiped a tear from her cheek. "Katie? Talk to me."

His eyes pleaded, and in their intensity she had to look away. Her heart was choking. Fumes of love that refused to be extinguished crowded in, consuming and confusing her. She gathered strength between long breaths. He deserved an explanation.

"My faith is important to me. I know you respect that, but you don't understand it. I've tried to explain that I need to be with a person who shares that faith. I have to be able to share my relationship with God and grow together. I can't do that if that person doesn't know God."

She paused to let the words soak in then spoke into the silence. "And there's more. I'm leaving for a few months. I won the Ally Peters scholarship to study abroad."

His body stiffened; his look hardened.

"How long have you known that?"

"Professor Hodges first mentioned the possibility in the fall. I only found out for certain last week."

"Why didn't you tell me sooner?"

"You almost got it out of me, remember? The first time we went to The Grill?" Katie twisted her fingers together in her lap. "Would it help if I told you you're the first one to know?"

His jawed clenched. This was the first time she had seen him upset, and she hated being the cause. "I mean, it wasn't for sure... I didn't think I'd even be selected."

She waited through the hard silence, but it lasted longer than she could bear. "Hey, I'm sorry I didn't tell you sooner, okay?"

"Didn't you think I had a right to know? I mean, I thought we were pretty close. Did you think I was just putting in time?"

"What do you mean?"

"These last four months... did you think I didn't have anything better to do?" He shook his head. His chest rose and fell, as if he'd been running. "So, when do you leave?"

"End of semester, mid-April."

"Where are you going?"

"Paris."

He blew out a breath. "Wow. For how long?"

His voice already seemed far away.

"A year."

In the silence, blood pounded in her ears. She tried to swallow, but her throat was too dry to allow it.

"I guess I should say congratulations." He rose and gathered his Valentine decorations and stuffed them into his backpack.

When he'd finished, he brushed past Katie, not bothering to look at her.

For a long time, she stared at the doorway where he had disappeared, her chest filled with the ache of loss.

———

The cake's frosting tasted bitter. Justin opened the trash can and tossed the remains in the garbage, wishing he could rid himself of the memory of the look on Katie's face as easily.

He dragged a hand through his hair and slumped on a chair, replaying the disastrous evening in his mind. *How could I have been so stupid?* What had he been thinking? His behaviour these past few months had been so uncharacteristic of him. And now it seemed ridiculous and a total embarrassment.

You are a fool, Justin.

His cell phone rang. He plunged a hand into his front pocket, fighting the hope it might be Katie.

"Hey, Justin." The voice sounded far too cheerful against the backdrop of his gloom.

"Hey, Melissa."

"I tried texting you. A few of us are at Fed Hall..." The connection was poor and made worse by the loud music and voices in the background. "... celebrating. Come over."

"I'm not really into it."

"Great. See you in... minutes."

"Melissa... you still there?"

No answer. Justin gave up and stuffed the phone back into his pocket. Nine-thirty on a Friday night. Valentine's Day, and he was at home alone. It might be good to get out, see some friends, have a beer, and disappear in a noisy crowd. He pulled his coat back on and stepped outside, shutting the door on his house and on all thoughts of Katie Banks.

Rachael's legs ached. She lowered herself onto a bench inside a bus shelter to block the biting wind. Her hands were numb; she was numb. Tears were frozen to her eyelashes, the cold air oblivious to her sorrow, the darkness neglectful of her aching heart.

Overcome with a desire to escape, she had run from the dorm and, in a desperate rush, had left without gloves. She had yanked her coat sleeves over her hands as cover from the stinging cold and now pulled one up to check her watch. It had been almost two hours since she had phoned Zack to tell him she wasn't feeling well—which wasn't exactly a lie—and she was still aimlessly wandering around the campus.

A harsh emptiness scraped at her insides. The purposeless walking brought no relief to the question that turned relentlessly in her mind: *What am I going to do? What should I do?* She sat in the darkness, feeling like a frightened child who had lost her way but was incapable of asking for help.

I'm so stupid. How could I have let this happen? She struggled to think through the haze of confusing thoughts that swirled in her mind, desperately wishing she could turn back time.

Barely any traffic passed by as she sat inside the covering, until a bus slowed, nearing the curb. Rachael waved the driver on before the vehicle had fully stopped. Diesel fumes spilled out of the exhaust pipe and filled the glass shelter. Black smoke swirled and then dissipated. Rachael stared at a few stray snowflakes and pressed boot prints into the thin layer of slush underfoot. Eventually she stood, pulled up her hood—and whatever semblance of courage she could muster— and trudged back to the school campus.

The club's dance floor was overflowing. All the tables were occupied, the bar was completely camouflaged by the crowd, and bodies crowded every other available space, swaying to beating music.

The first beer went down easy, the taste and coolness coating the inner bitterness. Halfway through the fifth, Justin was feeling good—by the time he lost count, his mind was numb and beginning to forget he had ever cared.

It's been a while since I've had this much fun. It felt good to be with old friends again. Chris and Sarah sat across the table, Zack and Melissa on either side of him, with Tom-Cat at the end, ordering another round.

"Where's Rachael?" Justin yelled, leaning close to Zack to be heard above the music.

"She's not feeling well. She told me to go without her."

"Hey Justin, where's Katie?" Tom-Cat called from the end of the table, his words slurring.

A server arrived and set a full tray on the table, allowing Justin to feign distraction. Melissa stood and distributed the shot glasses.

"I propose a toast," she shouted, her glass dangling from a thin, raised arm. "To Justin. We're honoured he joined us tonight."

"To Justin," they all chimed in, clinking glasses in the centre of the table.

"Happy Valentine's Day everyone," Melissa said, her eyes focused solely on Justin.

———————

Rachael closed the door to their dorm room softly and stepped forward into the darkness.

"You don't have to be quiet. I'm not asleep." Katie rolled over and turned the switch on the bedside lamp. She squinted to check the time on her phone. "It's late," she said. In the pale light, Rachael's face was swollen and tear-stained. Katie pulled herself up in her bed. "Do you want to talk about it?"

Rachael dropped down beside her. "I'm pregnant."

CHAPTER
Ten

MADNESS FILLED AIDEN WITH EVERY THOUGHT OF KATE. It drove him to another and another, but it was all emptiness. The memory of her was like slow poison. The girl who had shared only a fragment of his life was now a relentless echo that sucked the here and now away. Would he always be riddled with remembrances of Katie Banks? They came unbidden, seeping into his thoughts like a disease he could never quite be cured of. Even tonight, as he dressed for another date, he caught himself thinking of her. The others were temporary remedies, their bodies a way to forget. But she was somehow carved into part of his being. He wanted to sear her away and start over, as if they had never met in what seemed another lifetime.

It had been over a year and he still couldn't completely let her go. Sometimes weeks would pass without a single thought of her, and then suddenly he would be hit with memories again. Thoughts would flood his feelings and torment his being. Her smile haunted him, even as it warmed him as though it were yesterday and they were once again sitting beneath the summer sun on their bench. He could still hear her laugh, feel her touch, the curves of her body; he would never find such intense beauty and love like that again. It was as though she was etched into his existence, like a tattoo in the skin, marking him for all time.

"Stop!" he shouted at the mirror in disgust, raking his fingers through his hair.

How could he have known that a few small decisions would cast him into this state of perpetual bondage? Why had he let her go? How had the words of agreement ever come out of his mouth? The questions poured in, riddling his mind with accusations.

Then there was the quiet, persistent nagging that plagued and pressed at his soul. It frequented his mind uninvited, illuminating the dark, empty cavern in his heart, speaking into the desolation and identifying the desire for it to be filled. A gentle yet relentless beckoning, drawing him in like a peaceful current, ready to receive and wash over him. Its ripples shimmered with invitation and held the promise of reconciliation and the assurance of rest.

But he hid from it.

To face it was too much. To receive it, utterly frightening.

He saw it for what it was even then. The intensity of Kate's faith was unnerving. He retaliated by closing himself off from it, trying to contain it. He attempted to keep her from God in order to keep her for himself. A jealous repulsion welled up in him at this faith that had ultimately taken her far from him.

He had let it happen. Even as every part of his insides screamed insanity, any fool could see there was no place for him in her life anymore. She had forsaken him to pursue this irrefutable passion, believing it was more important. Out of resentment he resisted its every call. He would never allow himself to follow this covetous love. A love that had stolen Kate.

They hadn't seen each other since; their lives had split in two separate directions. He left town that fall to study at the University of Western Ontario, hoping to forget her.

He was still waiting.

———

Zack felt helpless. Rachael wasn't herself at all. She wouldn't answer her cell phone or return his text messages. She had been suffering with a stubborn flu virus, but she should be over it by now. A vague thought seeped in. Was she deliberately ignoring him? He took a brief inventory and decided he hadn't done anything to deserve the cold shoulder. As far as he was concerned, they were having fun.

She was great in bed. The last time they'd hooked up, they'd stayed up half the night. It wasn't unusual for her to stay over on a Saturday night. They'd slept in, had breakfast together, and spent Sunday on schoolwork. They enjoyed being together. He couldn't think of anything that had gone wrong.

He *had* been a bit distracted lately. After several weeks of intense interviews, the job offers were coming in. Had he been too focused on which company would be the best fit? He frowned. That was important. After all, the culmination of his last year of university was just a few short weeks away, and he wasn't going to miss any opportunities to start his career. His plans were shaping up nicely. Even if he had been a bit driven as of late, he had managed to make time for Rachael. Was she angry with him for his divided focus? Was that why she was uncommunicative?

He had been patient but was getting tired of guessing. Zack reached for his leather jacket and thrust his arms into the sleeves. Time to go find out why his girlfriend was suddenly distant and unresponsive.

Aiden woke up in a fog. What was her name? He had forgotten—or had he even asked? He slid out of bed, careful to not disturb the woman beside him. His head swam and the room spun. He leaned on the bed frame to steady himself. His stomach lurched, and he stumbled to the bathroom in time to purge his insides.

Temporary relief swept over him. Relief from the sickness of too much. Followed by that staggering, insatiable emptiness. No amount of drinks, bodies, or accolades could fill it. Would he ever be rid of it? Tonight had been another vain attempt.

As he pushed himself up from the cold porcelain, a memory flooded in, of a time when Kate had stayed with him through a day like this. He had already vomited several times before she arrived. The look of disappointment in her gentle eyes still plagued him.

At first, he had tried to give up the weekend binges with his friends. She was too good for that, too good to be true for that matter, and he had wanted to be good—for her. She was so kind, so patient, so trusting. He couldn't believe she belonged to him. She made him want to be a better person, and he wasn't about to mess up. But he had. He lowered the toilet seat cover and slumped down on it.

The inevitable came. She tried to break it to him gently. That was her way. But in the end, he let her walk away. Residual pain pierced deeper, joining the ever-present ache. At least he could be thankful she left without knowing all of it. He'd never want to hurt her that way.

At the sink, he turned on the faucet. The cold water felt good on his face. A small tap sounded at the door.

"Aiden? You okay in there?"

He opened the door and the stranger stood before him, unclothed.

"Yeah, I'm fine."

"Fine enough for another round?" She smiled and tossed him a towel.

He dried his face, wiping away the wetness, and the thoughts of Kate, before following his date back into the bedroom.

"Oh Rach." Katie swung her legs over the side of the bed and sat beside her friend.

"I know. What a mess, right?" Rachael blew on her frozen hands. "I'm so stupid."

"Does Zack know?"

"No, and I'm not going to tell him."

"Why not?"

"It's not his problem."

"You didn't get pregnant by yourself."

"I know that, but we were careful. This shouldn't have happened."

"How are you going to keep it from him?"

"I'm not going to have it."

Katie swallowed, forcing back the words she wanted to say.

"Don't look at me like that. I knew you wouldn't agree, but I have no choice."

"Of course you do."

"Raise a baby by myself with no education? Yeah, some choice."

"I know things look bad right now, but don't rush into a decision."

Rachael sniffed and swiped a tear from her cheek. "The longer I take, the worse it will be."

"What about talking to someone who deals with this sort of thing? Maybe they could help."

Rachael shook her head. "I don't want some self-righteous religious person telling me how to live my life. I messed up, I need to fix it."

Katie wrapped her arms around Rachael's shoulders and pulled her in for a hug. At first Rachael resisted then she collapsed into tears.

For a long time, Katie held her friend, weeping along with her, not just for Rachael, but for the innocent baby she carried. *God, please help her.*

CHAPTER
Eleven

THE TERMINAL BUILDING GREW SMALLER AS THE PLANE taxied down the runway. Screens on the seatbacks displayed a safety video. A few rows behind Katie a baby cried, the man in the seat beside her coughed while unwrapping a throat lozenge, and a flight attendant with bright red lipstick brushed by. The smell of over-brewed coffee filled the cabin.

Katie opened her backpack and pulled out her itinerary. Her new address was scrawled across the top. The university admissions office had given her a few leads for housing arrangements, and she had managed to find a building in close proximity to the AUP. There were still a few unknowns, but her heart beat faster every time she contemplated the changes in her life, the opportunity for a fresh start. The thought brought a wave of relief in the shadow of the last two months.

It had been difficult to leave. A part of her felt as though she was abandoning her best friend, but Rachael didn't want her help. Once again, she thought about the decision Rachael had made and swallowed back the sudden urge to cry. How would her friend cope?

It could have been her less than two years earlier. She thought of the inconclusive pregnancy test, the dreaded trip to her family doctor, and the pink birth control pills the doctor had handed her afterwards. She remembered Aiden's relief matching her own, and the feeling of being extricated from a disastrous circumstance. Again she was struck by how entirely different her life could have been. Could she really blame Rachael for her decision to get an abortion?

The plane lifted off. Katie stared out the miniature window as Pearson International Airport grew smaller and smaller. The long lineup of commuter traffic on Highway 401 looked like far-away freight cars strung together, slowly slinking their way home. As the plane continued its ascent, thin clouds shrouded the view of the CN tower downtown, even though a late-day sun shone brilliantly over Lake Ontario and through the window of the 747, warming Katie's shoulder.

She leaned her head back and closed her eyes. At least leaving would ensure she wouldn't make the same mistake twice, and hopefully the vast distance would help her to forget.

Lord, give me the strength to enjoy whatever lies ahead and the wisdom to make sure I let go of whatever is not your plan for me. Don't let anything hinder my potential for growth. Please help Rachael deal with her choice. And help me to let go of my feelings for Justin.

"Excuse me Miss, would you like a blanket or a pillow?" The bright-lipped flight attendant stood beside her, smiling.

"Both please." Katie positioned the pillow behind her neck and opened the insubstantial cover, preparing herself to endure the time change and the eight-hour, red-eye flight.

She would be in Paris by morning.

Katie turned the thick key in the brass opening and pushed open the heavy door so she could wrestle her cases into the small apartment. It smelled musty, as if two hundred years of memories had soaked into its ten-foot high ceilings and scrawled their signature on the thick, raised wallpaper. Pushing the door shut with one foot, she wheeled her cases just inside the small bedroom that stood off to the right of the tiny vestibule. Sun shone through the window and onto the bed that dominated the room, leaving just enough space for an armoire on one side and a small dresser on the other.

Returning to the entryway, she tossed her key on the miniature marble table by the door. On the other side of the narrow hall, across from the bedroom, a thickly-painted door opened into a washroom with a pedestal sink, claw foot tub, and colourful mosaic floor tiles. She opened a second door to reveal a separate, closet-sized space housing nothing but a toilet with a pull chain hanging from a tank near the cracked ceiling.

Three steps from the bathroom and Katie stood at the opening to the kitchen that included a gas stove, half-fridge, and little breakfast nook facing into the main living space. There, a loveseat and chair, separated by a side table, occupied the narrow rectangular room. An antiquated television stood in the corner of the room on a simple, wooden stand. Tall glass doors flanked a pillar on the far wall facing the front of the building, making the small space feel surprisingly airy.

After pulling back the yellowed lace sheers, Katie smiled to find a quaint balcony with an ornate ironwork railing. She swung open the doors and stepped onto the terrace. The sun was rising above a row of apartments facing hers and seemed close enough to reach out and touch. Clothing hung over one railing of the adjacent building and a pair of sneakers sat outside the balcony door of another. Her neighbour's corner unit balcony uniquely curved to grace both sides of the stone façade, its glass doors propped wide open to reveal a man ironing inside.

She leaned out, peering down on the narrow street below where a man in overalls swept up debris. A flowering tree grew out of the cobbled sidewalk reaching just below the balcony. Birds sang from newly budding branches, from metal railings and heavily shingled roofs, finding their nesting places in the middle of the crowded city.

Katie would need to learn her way around Paris sooner rather than later. Classes began in a week. Before that, she planned to familiarize herself with the school, sorting out her courses, doing a bit of sightseeing, and finding a part-time job. A nervous excitement welled up inside her at the thought of the days ahead. Propping her elbows on the railing, she rubbed her hands together. Time to begin this new phase of her life.

———————

Rachael absently sprinkled flakes into Dumpling's bowl. Yesterday had been difficult for her. Katie had left for Paris, and now she was leaving too. The way her first year of university was being thrown away pinched at her mind. *It's for the best.* Her second semester grades had dropped substantially, and she would probably fail most of her courses anyway, but most of all, she needed to leave before the pregnancy became too obvious.

She could feel Zack's eyes on her as she pulled her photo frames from the windowsill and dropped them in the suitcase on top of her clothes. She could only hope her actions had convinced him that she no longer cared about him. When he had broached the subject the week before, she was purposely unresponsive. What if she opened her mouth and the truth spilled out? Besides, what could she tell him that might come close to making any kind of sense? What words were there to tell him how much she loved him, but that she had made a terrible mistake she couldn't let him pay for? That to keep it from him was tearing her apart, but to tell him would risk ruining his whole life and any future they might have built together? It didn't matter that this was making her more miserable than she thought humanly possible. That every time she looked at him she felt as though her heart was withering from some incurable disease. She'd make sure he never knew. She'd manufacture a lie, back it up with actions, and instead of a reciprocated fondness, all Zack would see was the growing distance between them.

When she refused to discuss her feelings with him, he grew angry. He tried to convince her she was making a foolish decision by leaving but finally gave up, clearly exasperated at her stubborn resolve and lack of attempt to communicate. Even now, as he watched her packing the last of her few belongings, he was still obviously struggling to understand why she was leaving.

"Are you sure about this, Rach?" He pulled a textbook from a cardboard box, only to flip through it and return it to the box seconds later.

"For now... until I decide what I'm going to do. Turns out Business wasn't the right program for me."

"You know I hope you come back and finish."

"I know." She smiled weakly, concentrating on zipping the suitcase.

"I love you, Rach."

She nodded, avoiding his gaze, and turned her back on him to make sure he didn't see the tears that sprang into her eyes without warning.

"There. That's the last one." She sealed the box with several strips of tape. Would he pick up on the fact that the action was more as a distraction to fill the awkwardness than a necessary task? When the risk of a full-out emotional breakdown had passed, she lowered herself onto the bed to rest.

"Hey, you two." Justin strode into the room, sidestepping a box that held open the door. He tossed a wrapped sandwich to each of them. "Thought you might be hungry."

"Perfect timing. We just finished." Rachael patted the bed beside her. Justin offered the spot to Zack and pulled up a chair by the desk.

Zack sat next to Rachael, tore the paper from his sub, and took a bite. Rachael left hers on the bed. "Excuse me for a moment." She closed the bathroom door behind her and clutched the sides of the sink, taking in several full breaths until the urge to vomit had passed.

Looking in the mirror, she tugged at her sweatshirt, trying to place it just right around her thickening waist. She was getting out of here in the nick of time. Any longer and she wouldn't be able to conceal her condition anymore.

Rachael sighed as she opened the bathroom door. Working to appear unfazed, she contemplated the sub, sitting in its wrapping on the bed. Just the thought of it made her want to vomit again. She swallowed instead.

Zack turned to Justin. "I'm worried. Can you talk any sense into her?"

Rachael glanced over at Justin. He wouldn't betray her. Would he?

"She just needs a bit of time to figure things out, right Rach?" Justin tossed his sub wrapper in the trash and stood. "You guys need a hand taking this stuff out?"

"That would be great. I already pulled Rach's car up to the back door."

"Finish eating. I'll get started." Justin hefted one of the boxes onto his shoulder and headed out the door.

Justin carried the box outside, grateful to be away from the tense atmosphere inside. It was hard to witness Zack's frustration with Rachael and keep quiet about its cause. Since his break-up with Katie, he and Rachael had grown closer. Initially, it was the result of him trying to make sense of why Katie had pushed him away. He had hoped Rachael would be able to offer a little insight to provide some relief to his misery. They talked for hours at the quiet pub, or in the girls' shared room while Katie worked longer hours than before at the studio. On one visit, Rachael had confided over coffee.

"I'm quitting school after this term," she announced, catching him off guard.

"What? Why would you do that?"

She bit her lip. "Promise you won't say anything?"

"Of course not."

"I mean... not to anyone, most of all Zack." She leaned over the table, staring intently at him.

"What is it, Rachael?"

"Promise me."

"Okay, I promise."

"Well..." she began, but the words didn't come. He waited, concern rising in the wake of her intensity. Her eyes were suddenly brimming with tears.

"Hey..." He reached across the table. "Are you okay?"

She shook her head. "I'm pregnant."

"Oh man, Rach, really?" He hadn't seen that coming.

She nodded, tears falling down her face.

"I found out in February. I'm almost three months along." She wiped her cheek with her sleeve and glanced around the coffee shop. "Thus the lovely sweatshirts." She laughed through her tears, tugging on the bottom of her bulky garment.

"And you haven't told Zack?"

"No. I can't."

"Why not?"

She looked at him as if asking if she really needed to explain the obvious. "He has his whole life ahead of him. I mean, he's doing so well, he's incredibly smart, and he'll totally make something of himself... but not if he has a baby to worry about."

"But what about you?"

She took a deep breath and shrugged. "I'll be fine."

Justin studied her. Her forehead was etched with deep lines, and dark shadows rimmed her eyes. "Rach, there's no way you can keep this from him."

"Yes, I can. I already have."

"Don't you think he deserves to know?"

"There's no way I'm going to mess up his life."

"Why don't you let him be the judge of whether a baby would mess up his life?"

"Look Justin, I've given it a lot of thought." Her eyes flashed. "I've made up my mind. And I don't want any pity."

"What's that supposed to mean?"

"Zack might feel obligated."

"Rach, you can't do this alone."

"Don't you get it? I don't want him to be with me because he thinks he *has* to be. You can understand that, can't you?"

He nodded, working through the possibilities in his mind.

"Have you told your parents?"

"Are you kidding? My mother would go crazy."

"Does Katie know?"

She nodded. "She was going to stay. Can you imagine? Giving up that kind of opportunity to help a dumb friend through a stupid mistake."

He could imagine it... all too well.

"You're not dumb, Rach."

"How could I have let this happen to me?"

He squeezed her hand. "There's not a person out there who hasn't made mistakes. That doesn't make you dumb—it makes you human."

"But this? I mean, this isn't just any mistake."

"Yeah, it's a tough one, but I know you'll get through it."

She exhaled, not looking up from her mug. He hated how defeated she looked.

"How did you convince Katie to go, anyway?"

"I told her my plans."

"What plans are those?"

"To have an abortion."

He blinked. "But, you haven't yet, right?"

"No. I guess I've been procrastinating."

Justin watched as she traced the scratches in the wood laminate table then, with shaking fingers, brushed away the tears that fell and filled the carved crevices.

"Listen, Rach." He handed her a napkin and spoke as softly as the noise in the room allowed. "Whatever you decide is okay. It's up to you. You have a choice, right?"

"I guess."

"I'll be there for you. I'll even go with you if you need someone to come. Just do what's best for *you*. That's what's most important."

"That's the problem. I don't know what's best." She dabbed at the endless flow. "But you're a sweetheart for offering."

"Are you sure you don't want to tell Zack?"

She tossed the crumpled napkin onto the table. "That's one thing I am sure about."

Before they parted, she had made him promise once more to keep her secret. He'd assured her he wouldn't say a word, but as Zack's confusion escalated, Justin began to think he had made a poor decision.

Zack joined Justin at Rachael's car, weighed down with a couple of boxes.

"So you're staying here for the summer?" Zack placed the boxes on top of the closed trunk.

"Yep. I start work on Monday."

"At the place here in town?"

"Bridgeman Engineering, yes. They're doing some pretty cool projects, so it should be good. How 'bout you?"

"I'm heading out in a few days. No big rush, but no sense staying around here either. I don't start at Coldwell Banker until next week." Zack flipped the passenger seat forward.

"Commercial Real Estate, right?"

"Yeah, in Toronto. See if I can pay off these last four years of school."

"No kidding." Justin winced, thinking of his own mounting debt.

"This isn't exactly how I pictured this year ending."

"I know what you mean."

"I don't get it." Zack shook his head and reached for one of the boxes. "Why the 180 degree turn?" He loaded the container into the back seat.

"Hey, I wish I could help you, but apparently I'm no expert myself."

"Has Rachael said anything to you? I mean you two have been hanging around together lately and she's definitely not talking to me. She hasn't been herself for weeks, though. Any idea what she's thinking?"

Justin chose his words carefully. "I know she's having a hard time right now."

"Yeah, I think so too. Getting sick during midterms didn't help. I know that has something to do with it. Plus, I don't think things are very good at home. But to change so much?" He let out a long sigh. "Maybe I should just let her go."

"Give it some time. Pretty sure she needs a friend right now."

"You seem good at that."

He wasn't sure how to take the accusation he heard in Zack's voice and decided to ignore the comment. "Are you going to visit her?"

"I would, but she says she doesn't want me to. I asked her if we can meet for dinner sometimes and she said she didn't know. We've been dating all year, and suddenly she doesn't know? What am I supposed to do with that?" Zack shoved the second box into the back seat with a little more force than necessary.

"Keep doing what you're doing. Don't give up on her."

"She's not giving me much to go on. It takes two."

"Yeah, but sometimes one has to carry the other."

Zack shot him a sideways glance. "Very profound. How'd you get so smart?"

"Watching my parents mess up." Justin slammed the car door, relieved that, for the moment, the conversation had moved away from Rachael.

"Maybe you should take some of your own advice." Zack slapped him on the back as they turned and headed back for another load.

Justin thought about the irony in Zack's comment. He did have a proud stubbornness that rendered him incapable of taking the action his heart most desired. It was easier to look at a friend's situation and pass on advice than risk taking it himself. He shrugged. It didn't matter now; Katie had given him no choice.

Once the vehicle was fully packed, the three of them stood in the empty dorm room, delaying the impending goodbyes with small talk. A solitary nail, the one that had held Justin's photograph of Katie, poked out of the bare wall, a stark reminder of their fleeting relationship. All that remained were two beds in a plain room that now looked like it belonged to no one in particular once again.

"Justin, before you go, I have to give you something." Rachael went to the barren-looking window ledge and picked up the fish bowl. Turning, she held it out to him.

"I can't take that." He held up both hands. "You said she asked you to look after it."

The fish circled the glass enclosure, its mouth rhythmically opening and closing.

"And I'm entrusting him to you," she said, thrusting the fish bowl into his arms. "Whatever you do, don't overfeed him."

"Great. We better write his last will and testament now." He relented and took the bowl from her outstretched hands.

Rachael laughed and hugged him goodbye. "Thank you. You're a good friend."

Justin turned and gave Zack a brotherly slap on the back before heading out of the room and leaving them alone, standing together in the middle of the barren room.

CHAPTER
Twelve

SPRING IN PARIS WAS MAGICAL. THE AMBIANCE OF THE bustling city was energizing. Katie faced her first full day with the same wonder a young child might on Christmas morning. She woke at dawn and, wrapping her robe around her, carried her cup of tea out onto the balcony. Two dainty wire chairs waited like old friends eager to spend time. She picked one and sat in the golden glow of early morning, watching the city wake up. She soaked in the sights, everything so new it made her feel that all kinds of adventures awaited her.

Yesterday, she had unpacked and organized her clothes into the drawers and armoire, making the best use of the limited space. She went for groceries and found the area surrounding her apartment had the feel of a small village within this great city, filled with its own distinct character. The narrow streets were lined with small, quaint shops; a few vendors, temporarily idle, stood outside their doors welcoming the spring sun and passing customers. Petite cafés jutted out onto the sidewalk. Servers decked out in white shirts and black vests, aprons tied around their waists, prepared tables and opened umbrellas to shade the tidy place settings from sun or sudden rain.

Katie took a bit of time to memorize the streets and their names to familiarize herself with at least this part of the sprawling city. At a newsstand, she bought a map of Paris and went to the nearest underground stop to obtain another that would show the routes throughout the city. She would learn the way to her new school and other attractions she would visit in this week before classes began.

This morning she planned to visit the university to make sure all her courses were in order and wander through the school to learn where all her classes were offered. Tomorrow, she would go to the Louvre, and the following day Musée d'Orsay. She planned to walk to the Notre Dame Cathedral, which she had experienced only in her art history textbook, and then take a boat tour along the Seine River to visit the Eiffel Tower and L'Arc de Triomphe. Another day would be set aside to visit Montmartres, the famous art district. All of which she had only ever hoped in a far-off dream to see.

Such a sense of excitement rose in her that she had to force herself to linger on the balcony, knowing it was too early for anything else. Peering down at the street below, Katie watched as a woman on a bicycle came bumping along the cobbles and stopped outside a shop door. She leaned her bicycle to one side to hop off, and from the basket fastened in front, picked up a bundle wrapped in brown paper and tied with string. After fumbling in her coat pocket for a moment, she produced a set of keys. A bell clanked against the door's glass front as she disappeared inside.

Moments later, a stooped man with hands clasped behind his back meandered past and paused in front of the window. With some effort, he lifted his arm and waved at the shadow of the woman inside.

All these people living their lives, so different from her own. Katie sighed. *How quickly will I become fluent in French so I can communicate with them?* After taking a last sip of tea, she gathered her robe in tighter and, shivering from the slight chill in the morning air, moved inside, filled with anticipation for the day ahead.

———

Rachael sat on the edge of her bed and took one last look around the room where she and Katie had spent their first year of university, still dabbing her cheeks with a soggy, disintegrated tissue. She had managed to say goodbye to Zack without shedding a single tear—had kept from him the truth of the agony she was in, and the baby she carried—but now they came, pure misery pouring out of her body.

She tried to take solace in the fact that she had managed to successfully release him. Now he could pursue the life he'd so carefully planned. The look on his face these past weeks, as she'd attempted to convince him she no longer had feelings for him, haunted her, but she told herself it was for the best. He had his life ahead of him, and she loved him too much to take that away. Now alone, and feeling the choking weight of her circumstance, she crumbled under the exhaustion and months of pressure.

A hard knock startled her and she leapt to her feet. Thinking it might be Zack returning, she mopped her cheeks dry. "Come in." When the door opened, there stood the last person she wanted, or expected, to see.

"Hey Rachael. Havin' a bad day?" He swaggered into the room.

"Tom." She couldn't keep the coldness from her voice. "I've had better." She stuffed the tissue into her sweatshirt pocket. *Why is he here?*

"Figured I'd stop in and say goodbye. Zack told me Katie left for Paris. Thought maybe you'd be takin' it hard."

Rachael blinked. That was uncharacteristically kind of him. "Yeah, it's hard. She's been my friend a long time."

"Zack said you two split up."

Rachael's stomach tightened at the words; they had such an edge to them, a finality. Slightly nauseated, she sank onto the edge of Katie's bed. "Yeah, I'm not coming back next year."

"Too bad. I wanted to ask you out sometime... thought maybe we could finish what we started."

Rachael's head jerked. "What did you say?"

"It'd be nice to finish what we started." He crossed the room and sat down beside her, leaving no space between them. She inched away.

"What do you mean by that?"

"New Year's Eve? Don't tell me you don't remember."

Rachael's face grew hot, and she squeezed the damp, crumpled tissue into a ball inside her pocket. Panic rose, licking at her raw nerves.

"What about New Year's Eve?" She struggled to sound calm.

Tom-Cat squeezed her knee and smiled. "No need to pretend anymore, Rach."

His hand inched up her leg, and Rachael pressed her own over his to stop it.

"I don't know what you are talking about." Bile rose in her throat, but she swallowed it back. All she remembered of New Year's Eve was that she'd had a few too many drinks and passed out before midnight.

"Don't worry, I never told Zack."

"Never told him what?" Her legs began to shake.

"Thought I'd keep it to myself, you know, just between us. But we had a good time."

His crooked smile broadened and she could smell the alcohol on his breath.

Unable to hold back the sick feeling, she covered her mouth with her hand and ran to the bathroom. A horrible coldness swept through her, then a dizzying, rushing heat. She reached for the vanity but missed and fell to the floor.

CHAPTER

Thirteen

ZACK TURNED THE KEY TO THE FRONT DOOR, BALANCING the bag of groceries he'd picked up after working out at the campus gym on one hip. Just before entering, he noticed the garage door ajar. Exhausted from his paltry parting with Rachael, he made a mental note to close it before dark and went in the house.

He placed the grocery bag on the counter and dropped onto the couch. The exercise had failed to provide the usual rush of endorphins. Disappointment had turned to anger, which, having no outlet, had left him entirely drained.

When had he ever let a girl get in the way of his plans? If he was going to fall in love for the first time, why did he have to go and choose Rachael as the girl? He had dated many, known most of them intimately, but Rachael was the first he'd ever envisioned a future with. It figured she had to be the woman who didn't see one with him. Maybe if he'd realized it sooner, if he hadn't waited until he had lost her to figure out he loved her, he could have done something to save their relationship. Now it was too late.

He forced himself to get up off the couch and return to the kitchen to unpack the groceries. The job devoured all of three minutes. For lack of something better to do, he dragged himself upstairs to his room. Maybe he could go through his notebooks and pack a few things.

Sorting through the piles of textbooks and binders brought the last four years of his life into sharp refocus. He had worked hard to get where he was, not letting anything else in his life spiral seriously out of control. Rachael had been a wild card—unexpected and exciting. But maybe it was just as well they ended it now. *Better to start out in the real world with a clean slate.* Unfortunately, in his current state of mind, the piles of books representing untold hours of toil felt as pointless as the past eight months of his life with Rachael.

An hour later, he headed downstairs with a bag of garbage. He was about to drop it in the entryway to take out later when he remembered the garage door. Exhaling loudly, he grabbed the bag and stomped out to the garage. Grasping the handle, he heaved on the rusting door that grinded heavily on its rollers, protesting the very operation it was designed to perform.

He saw the feet first. Looking up, the incomprehensible reality struck like an agonizing blow, knocking the breath from his lungs. His roommate hung from the crossbeam, his face grossly distorted and barely recognizable.

A primeval sound clawed at Zack's throat as he dropped the garbage bag and ran to Tom. He wrapped his arms around the dangling legs to hold up the weight of the body. Then, craning his neck, he held on, screaming for help, waiting for someone to hear him.

———————

Rachael woke up face-down on the cold floor. She struggled to sit up. *How did I end up in the bathroom?* A shudder convulsed her body and a pulsing pain pounded at the side of her head, blocking out any recollection. She reached up to touch the painful spot. When she held out her hand, it was covered in crimson.

Fighting the urge to scream, Rachael held onto the side of the bathtub for stability and pulled herself up. Once standing, she wavered a moment then rested her head against the wall, waiting for the dizziness and throbbing to subside. When the room stilled, she staggered to the sink. At the sight of her reflection in the mirror, she cried out. Her hair was matted and saturated with blood, and the bathroom tiles had left an imprint on her face. With an unsteady hand, she turned the cold water tap and reached for a facecloth. Pressing the cold, wet cloth over the place it hurt most, she began dabbing. The dried blood in her hair was stubborn and took more work to remove.

As she scrubbed, she searched her mind, trying to unlock what had happened. She remembered saying goodbye to Justin and Zack, but nothing else. The redness swirled around the sink as she squeezed and rinsed the facecloth.

She resumed wiping the side of her face. The room felt so cold. She shivered uncontrollably.

———————

Katie stood at the front of the crowded tour boat as it motored along the Seine River. Like many of the other boats, it was filled with tourists whose voices competed with the tour guide's blaring over the crackling speaker. She tipped back her face to the warmth of the spring sun, favouring the open air to the cramped, glassed-in quarters. From the vessel's bow she soaked in the many sights, seeing the Eiffel Tower and Notre Dame Cathedral properly for the first time. Even at a distance, they were both more magnificent than she had imagined. She could hardly believe she was living in Paris and would have months to explore and enjoy it.

From her brief first visit, the university seemed an inspiring place to study. The campus was a cluster of historic buildings in close proximity to the Seine and Eiffel Tower. Even though this was only her second full day in Paris, the University of Waterloo, and her short time there, seemed so far away. In the excitement of travel and settling in, Katie had managed to push aside thoughts of home. But now memories of Justin floated at the edges of her mind, competing for space like the barge boats bobbing at the sides of the Seine. Hopefully the stubborn memories would soon be crowded out altogether by the noise of the larger, more pressing happenings in her life.

———————

Rachael opened the bathroom door. She struggled to make her way to the hallway that was just three steps away and much closer than the phone.

Open the door, just open the door. Her head felt thick and dull, her mind swimming, her thoughts trickling out slowly like the crimson fluid seeping from the side of her head. Everything was growing dim and strangely far away. Using her last remnant of strength, she tugged the door open and collapsed into the hall.

———————

Zack sat across from the police officer. He had told the paramedics the little he knew, then allowed the officer to lead him back inside, away from the desperate scene. His hands still shook and he squeezed them together in an attempt to still them. The image of Tom's twisted face would not flee but kept flashing before his eyes until, in complete despair and helplessness, he dropped his face into his hands and wept.

He sobbed like a child, his insides groaning. It didn't matter to him that the uniformed man sat across from him, waiting to question him. Why hadn't he seen it coming? Why couldn't he have been there? The questions scraped the recesses of his mind. He should have known; after all, he was Tom's roommate. He was ashamed to admit that he hadn't noticed a sign of anything wrong. Tom had been his old self that day. In fact, earlier he had seemed even happier than usual. Zack hadn't noticed anything different, he told the officer, whose gaze was steady but sympathetic. Still, he felt tortured.

The officer closed the door behind himself on the way out. Zack stood, a frozen figure in the front window, watching as the paramedics wheeled the gurney out of the garage. They hoisted the stretcher and placed his housemate into the back of the ambulance. The doors closed, slamming in finality, as if shutting off Tom's life. Then the ambulance drove away. No lights. No urgency. Nothing.

———————

Early Wednesday morning of her first week, Katie stepped onto the balcony with her cup of tea to watch the world wake up. The woman arrived on her bicycle, the old man scuffed along the street and waved to her from the sidewalk. A few minutes later, when the same woman placed trays filled with beautiful pastries in her front window, an idea struck Katie and she decided to visit the bakery later that afternoon.

The day turned busy, much of it spent at the university where she purchased her books and art supplies and further acquainted herself with the campus. She returned home to read through her course material, and by the time she finished, it was growing late in the day. She set aside her papers and headed outside, running the idea she'd had earlier over in her head.

The afternoon sun was beginning to cast its soft, orange glow onto the buildings. Standing outside the bakery window, Katie contemplated the remnants of jelly and chocolate stuck to the parchment paper where once fresh pastries had beckoned. She took a deep breath, pushed open the door, and entered the shop. The bell banged against the wooden frame of the glass door, louder than it had seemed from the balcony and rudely announcing her arrival.

The woman working behind the counter with quick, deliberate movements looked up briefly as Katie entered. "Bonjour. Puis-je vous aider?" she said, asking if she could help Katie while closing a plain, white box around a delicate cake.

"J'ai besoin de travailler. Can I be of some service to you?" Katie asked her as boldly as she could.

"Êtes-vous une boulangère?" The woman stuck a gold embossed label over the folded opening of the box.

No, she wasn't a baker. Katie shook her head. "I am willing to do any job you require, though." Was her French okay? Could the woman understand her?

The woman pursed her lips. "Where are you from?" she asked her in French.

"Canada."

The woman smiled broadly, her double chin tripling. "I have a niece who moved to Canada. She lives in Ontario, a city called Oakville, do you know this place?"

"Yes, very well—it's about an hour from where I live."

"What brings you to Paris?"

"I am going to study at the AUP."

"Très bien! How long will you stay?"

"Just a year."

"And you need some work to help with your studies?"

"Yes, ma'am." Katie hadn't been sure it would, but the more she spoke in French, the more it came back to her.

"Well, you seem to know enough French to get by, and your English would be helpful with the tourists. I could use some help behind the counter and with deliveries and clean up. I can only give you fifteen hours a week though."

She spoke in French, but Katie managed to decipher most of her words. "C'est parfait!" Katie clapped her hands in unconcealed excitement.

CHAPTER
Fourteen

RACHAEL STOOD AT THE BOTTOM STEP THAT LED TO THE abortion clinic, staring up at the nondescript brick building. *I wish Katie was here.* The wound on her head was almost healed, and only a slight scab remained in place of the removed stitches. The bruising around her eye had changed from blue to purple then yellow and could now be concealed with well-applied liquid foundation.

She shuddered, remembering how she had awakened in the hallway to the sound of a blaring siren. When next she gained consciousness, she was riding in the back of an ambulance. Her eyes had flown open as she pressed a hand to her stomach. Her mother or Zack would discover the truth about the baby! She had struggled with the straps around her hips. When she couldn't release herself, she began to scream and kick. The paramedic had spoken quietly yet firmly, attempting to comfort her while lowering her back down onto the gurney. The exertion had slipped her back into unconsciousness.

When she woke up, she was in a hospital bed. A nurse stood over her, checking her blood pressure. A voice drifted across the room. Rachael slowly turned her head on the pillow as a doctor moved towards her, lowering a chart he had been checking. He stopped at the side of her bed and sat down on a stool.

Hello, Rachael." He had a kind face and spoke to her gently, looking directly into her eyes. "I'm Dr. Milton. How are you feeling?"

Something about the way he had spoken and the concern in his eyes made speech impossible. Her eyes filled. He had already discerned her situation. She wanted to turn away, but the tubes and blood pressure cuff around her arm prevented it, multiplying her sense of lost control.

"I'm glad you're awake. You're at Grand River Hospital."

The nurse undid the Velcro fastener, tugged the strap from her arm, and left the room.

Dr. Milton rested a hand on the bedrail. "We were a little worried about you and your baby. Can you tell me how you got hurt?"

She closed her eyes in a vain attempt at shutting out the world. The pain in her head was intense and she fought to manage it alongside the inner pain of her circumstances.

"Rachael," the doctor softly urged. "Can you tell me what happened?"

She had managed only a slight shake of her head. The doctor sighed. After a moment, he left the room, though Rachael could hear him speaking with the nurse in a low tone outside the door. He instructed her to check on Rachael frequently and said he would follow up again before his shift ended.

She had turned and drawn her knees in toward her chest. *How did I end up on the bathroom floor?* The last face she remembered seeing was Zack's, filled with a mixture of disappointment and sadness.

If only Katie had been there—she would have done the talking for Rachael. She would have explained everything and stayed with her. Instead, Rachael had felt the cold arms of loneliness envelop her, just like she did at this moment, as she faced the door to the abortion clinic without Katie. Swiping away a few stubborn tears, she drew in a deep breath and pulled open the door to the clinic.

Her eyes widened at the number of women in the waiting room. Rachael found a seat next to a table with magazines fanned out on its top. Grateful for a distraction, she pulled one into her lap and opened it. The words and pictures blurred as she flipped through the pages. What would Katie have said if she was still here? Like Justin, would she have offered to come with her? Rachael thought of how one of their last conversations about the pregnancy had ended.

On the night she told Katie she was pregnant, they hadn't slept. Katie hadn't spoken much, just listened quietly, for which Rachael was grateful. It gave her the chance to sift through her emotions and the space she needed to try and make sense of it all.

Two weeks later, as Rachael ate in silence across the table from the father of her unborn child, she listened to words that seemed make-believe.

"Justin told me Katie's leaving in April," Zack said.

The news came as a secondary jolt, like the aftershocks of an earthquake. Katie leaving in the spring to go to school in Paris? Realization flooded in. Wrapped up in her own misery, Rachael hadn't given Katie the chance to share her news.

Zack frowned. "You didn't know? I'm surprised she didn't tell you."

"Yeah, me too," Rachael had mumbled, before changing the subject.

That evening at dinner, she had confronted Katie.

"Zack told me yesterday that you're leaving in the spring. When were you going to let me know?"

"I wasn't," Katie replied.

"Why not?"

She shrugged. "I decided not to go, so there really wasn't a reason to say anything."

Rachael had watched her play with the spaghetti on her plate, twisting it in relentless circles. She saw the movement for what it was, a vain attempt to hide how much that decision was costing Katie, and she pushed back her shoulders.

"I don't need your help on this one, Kat." She reached for her glass of water. "I've decided for sure not to have it."

"Not have the abortion?"

Her friend's face brightened and a stab of pain shot through Rachael. She wished she had even a small measure of Katie's hope and courage. "No." She shook her head. "The baby."

The light faded from Katie's face. Rachael waited for what she might say or how Katie might inflict her morals on her. But she said nothing. At least, not then. How could Katie understand that it felt as though the last reserves of strength were being sucked from her soul alongside her dreams, or that she had searched her mind for another option but found none? Unable to put it into words, Rachael could only stare at her friend.

"It's my choice," she finally forced herself to say, attempting to sound more certain than she felt. "It's my life."

"But, Rach, it's a human b—"

Rachael flung up a hand. "I don't need a sermon. Can't you for once just listen and not judge?"

The words had their intended effect, and though a part of her was instantly sorry, she continued, gathering angry momentum. "I can make my own decisions without your input. And, in case you haven't noticed, we're not kids anymore; you can't save me this time." Her words ended in a choked cry, and she stood abruptly, pulling on her jacket.

"Rach..."

She paused at the door. "And don't bother cancelling your trip."

The words had spilled out much harsher than she had meant them to. Katie hadn't deserved to be the target of her frustration. It wasn't her fault that Rachael was in this mess. Even so, why couldn't she just understand?

Now, after pushing Katie away, Rachael needed her more than ever.

———

Even though it added to her already full schedule, Katie loved her job at the bakery. Despite the pressure of juggling work and school, when Madame Bonnard asked if she could increase her hours, she agreed to continue with three weekdays, add on the busiest part of the day on Saturday, and still have Sundays off.

Katie admired Madame Bonnard's work ethic and appreciated the way she enjoyed her customers. Although perpetually in motion, she always took time to listen to customers' stories, and Katie's respect for the woman who laboured unceasingly without complaint grew.

With her increased work hours, Katie disciplined herself to make it to school early enough to fit in two hours of painting before classes began. Relishing the stillness of the morning hours, she used her studio time wisely, painting every spare moment. After she finished work at the bakery, the evening was set aside to complete any outstanding coursework.

She had little time for much else. Less and less frequently did she think of what her life had been just a few weeks before. During the occasional quiet moment, unwelcome reflections still came, arriving between customers at the bakery, disguised as a stray thought over a sentence read too many times, showing up between classes, mid brush stroke, or before sleep—bringing unmet longing and its close companion: loneliness.

During those times, her thoughts often turned to Rachael. Her heart ached for her friend's troubles, and the child she would never know. Katie channelled any disappointment over Rachael's choice to abort her child into school and work, making every effort to learn the language and culture. French language courses were a requirement at AUP, and she was determined to become fluent in the Latin-based language.

In spite of these purposeful distractions, she would at times catch her mind lingering over a moment spent with Justin. The simple, everyday things would come to mind. The way he liked to spend time in her cubicle and watch her paint, how he told jokes until it became difficult to steady her brush, the way he brought her hot chocolate with whipped cream, or the warm feeling that rose inside when she caught him studying her when he was supposed to be studying his books.

How had he adjusted to their break-up? Had he settled in at his co-op placement? Most of all, had he met someone else? The latter was a hard thought for her, and although she wasn't meant to be with him, it niggled at the back of her mind. At times, she could clearly see his dark curls hanging carelessly around his face or over his warm brown eyes. Other times, she could scarcely remember his features at all. Katie wasn't sure which of those was harder for her to bear.

CHAPTER

Fifteen

RACHAEL'S HEART POUNDED. SHE PLACED A HAND ON HER chest, took in a deep breath, and exhaled slowly. Was anyone else conflicted by this decision? No amount of distraction could mask the solid lump that had settled in her chest. It had been there for weeks, and now dread added its grip.

What if I got up and left?

Scanning the waiting room added to the chaos churning inside her. A girl who appeared no older than fifteen gazed at the hands she had clasped in her lap, fiddling with a tissue. A fashionably-dressed woman who looked to be in her mid-thirties leafed through a magazine, and a teen to the right of the woman slouched in her chair texting and smacking her gum.

"Rachael?" A nurse called into the waiting room.

Rachael followed her through the reception area on legs that behaved like lead posts, and into a stark, sterile room where the nurse instructed her to undress before leaving the room.

Rachael pulled off her socks and shoes. When her bare feet met the tiled floor, a shiver swept up her spine. She unfolded the crisp white gown and placed it on the table before yanking her T-shirt over her head. Her protruding belly jutted out above jeans too tight to fasten the top button, a visual reminder of the mistake she was about to reverse.

She slid onto the examination table and sat with her legs hanging over the side, waiting. Her heart thumped so hard now she could barely breathe. *I should have asked more questions.* She hadn't wanted to know the details. She just wanted it to be over. They had said she could return to most activities the next day. She wouldn't even have to miss work. *No one will ever have to know.*

Rachael looked up when a small tap sounded on the door. The doctor entered, a nurse behind him. The doctor glanced at the chart in his hand then removed his glasses. "Rachael Meyers?"

Rachael nodded.

"I'm Dr. Stafford. Nice to meet you." He held out his hand. "This is my assistant, Jennifer. Do you have any questions before we begin?"

"Yes." She clenched her jaw to keep her teeth from chattering. "Will it hurt at all?"

"The fetus or you?" Jennifer asked.

For the first time Rachael considered the baby's life.

"Uh, both?"

"You may experience some discomfort during the procedure." Dr. Stafford shot the nurse a stern look. "But the fetus is virtually unaffected at this stage." He began washing his hands.

Virtually unaffected.

The nurse helped position the pillow behind Rachael's head and placed her feet in the stirrups. Lying with her legs stiffly separated, staring at the various steel instruments while Dr. Stafford switched on a lamp, fitted his face mask into place, and pulled on latex gloves, increased Rachael's dread. As soon as this was over she could put it all behind her, return to school, and move on with her life. It would be like nothing had ever happened.

———

"Are you ready to begin?" Dr. Stafford moved to the end of the table and sat down on a stool. He reached for one of the instruments on the stainless steel tray.

"Take a few deep breaths and just relax," Jennifer said. "Would you like a stress ball to squeeze?"

Would she need one? "Um... yes please." Rachael took the ball and automatically squeezed even though they hadn't started yet. She wanted to look away, but she couldn't take her eyes off the tray of instruments. She began to feel nauseated.

"Are you in school, Rachael?" Jennifer asked.

"No, not at the moment."

"So, you're working then?"

"Yes." She ran her fingers across her damp forehead.

"Are you feeling okay?" Dr. Stafford asked, glancing up from the tool he was removing from its plastic wrapping.

"Actually, I don't feel very good. Can you give me a second?"

Jennifer helped her sit up and reached for a small plastic bowl. Panic rose in Rachael. She didn't know if it was a result of the nausea or the procedure. Her heart raced and she couldn't find her breath. The room was getting smaller.

Jennifer slid something around her upper arm. The voices in the room grew distant and Rachael felt dizzy. Dr. Stafford was standing beside her asking her something, but his face was blurry and his words wouldn't register. She heard her name being spoken from far away and then the darkness took over.

———

"Rachael? How are you feeling?"

Rachael opened her eyes. Jennifer stood beside the table. Where was Dr. Stafford? Was the procedure over?

"You weren't feeling well. Dr. Stafford stepped out for a moment. He'll be back in a few minutes then we can continue."

Rachael sat up and her head felt light. Jennifer reached to steady her.

"Your blood pressure was a bit on the low side. I'll just check it again."

"No, it's okay."

"I need to before we proceed."

"I've changed my mind. I don't want to go ahead."

"Oh, I see." Jennifer frowned. "I understand it can be a confusing time. Maybe it will help to remind yourself why you made the decision to begin with."

Rachael swallowed. "I'm not sure they were the right reasons." What had changed? Why was she saying this? She reached for her clothes. Jennifer refolded the blood pressure monitor and slid it into the holder.

"Well, maybe you just need a bit more time to make sure. But I'd advise you not to wait too long." She slid the table holding the tools to one side. "I'll let Dr. Stafford know. Do you need a hand getting dressed?"

Rachael shook her head. Jennifer handed her a brochure before closing the door behind her. Rachael exhaled. She slid off the table and began to dress with a faint feeling that she had somehow escaped disaster.

The waiting room was fuller than before. None of the patients were the same. The frosted glass door swung shut behind her as she stepped out of the clinic into uncertain confidence. For a moment she stood on the sidewalk then her legs gave out beneath her and she sank down onto the steps as tears of relief and hardship poured out.

CHAPTER
Sixteen

THE EARLY MAY SUN WARMED KATIE'S BACK THROUGH THE
bakery window as she tied her apron around her waist. Madame Bonnard whisked
past. "Katie, I need three orders delivered, including one to Café Pierre. Très
important... a new customer." She pointed to a stack of boxes on the counter.

Katie untied her apron and scanned the order forms, noting the address
of the new place. She'd walked by Café Pierre but had never gone inside. She'd
go there first. After folding her apron and tucking it beneath the counter, she
reached for the first stack of boxes. She transferred the majority into the small
trolley attached to the back of Madame's bicycle. The remaining white boxes,
held closed with delicate, gold-embossed seals, she secured in the front woven
basket. Katie cautiously balanced the bike between her legs as Madame Bonnard
rushed out the shop door.

"Pour toi." Madame handed Katie a croissant, partially wrapped in a napkin.
"You need more ici." She pointed to Katie's hips then motioned with her hands
for Katie to take a bite, watching to ensure she obeyed.

After swallowing a mouthful, Katie patted her stomach. "Délicieux." Madame
Bonnard beamed as Katie tucked the rest down the side of the basket to finish later.

It had been some time since Katie had ridden a bike, and never one laden
with precious pastries over cobbled streets. She took a deep breath and pushed

off. It took some careful manoeuvring through the clusters of people and cars that occupied the uneven side street, but she gained confidence with every block.

She arrived in front of Café Pierre minutes later, relieved that her load remained unscathed. Propping the bike against the side of the stone building, she began to unload. Balancing several boxes in her arms, she reached a hand from underneath her pile and pushed the door handle. When it failed to open on the third try, she banged on the door with her foot and waited. No one answered, so she adjusted the boxes, balancing them in one arm and propping them against the door for extra stability. She knocked again.

Without warning, the door flew open. As if in slow motion, her precious load landed at the feet of the man before her. Katie groaned. Madame's beautiful tortes were a magnificent mixture of chocolate, cream, and cherries, randomly infused with candied orange and berries and partially buried in white cardboard and gold seals.

Katie stood in the doorway, clinging to the only box that hadn't made a quick descent, heat rushing into her cheeks. She gaped at the mess on the floor, and at the man's cream-smattered black trousers and shoes, trying to summon the courage to make eye contact with Madame's new customer. Before she could, she heard a low sound that grew from a chuckle to a full-blown laugh. Katie looked up. Lines creased the corners of the young man's brown eyes as his mouth curved wide open and he threw back his head. The sight of this was all the relief she needed and, without restraint, her laughter joined his.

When their laughter faded, he pulled out a handkerchief and made a wiping motion beneath his bearded chin. When she didn't move, he reached for her. Katie instinctively pulled back, but when his handkerchief came away with a lump of cream, she understood.

She muttered an awkward "Merci" and placed the cake box on a nearby table, then bent down to try to undo the mess. "Je suis sincèrement désolée."

"Non, non, Mademoiselle. C'est rien."

She stood again, expecting to be handed a cloth. Instead, the man took her by the elbow and led her away from the mess and into the restaurant. He stopped in front of the bar, pulled out a stool, and motioned for her to sit.

"I'm fine." Katie spoke in careful French as she waved her hands in front of her.

He was insistent, and she slid onto the stool as he spoke a quick word to the bartender, who must have seen the whole thing. To her relief, the bartender behaved as though he hadn't noticed and simply asked her if she would like a drink.

"No, thank you." She shook her head emphatically. She'd caused them more than enough trouble already.

Moments later, the man in the black trousers returned with a bucket of cleaning supplies. Katie jumped off the chair to help, but he smiled and waved her away. "A sparkling water for the young lady," he instructed the bartender in French. The bartender nodded and set the cold drink in front of her.

It took all her might to watch the clean-up effort without helping. The man showed no sign of aggravation and set about wiping the floors on his hands and knees as if he did this sort of thing every day. Moments later, he stood beside her—the floor spotless, his trousers and shoes the same—offering a smile while brushing aside the flow of apologies.

"Let me ride back to get replacements for you," she offered.

"No need to worry. I called Madame Bonnard and ordered more cakes. Finish your drink. I will go and get them while you continue with your other deliveries."

She stared back at the stranger, dumbfounded by his kindness, amazed at his graciousness, and sorry that "Merci beaucoup" didn't seem sufficient thanks.

––––––––––

"I used to come here a lot during school. Introduced Katie to the place, too."

Justin could now say Katie's name without his mood darkening. Most of the time. The ending of their relationship had been like a slow recovery from a debilitating sickness. He told himself he was over her now—a little scar tissue, perhaps, but nothing too severe. He had moved on to a new stage in his life and, despite forced optimism, looked toward the future. He and Rachael were even keeping their promise to stay in touch by meeting at The Grill for lunch.

"Thanks for bringing me here. I had the worst craving for a greasy burger."

Justin laughed. "This is perfect then. How have you been feeling?"

"The sickness is mostly over, but honestly… I feel fat."

"You look great, Rach."

"Thanks. I'm trying to walk every day after work, but sometimes I'm just way too tired."

"I bet. It can't be easy being behind a counter on your feet all day."

"It's not that bad. Helps me keep in shape."

"And how are you feeling about your decision?"

Rachael had called him when she arrived home from the clinic three weeks earlier. He listened to her brief explanation about why she had changed her mind, made sure she was going to be okay, and asked if she wanted him to drop by. She didn't want any company, but requested he stay on the phone a while, which he'd been happy to do.

"Okay to have the baby for sure, but the rest is the tricky part, you know?"

"Then maybe I should be asking how you are feeling about your decision not to tell Zack."

She frowned. "Give it up, Justin. I made up my mind on that, and I'm not going to change it."

"Even if it makes you miserable?"

She shrugged. "How's your job going?"

Okay, I get it. You don't want to talk about it. He sighed. "I really like it. They've got me working on a condo project, so I'm busier than ever. But I don't mind, it keeps me occupied."

Rachael reached across the table and covered his hand with hers. He could pretend he was over Katie, but so far no amount of work could completely erase the feelings he had for her. And Rachael could clearly see that.

"I talked to Katie this morning."

"Oh yeah, how is she?" He tried to act casual by gently pulling his hand out from under hers and sipping on his drink.

"Doing really well. You know Katie—she could fit in anywhere. She's working part-time at a pastry shop and said the school is excellent."

"That's great. I'm happy for her."

"It's hard though, isn't it?"

"I guess. But not as bad as it was at first."

"Do you think you two will ever get back together? I mean, when she comes back?"

Justin shook his head. "It wasn't so much her going away, but more her perspective on life. It was a big deal to her that I'm not into going to church."

"I know what you mean. She had an experience a while back and it changed her in a big way. She's pretty serious about it, too; she told me she'd never marry a guy who didn't share her faith."

"She told me that early on too, and even then it sounded kind of exclusive."

"It does, doesn't it?"

"I guess I thought I could get her to change her mind." He let out a short laugh. *What a fool.*

Rachael shook her head. "Not Katie. Sweet, but stubborn. Did she ever tell you about Aiden?"

The server, a young woman with a blonde ponytail bouncing between her shoulder blades, slid the burger and fries onto the table in front of Rachael and handed a turkey wrap to Justin. "Do you need anything else?"

"A refill please." Justin held up his empty glass.

"And mustard," Rachael added.

When the server had gone, Justin leaned in. "So what about this Aiden guy?"

"Well, they were really serious the last year and a half of high school, even though they were total opposites. I was surprised she went out with him at all. She was one of the most popular girls in school, if not the most, even though she was a "good girl", if you know what I mean. And Aiden was a real partier. Well, whether she got tired of being so perfect or what, I don't know, but when I saw her with him for the first time, I nearly died."

The server set the mustard beside Rachael's plate and smiled at Justin as she handed him his drink and turned to go back to the kitchen. Rachael squeezed the mustard on her burger, reassembled it, and took a bite. "Sorry, I'm starving."

"No, go ahead. You're eating for two."

"Sadly, yes. Who knows what I'll look like when this is over?"

"Just as beautiful as before."

"Thanks. You're good to have around," she said, taking another bite.

"So what happened?"

"They went out for the spring and summer and then she moved to England."

Justin's forehead wrinkled. "She never told me any of that."

"I'm not surprised. I'm only bringing it up 'cause I think it might help a little. After about five months or so, she moved back here to be with him, and they picked up where they'd left off. She was living with this family who went to church, and she went some Sundays, too. One week she came back all excited and talking about how she was *saved*. From then on, it was downhill. Aiden was ticked off and didn't want her going to church, but she was super stubborn about going. From what I could tell, he was a pretty jealous guy and didn't want to lose her, but not long after that, maybe two or three months, they finally called it quits."

Justin raised an eyebrow. "You mean *she* called it quits."

Rachael waved a fry through the air. "She said it was mutual. Anyway, I'm telling you because she decided right there and then that her faith was more important than anything else. She picked *it* instead of him. She explained everything to me at the time, and even though I don't quite understand it, I admire her for it."

Her voice held a wistfulness that he understood. Rachael missed her friend. "I get it. It means I lose." He smiled then, trying to lighten their shared loneliness. How had Rachael managed to see through his facade and the lingering feelings he barely admitted to himself?

"She reads her Bible every morning and night, and prays a lot. And she's really disciplined and self-controlled."

"You can say that again."

"Sometimes I don't agree with her, and she can come across as close-minded, but she's still the best friend I'll ever have."

They were both silent for a moment then Justin cleared his throat. "Thanks. That sheds some light on things." Katie's words ran through his mind: *I'm a Christian... I can't get serious with someone who doesn't understand or share my beliefs.*

Rachael set down her burger. "You okay? Maybe I shouldn't have brought it up."

"No, I'm glad you did. It helps."

"You better eat. You're making me look bad."

"Sorry." He took an absent-minded bite of the carrot he'd been turning around between his thumb and finger.

"Have you heard from Zack?"

"He called me a couple of weeks ago. He's enjoying living in Toronto and likes his job but says it could be a little more challenging. He even talked to me a little about what happened with Tom."

"What happened with Tom?"

"I didn't tell you? No, I guess I never did. It happened around the same time you went to the hospital, and I didn't want to upset you, so I didn't tell you about the funeral."

Her head jerked. "Whose funeral?"

Justin hesitated. "Tom's."

Her eyes grew huge. "Tom's dead?"

"Yeah. He hung himself, Rach."

She slumped back as if his words had pushed her against the booth. "That's horrible; do they know why?"

"I don't know, but Zack was pretty hard on himself about the whole thing. This was the first time he talked to me about it."

"Poor Zack."

"Yeah. He was the one who found him. Shook him up pretty badly."

Rachael leaned her head back against the booth and closed her eyes, but the tears found a way out. He took her hand. Her life was hard enough right now, without this added burden. As much as he disagreed with her decision not to tell Zack about the baby, he admired her strength and the way she loved Zack enough to let him go. Her reaction to the news, and obvious concern for Zack, confirmed to him that she was still struggling and still very much in love with him.

"Are you okay?" He let go of her and handed her a napkin.

She nodded, dabbed at her face, and produced an almost-convincing smile.

———————

Zack sat at his desk, clenching a pencil so tightly that it grooved deep indents in two of his fingers. He understood he was the new kid, but he already had two considerable deals on the table and several others in the works. Why would his bosses not give him more authority? It seemed those in upper management were trying to hold him back and force him through the ranks of some unspoken hierarchy. The pencil snapped in two and he tossed it onto the desk. Climbing the ladder one painful rung at a time just wasn't his style.

He was accustomed to diving into projects, having full control, and seeing them through to fruition. Maybe that's why the post-university job interviews and aptitude testing had suggested he would be difficult to manage. Still, being held back from doing what he had been hired to do made no sense to him. His aspirations were too high to be suppressed. He needed—no, craved—a challenge. He also needed patience.

Adding to his frustration was the fact that Rachael had no desire to keep in touch. Early on, he'd tried her number and listened to an automated voice tell him, "This number is no longer in service," with no forwarding number to call. His pride prevented him from asking Justin for her contact information. For someone who relished a challenge, and had a knack for making things happen, having two parts of his life so out of his control was enough to drive him out of his mind.

Falling in love hadn't been part of the game plan. He'd nearly managed to make it through school without getting serious with anyone, to stay focused, until Rachael. Things had gone well with the two of them, until it hadn't. He was still bewildered as to how things had suddenly turned sideways. Was there an easy way to by-pass this hurt? Sometimes anger displaced it, until he would recall a moment shared with her and his heart refilled with the empty ache and longing. Good thing work offered a distraction.

Flipping open his laptop, he adjusted his tie—and his attitude—for another day at the office. He would pay his dues like everyone else and wait for things to fall into place.

CHAPTER
Seventeen

THE MID-JUNE SUN SHONE THROUGH THE LACE CURTAINS, and Katie pulled them aside to step onto her balcony with her morning tea. The quaint space was her own little piece of Paris, an outcrop from which to reflect and watch the world go by. On this one day there was no work, no rushing, only the beautiful ease of a quiet day.

Summer term was in full swing and, despite the full course load, Katie had managed to stay several days ahead of completion dates. Sundays were still her day off. After church she visited galleries, the local park, or enjoyed various sidewalk cafés. By her fourth visit to the Louvre, she knew the location of certain paintings without consulting the floor plan. Even though it meant staying up late during week nights, having one day off a week was worth it.

In the stillness of the early morning, she closed her eyes and prayed, lingering and letting the sun's warmth soak in. She would go for a run before the streets became busy then go to Sunday worship. After that, she planned to visit Café Pierre. Despite their initial awkward meeting, the proprietor, Jean, always received her warmly, and offered her a cold drink and friendly discourse on her deliveries. There was nothing romantic in their interaction, but they were rapidly becoming good friends. When he found out she was studying art, he told her she must visit Montmartre and offered to take her this afternoon.

Jean possessed a carefree manner and warm smile that made it easy to feel comfortable in his company. He made running a busy café look simple. Katie hadn't asked Jean's age but guessed late twenties. She was thankful for his offer of company. No better way to learn about the culture and city than being escorted by a local.

Gazing up at the pale morning sky, Katie's thoughts drifted to her mother and their phone conversation the day before. Her mother was putting their house up for rent in order to stay in England and help Katie's grandmother. Her chest ached for her mother. How had she managed both the pain of being left by her husband and coping with a young daughter on her own?

Katie leaned back in her seat. Where was her father now and what had his life been like since he left them? Was he still alive? Did he ever think about her? Why had he never tried to contact her?

As she always did when the loneliness threatened to overtake her, Katie closed her eyes and prayed, thanking God that he was with her and had promised to never leave.

———————

Jean took on the role of tour guide, telling Katie all he knew about Montmartre and the area. She was delighted to learn how much he knew of the great artists such as Toulouse-Lautrec and Picasso, who had frequented the then "shady" area of town. She marvelled at the looming Sacre Coeur, taking in the spectacle of architecture, the street artists, and crowds of tourists. Jean introduced her to his acquaintances who worked at nearby restaurants or gift shops and took her to his favourite crêperie.

Mid-afternoon, Jean ushered Katie onto a street artist's stool. "Sit nice and still."

The artist affixed a fresh sheet of drawing paper to his easel then began her portrait. Under the scrutiny of the artist's careful eyes, Katie concentrated on not moving. It didn't help that Jean made silly faces at her from behind the artist's back. When she burst out in laughter, the artist muttered something in French she couldn't discern.

Although under the shade of a large umbrella, the afternoon heat and forced composure tried Katie's patience. *Why is he taking so long?* When the artist looked from her face to his drawing, she rolled her eyes to show her exasperation. To her relief, Jean caught on and began fanning her with a menu from a nearby table while telling her a joke. At the punch line, they stifled their laughter like misbehaving schoolmates in trouble for fidgeting in class. The artist gazed at Katie over his spectacles. The charcoal in his blackened hand trembled.

Katie tilted her head. "Est quelque chose de mal?"

At first he didn't respond. Did he think she was speaking to Jean? Was he angry? After she repeated the question, asking him if he was unwell, he shook his head and muttered under his breath, returning his attention to the paper.

———

At her apartment, Katie unrolled the thick drawing paper and stared at her half-finished portrait. The artist hadn't charged her. Midway through the project, he'd excused himself, saying he was not feeling well. "You will return another day, mademoiselle?" he'd asked, the unfinished drawing shaking in his outstretched hand. He'd looked so chagrined, she could not refuse. What he had completed was excellent, and clearly her. How many portraits did he draw every year, and did he make a decent living from it? She rolled the paper back up, slid the red ribbon around the roll to fasten it, and placed it in her side table drawer.

———

Katie sipped her punch and tried to appear confident and composed. Standing inside the gallery's entrance at the student exhibit, her insides were in knots over what the general public, not to mention the discerning critics in Paris, might have to say about her abilities as an artist. What if they hated her work?

Jean called out to her as he entered the gallery with a broad smile. He kissed her on either cheek and grasped her hand. "How are you doing?"

"Very nervous."

"I can tell." He chuckled and squeezed her trembling fingers. "So, which are yours?"

She glanced around before pointing discreetly. "They're over there."

Jean studied the growing crowd gathered around the central wall.

"How did you get the prime location?"

"My classmates decided. They didn't give me a choice."

He let go of her and joined the crowd, moving in close to each piece, slowly backing away, and finally returning to where he had left her.

"Kaitrin, they're amazing. I had no idea you were so talented."

"Merci. But I still have much to—" To her horror, he grasped her hand and pulled her into the middle of the crowd. "What—?"

He pressed a finger to his lips. "Listen."

Katie tried to tug her hand free, but he held on tightly until she stilled and began to take in the discussions and compliments being made about her work. When she started to turn away, embarrassed, he pulled her to his side and began introducing her to people in the crowd.

Between fielding questions, Katie caught a glimpse of a man in a high-collared white dress shirt and tailored suit who appeared to pay no regard to the crowd's chatter as he stood in front of her paintings. He showed particular interest in the one entitled *Luminous Horses*.

During a reprieve in conversation, Katie turned to join her classmates at the dessert table. As she made her way across the room, she was intercepted by the man in the suit. "Excusez-moi. Can you tell me how much for that one?" He pointed to *Luminous Horses*.

Katie floundered for an answer. This was meant to be an exhibit, not a sale. She had no idea what to ask for her work. After a short pause, he offered his own price, clearly taking her silence for a negotiating tactic. "Will you accept one thousand euros?"

Katie fiddled with one earring. Was the man serious? She met Jean's gaze, but he only shrugged.

The man who'd been looking at her painting frowned. "I'll give you one thousand, five hundred euros."

Just as she was about to accept his offer, a voice from behind interrupted the negotiation.

"Two thousand euros."

Katie turned to face the street artist from Montmartre. He studied her with the same strange expression he'd worn the day he'd drawn her portrait. "Your work is remarkable. So beautiful and well-executed."

Katie shifted awkwardly. "Merci beaucoup."

"We share the same passion."

She contemplated his bright blue eyes beneath grey eyebrows. Why did he look so familiar? As far as she knew, she had never seen him before, other than the day he'd tried to paint her portrait. After several long seconds, the artist turned his attention to the man in the suit.

Katie stood and listened as the two men jostled over the painting. Jean stepped to her side and whispered in her ear. "What's he doing here?"

Katie shrugged.

"Do you want to sell the painting?"

She managed a nod. That amount of money would help pay for much-needed art supplies.

At her consent, Jean took over and organized the bidding that had escalated to three thousand. Eventually, the man in the white shirt dropped out, and Jean announced, "Sold, for three thousand, five hundred euros to the gentleman in green."

CHAPTER
Eighteen

RACHAEL LOOKED DOWN AT HER TUMMY AND GROANED. At seven months she had thought she was huge, but now, only two weeks from her due date, she couldn't imagine her belly getting any bigger. *I'll never wear a bikini again.* Pulling at her sweater in an effort to stretch it, she bemoaned how tight it had become.

Just yesterday, she had received a message from Katie. Her friend's inspiring news and stories about Paris always made her smile. Rachael looked forward to seeing Katie's posts with pictures of the places she visited. She was happy for her, even though she continued to fight the painful tug of loneliness from her absence. It grew especially difficult when she saw photos of Katie with Jean or her new university friends. The feeling had intensified the past few days, knowing she could go into labour at any moment and would face the experience alone.

Justin had been amazing and had done so much for her. She didn't know where she would be without him. But anxious thoughts and uncertainties plagued her. Most days she coped hour by hour, any more than that was too much. She spooned a few mouthfuls of cereal into her mouth, struggled to tie her shoes, and rushed to catch the early-morning bus. For the third time that week, she would work a ten-hour shift at the grocery store checkout, in addition to the other three eight-hour ones, and try not to think about how she would pay her bills this month.

———————

A meticulously-manicured poodle and its owner brushed by Katie's table outside Café Pierre. Katie wiped the charcoal from her fingers and took a sip of coffee, taking a break from the street scene she had been drawing. Jean was working the Saturday afternoon shift, bringing her refills of coffee between customers. Passersby paused to regard her work, and patrons called to her by name. Katie rarely missed a sketching opportunity, and since Madame Bonnard had given her the afternoon off, she was making use of the spare time while she waited for Jean to finish for the day.

Both managed busy schedules, but even in the little time they found, they had forged a strong friendship. She could always count on Jean to amuse her with a story or joke. At first his forthrightness unnerved her, but he was so good-natured that she soon grew to understand him and feel safe when with him. He had a way of disregarding her defenses and encouraging her to say what she really meant, instead of letting her give the politically-correct answer. He offered her counsel when she came up against a difficult choice or problem, and helped her look at life from a different perspective.

Every time Katie glanced up from her work, Jean was moving through the café, stopping at each table to visit with guests. He reminded Katie of a stagehand who, from the sidelines, made sure the show ran smoothly while supporting and encouraging those around him. She admired his work ethic, his relaxed manner, and his ability to put people at ease.

He seated a regular at a table next to Katie, and she caught him asking about her husband and making a fuss over the woman's purse-sized puppy, Chloe. *How does he remember all their names?* She watched him unfold a napkin with a flourish and pretend to tie it around Chloe's neck. The woman laughed and stroked the dog's miniature head with one hand while squeezing Jean's arm with the other. When he was satisfied she was settled, he came over and rested a hand on Katie's shoulder. "I can be done here in about twenty minutes. What do you want to do?"

"I don't know... why don't you show me another of your local haunts?"

"Oui, d'accord! I know just the place." He swept up a pile of dirty dishes from a nearby table and disappeared inside.

———————

"You're doing great, Rach! Keep breathing."

Rachael clutched Justin's hand, taking in several greedy gulps of laughing gas. The pain was so intense that she closed her eyes to shut it out, to concentrate, to will it to be over.

"Not long now. This one's almost over in 10, 9, 8..."

The counting was good—it gave her something to focus on.

"Good, now try to relax in between."

Easy for him to say. She drew in a cleansing breath and opened her eyes.

Justin brushed sweaty strands of hair from her face and smiled. "Are the pillows okay?"

She nodded, motioning for the cup of ice chips.

Justin grabbed the cup and held it out to her. "I'm so proud of you. Not long now."

She was grateful for his presence, and his encouragement, although she longed for Katie. Thankfully, Justin was a good substitute—he'd even come to prenatal classes with her. At that time, she'd wondered whether she would be embarrassed with him in the birthing room, but his presence seemed natural and comforting.

The last time she was in this hospital, she had been disoriented and suffering a concussion for a reason she couldn't explain. The baby was fine, the doctor had assured her, but he was frank about her need to take care of herself. She recalled his lengthy questioning concerning her head injuries and bruises, no doubt assuming she had been abused. "Here comes another one," she gasped, shoving the plastic face mask over her mouth and inhaling deeply. Less than a minute since the last contraction. Frantic breathing... more reassuring words that sounded as though they came from far away... then slow, momentary relief.

Between contractions, and just as methodically, her thoughts shifted to Zack. A vacant, aching place had been carved out inside her, reserved for mourning the beautiful relationship they had once shared. At first, it wracked her insides as deeply as these birth pains. Now, only from time to time did the ache drift through her body, painfully undelivered.

The day of the concussion and subsequent hospital stay was the last time she had seen Zack. Dr. Milton had been cautious about visitors. During Zack's short visit, the doctor remained in the room, scribbling on her chart and checking her vitals much longer than necessary. His kind face had transformed to a harder, less open one around Zack, his eyes betraying his watchfulness.

Thankfully, he had been discreet about her condition so that Zack left the hospital room and—at her bidding—her life, still unaware that she was pregnant with his child.

The tears had long since dried up, the ones shed for Zack at least, and although the months passed in emotion-numbing monotony, they hadn't yet disclosed how she came to need five stitches in her head. Time had managed to uncover emotions she had never before experienced, feelings that reached their climax the day she entered the Women's Choice Clinic.

Rachael sucked in a sharp breath. From behind closed eyelids she heard Justin's steady, reassuring voice as another contraction pressed mercilessly upon her. She squeezed his hand and moaned.

Justin spoke into her ear. "It's okay, Rach. The doctor's here. It's okay…"

Someone told her to open her eyes. It wasn't until she forced them open that she realized she was screaming. Seeing the doctor positioned at the foot of the birthing table, speaking sternly to her, shifted her focus from the pain to the man who would help bring her baby into this world.

"Okay Rachael, next contraction, I need you to push," he instructed.

She squeezed Justin's hand harder, forcing herself to find courage.

———

They took the RER, the express train connecting Paris with its outlying suburbs, in the direction of Orsay-Ville. Jean was secretive about where they were heading. He distracted Katie with questions about her week as they rushed beneath the streets of Paris. Three metro lines later, they alighted at École Militaire.

The magnificent day highlighted the splendour of the Eiffel Tower. The late afternoon sun spent its glory on the intricate structure that towered over the sidewalk, tall and majestic. It was a sight Katie could never tire of.

"I know you have been before, but I do not think you have seen it at night." He smiled, looking pleased with himself as he took her by the arm and led her up the steps toward the entrance. Thankfully, the queue was nowhere near as long as the one she had waited in five months earlier when she first saw the monument.

"You wanted me to take you to a local haunt," he said, a boyish grin animating his features, "Elevator or stairs, mademoiselle?" He bowed, indicating the tower with a flourish of his hand.

She laughed. "Merci, monsieur. The stairs, s'il vous plaît."

He bought their tickets and soon they were ascending the first level. Climbing had appeared daunting when she had first visited the tower, but once they got started, it was easier than expected.

"An hour before sunset is the best time to be here. You will see. But I think it is an amazing sight to look over Paris at night, too." Jean climbed two steps above her.

He was right. From the top, the late-day sun cast a hazy, dreamlike film across the Paris skyline. Cirrus clouds, layered like soft waves and tinted with various pinks, blues, and oranges, formed a glorious sunset. *I wish I'd brought my camera.* Her phone would have to do.

Jean led her to each side of the tower, pointing out the different landmarks. Together they took in the world far below, appearing like a slow, soundless motion picture. Little by little, darkness wrapped itself around them, like a navy blanket being pulled into place. The lights below winked pale at first, but soon they shone and twinkled from all around, dancing, sparkling, and competing with the starry sky.

"You were right." She clapped her hands. "This is a sight to see."

They leaned over the railing, and the rest of the world seemed to stand still; the bustle from below felt like an altogether different universe.

"You had to see this while in Paris."

"Yes, it's amazing. Thank you, Jean." She squeezed his hand.

"What are you thinking?" he asked.

"I'm wondering why you don't have a wife or a girlfriend."

"I do." He lifted her hand to his mouth and kissed the back of it.

"Seriously," she said, tilting her head as she looked up at him.

"Okay, I will tell you my story of misery." He smiled, but Katie caught the tinge of sorrow it contained.

Jean pushed back his shoulders, as though mustering strength for a long journey he wasn't sure he wanted to take.

Katie bit her lip. Maybe she shouldn't have asked.

"Her name was Chloe. She was with me for three years. We planned to get married, but one day she arrived at the café and said she was done with us." He gazed out at the deepening skyline and shook his head. "She said she did not like the hours I had to keep at the café, that we did not have enough time together, and then she left."

The pain was palpable in his voice.

"I did work hard. The start up of the café took much time to make it successful. I was very focused on doing it well and had to make many sacrifices...

I guess some things just are not meant to be." His voice resonated with quiet remorse, then a soft sigh of acceptance, and finally, no words at all, his thoughts as distant as the ground below.

For a moment, a strange stillness settled over them, even as people moved past them like water around rocks. Katie's heart echoed his loss. She understood all too well the emptiness that followed a breakup and tumultuous weeks and months of letting go. Finally, Jean pulled back from the memories.

"And you, what is your story, Kaitrin?" He turned an endearing smile to her, his jovial spirit reclaiming his features.

"My story?"

"Yes, I want to hear it. But wait." He held up a hand. "Are you hungry?"

Katie pressed a hand to her stomach. "Starving."

"We'll go then. I know a place to sit and talk."

Jean led her along the dimly-lit streets as they threaded their way between meandering tourists. Within a few minutes, they were viewing the illuminated Eiffel Tower from a narrow side street lined with quaint restaurants. They stopped at one of several establishments where tables spilled out of the restaurant into the canopied sidewalk. The proprietor knew Jean by name and welcomed him warmly, making a fuss of pulling out the chairs and setting their table with fresh white linen.

Two hours later, the two sat at the cleared table, sipping coffee and sharing stories. Jean asked Katie questions in such a way that she found herself telling him more than she had ever told another human being. Some of it she offered hesitantly, the act of putting words to certain feelings daunting. To offer another person a look inside, to be as vulnerable as he was asking her to be—as he had been himself—meant establishing a whole new level of trust. Was she ready to be in that place?

"Why Paris?"

The question drew her from her musing. "You know why. For school." From his frank gaze, she wasn't going to get away with a comfortable answer. "It was an amazing opportunity."

"It is very far from home."

His comment floated between them like the foam that clung inside her coffee cup. She licked off her spoon and set it beside her saucer. "Yes, it is a long way."

"No one to keep you in Canada, eh?"

She smiled at the comic relief. "No, not really..." She adjusted the white napkin on her lap. "There were a couple of guys but... not really my type, I guess."

"And why not?"

She shrugged. Had she ever really considered what her type was apart from God-fearing? She opened her mouth to give a generic reply, but instead found herself speaking Aiden's name aloud for the first time in many months. It was impossible to tell her story without speaking of the ways God had led her, protected her, and loved her. This was, after all, the essence of why she and Aiden hadn't stayed together. She figured Jean wouldn't understand, but he had asked, and so she told him.

"You still love him."

She laughed, attempting to shove away the truth.

"You do. I can see that you do."

"Jean, it doesn't matter."

One of his eyebrows rose in doubtful speculation. "What about the other man?"

She shifted in her chair. "Not really worth getting into." Sweet, thoughtful Justin. She beat back the threatening sadness.

"Will you return to Canada?"

"Eventually, I suppose. I do love Paris, though, and AUP. I guess I'll know by the time the year's up where I will go next." She sighed.

"Well, if you happen to stay in Paris and become a starving artist, you can always count on a meal at Café Pierre," he teased. "But, given your great talent, there will not be much chance of that."

"Thanks. I'll keep that in mind, just in case."

"You know I can always use a little cake-tossing fun."

"Hey, it's not my fault your old door sticks."

"No, but it was very entertaining."

They chuckled at the memory.

Katie lifted her glass in his direction. "Thank you for tonight, and for being such a good friend. If I do decide to go back, I hope you'll visit so I can pay my debt and take you around to my favourite places."

He clinked his glass to hers. "It's a deal."

———

The dark void finally released its grip on the secrets it held. Rachael woke in the hospital from a nightmare so real it took a few moments to discern reality. She sat up and gathered her bearings, letting her surroundings register. The smell of antiseptic filled her nose. Her roommate snored. The clock on the wall read 3 am. It was the third night she had spent in the hospital, her newborn son in the nursery nearby, sleeping in an incubator and hooked up to oxygen until the fluid in his lungs drained.

Her mind insisted on replaying the nightmare she'd just awoken from. Although the room was warm, she shivered. She was riding a Ferris wheel at an amusement park. Tom-Cat sat next to her, laughing while she struggled to get off, to get away from him. But the ride was broken and they were stuck at the top. She managed to open the safety bar and begin climbing down just as the ride resumed. For a few seconds she dangled from the steel beams then she fell. She woke up just before she hit the ground.

Was it true that if you fell in a dream and didn't wake up before you hit the ground, you could die? Regardless, she had woken up and somehow her mind awakened with her body and unlocked months of fog and uncertainty.

Tom-Cat's words pierced her mind like a poisonous injection. *New Year's Eve... no need to pretend... never told Zack... just between us... we had a good time.* The sickening words flooded in, stealing security and robbing her of the very strength she had desperately struggled to assemble.

It was this truth Dr. Milton had unsuccessfully tried to pry the lid off, and that she herself had searched her mind to recall. Now it returned in relentless waves. She remembered his hand on her leg, his nauseating words, how she had run into the bathroom to vomit, and how the dizziness had overtaken her.

A second sick feeling, worse than the first, now descended on her. Had he had his way with her a second time, after she fainted? Her mind staggered under the weight of the newly-recalled information. She and Zack had always been careful to take precautions. Now her situation began to make sense.

Rachael turned her face into her pillow, not wanting anyone, including her roommate, to hear her cry. She woke to a damp pillow and her new baby, the result of Tom-Cat's crime, crying to be fed. A nurse in scrubs covered with brightly-coloured animals stood beside her bed, waiting to hand her the sudden stranger. Once he was placed in her arms, a consuming sense of detachment crept through her, numbing her emotions and the very hands that held the newborn child.

"Rachael, are you feeling okay?" The nurse frowned and moved closer to the bed.

"No." Her arms wilted as she stared at the tiny, helpless human screaming in her lap.

"Let me get you a drink of water. Do you feel sick?" The woman retrieved a thermometer from her tray and placed it in Rachael's ear. The nurse handed her a Dixie cup of water before strapping a cuff around her arm to take her blood pressure. It all happened in a matter of seconds, but Rachael still couldn't seem to find the strength to feed her baby.

"Take a drink and I'll get you some food. Maybe you need to eat. But right now your little one needs his momma's milk." She helped Rachael position the baby.

Rachael scarcely felt his lips latch around her breast as he greedily suckled the milk that flowed as readily as her tears.

———

Katie tucked the mail under her arm and unlocked her apartment door. After closing it behind her, she reached behind the bathroom door to grab a towel. Dabbing sweat from her forehead, she stepped out onto the terrace to cool down and stretch. She sifted through the mail and stopped at the sight of an unfamiliar logo above the return address on one of the envelopes. She unfolded her towel, draped it over the chair, and sat. Katie tore open the envelope—the owner of a local gallery had invited her to show her work in an upcoming exhibit.

She read the card again, this time more slowly, letting the words register. This was just what she'd been aiming for. Heart pounding, she set the card aside and methodically started her stretching routine as she soaked in the wonderful thought of having her own show. *I'll need more paintings.* Reality set in. Her schedule was already filled with classes, assignments, and work at the bakery. How would she find more time?

She held a stretch a long while, took a deep breath, and prayed.

———

The other side of Rachael's hospital room was crowded with guests who surrounded the new parents, laughter spilling out the sides of the curtain drawn between the two beds. Her roommate's husband regaled his audience with their birthing story. The assembled crowd laughed especially hard at the part about him thinking his wife had given birth to a blue alien. The sound of wrapping paper and excited exclamations drowned out the sobs of the nineteen-year-old girl behind the curtain in the next bed. Her heart cried out, a silent scream into the deafening loneliness, as she stared down at the tiny stranger suckling at her breast.

An hour later, the food tray had been removed, its contents untouched for the second time that day. The rattle of the meal cart grew fainter as the elderly gentleman who had come to collect her tray pushed it down the hallway. Rachael closed her eyes. At the sound of a gentle knock, she opened them again.

"Come in," her roommate called out.

"How are you doing, Rachael?"

"Dr. Milton..." The small voice that responded didn't sound like her at all. Even speaking had become an effort.

"Congratulations. How was the delivery?"

"Painful." She attempted a small smile.

"I heard it's a boy. Did you name him yet?"

"Yes, Jack." She fingered the plastic hospital bracelets, one for her and a matching one for Jack, and stared out the window to hide the tears that filled her eyes. The doctor couldn't know that she had purposely chosen a name close to what she had thought his father's was. To her, saying the name aloud now seemed like a farce.

"I like it. It's a strong name."

He waited a moment, maybe to give her a chance to speak, but she was beyond small talk.

"And how's little Jack doing?"

Rachael sighed and turned away from the window. "He has some fluid in his lungs. We need to wait until it clears before they'll let us go home."

"I bet you're restless to get out of here."

She shrugged.

He pulled over a chair and sat. "Rachael, when I saw you back in April I was a little concerned. You appeared to have a slight case of amnesia. Did you regain any memory of what happened that day? Did you ever figure out how you got that nasty bump on your head?"

"I'm pretty sure I fainted. I mean, I remember being in the bathroom and feeling dizzy."

"Was anyone with you at the time?"

She met his concerned gaze. Could she trust this man she hardly knew? She twisted the stiff, white sheets as a distraction for her trembling fingers.

"Yeah," she finally said.

He waited, but she offered nothing more.

"Let me be open with you. It's my job to make sure my patients are carefully treated and to ensure their well-being to the best of my ability. I need to be honest and say that the last time I saw you, I was a little worried about discharging you, and more than a little concerned about your situation. So, if you want to talk about it, I'm here to help, or at the very least, to find someone who can."

No one can help me now.

When she didn't respond, the doctor leaned forward. "Can I ask a personal question?"

She nodded.

"Are you with Jack's father?"

Tears slid down her cheeks, forming dark blue circles on the worn, blue hospital gown.

"Do you have anyone to help you?"

She shook her head, making futile attempts to wipe her face with her fingers.

"What about your parents?"

"They don't even know," she managed between sobs. "They think I'm still in school, but I left last spring."

"So you're obviously not living at home."

"No, I have an apartment. I worked right up to the last day and have enough money for another month's rent. After that…"

She looked down at her damp gown. *After that I have no idea what I will do.*

————

"Here we are." Jean stopped in front of a red brick building with a massive front window. After Katie had shown him the invitation, he'd told her he was familiar with the gallery and would take her there to see it. "It's a well-known venue, renowned for showing new or upcoming artists."

Katie's chest tightened. "Really?"

"Oui. Art lovers come here to see the most recent works of art, buying pieces before the artist became celebrated and the price of their work rises." He waved an arm in the direction of the window. "It has a great atmosphere. Very lively and current."

Katie could see what Jean meant as she peered in the front window at several large, bold pieces. He touched her back lightly. "Should we go in?"

She bit her lip. "Oh, I don't know. I'm not dressed …" She looked down at the jeans and running shoes she'd thrown on when Jean suggested walking to the gallery.

"You look lovely, as always." He pushed her gently toward the door.

Katie pushed back her shoulders. If she really wanted to be an artist, she needed to start acting like one. She pushed open the door and stepped inside to the light tinkling of bells.

A woman in her mid-forties, dressed in a chic white blouse and black pencil skirt, approached them. "Bonjour. Can I help?"

"Hi, I'm Katie Banks." Katie held out her hand.

"Katie, hello!" The woman shook her hand warmly. "I'm Noel Grise. You are one of our new artists, non?"

"Well, I'm not sure about that. But I did receive your invitation. Thank you."

"Of course. One minute. I'll get my husband." She went to the back of the narrow space and opened a frosted glass door. "Patrick?" she called, disappearing through the opening. Seconds later she returned with her husband and introduced him to Katie.

"We saw your work at the student exhibit. You caused quite a stir." His smile was kind.

"It was a great night for all of us."

"So, you received our invitation?" Patrick folded his arms over a beige turtleneck sweater.

"I did, thank you. It was a nice surprise and I was very flattered."

"No need to be. We would really like to show your work."

"I appreciate that. And I did seriously consider your offer, but I feel I need to stay focused on school at the moment and not add to my workload."

Patrick pursed his lips. "That's too bad. We were very impressed with your talent." He tapped his fingers on his arm. "Would you consider letting us take any pieces you make at school?"

Katie tilted her head. They actually thought her work was that good? "That would be fine, but there aren't that many."

"We'll take what we can get." He held out his hand.

Katie shook it, her mind racing. What pictures did she have ready that could possibly look like they belonged in a gallery in Paris, France?

———

Rachael was asleep. Justin crept into the hospital room. In one arm he held a light brown bear and in the other fresh flowers that he placed on the windowsill. He silently pulled up a chair and sat beside Rachael's bed. A frown creased her brow, even as she slept. He lightly ran his hand over her forehead and shivered. That was quite the ordeal he had watched her go through. Everything in him wanted to call Zack and tell him to come to the hospital to be with her and see their brand new baby, but Rachael had been adamant. From the beginning, she had made it clear that she never wanted Zack to know.

She stirred and blinked.

"Hey you." He gripped the bed rail. "How are you feeling?"

"Tired. Sore."

"I'm sure. I brought you these." He reached for the flowers and set them on her bedside table.

"Thanks. They're beautiful."

Her words held no emotion. He picked up the teddy bear and held it in front of his face as he spoke in a squeaky voice. "Hi there! I'm..." he fumbled to read the label, "... Cappuccino, but you can call me Cappy for short. I'm going to the nursery to visit Jack. Wanna come?" He was relieved to see a weak smile.

"It's okay, you go. I'll rest for now."

"Are you sure? Your little guy might be hungry and need his mama." He moved the bear's arms while he spoke, but his feeble attempt to cheer her was clearly failing.

She closed her eyes and nodded.

"Okay, I'll be back in a bit."

At the nursery window, Justin studied little Jack through the incubator glass. The baby was sound asleep, firmly wrapped in a receiving blanket so only his face was visible. Tubes led into his nostrils above his tiny mouth. The protective bond Justin had experienced when he held Jack right after his birth returned. He worried, as he had many times lately, how the little guy and his mother were going to make it. He had been Rachael's biggest cheerleader, but most times he acted more positive than he felt. *God, if you exist, you need to help them. Please.*

CHAPTER
Nineteen

AIDEN DECIDED TO MAKE THE BEST OF THE SITUATION. U of W wasn't so bad. He preferred Western's campus, but he could get used to the change. At the end of the previous year, he had been asked to leave the university. The partying had outweighed his work, and he had managed to fail most of his courses. Waterloo was his second chance and he was determined to stay focused. In the past, he had always managed to have fun *and* achieve above-average grades, but the freedom of university had proved too much. Things had grown a little out of hand. He needed to muster discipline, and fast, since he was attending this term on academic probation.

Purposely choosing a heavy workload, he tried to ensure he'd have no choice but to concentrate on school alone. He had goals that deserved a fair try and was painfully aware this might be his last chance at higher education. Having come face to face with the possibility of messing up his life, he didn't want to have to explain to his parents why he was being forced to drop out. This year would be different.

The worst part about being at U of W was knowing it was the university Katie attended. He hoped, by some miracle, he would never run into her. The break-up had been painful enough. To have to face her again might undo him.

If he did, he would appear detached and, if needed, would carry on that facade in her presence. He wouldn't let himself acknowledge the weakest part of him, the part that had yearned for her every day since they had said goodbye, the part that was now buried so deep within, it had begun to consume him from the inside out. It manifested itself in a variety of ways, but he always refused it an audience.

Eventually, it would go away. It had to.

————

Rachael struggled through the apartment entryway with a baby car seat swinging from one arm and a bag of groceries from the other. Six-week-old Jack was screaming, his cry echoing in the hollow space. Her chest squeezed. He was hungry. Given her dwindling savings, it was a relief that she was able to nurse him with the nourishment from her own body.

One day at a time. It wasn't easy. Thankfully, before she'd been discharged, Dr. Milton had given her the contact information of the director at the Pregnancy Centre, and they had helped her find a place at a non-profit housing complex. Before that, on one of his visits to the hospital, Justin had told her, "If you two need a place, Rach, you and Jack can stay at my apartment. I don't mind the couch."

It was a generous offer, but she couldn't take it.

Sometimes she let herself imagine how different her life might have been if she had been able to stay in school, get her degree, land a great job, and reach her goals. But those thoughts were futile reminders of her choices; this was her life now. There were other times, while feeding Jack in the early hours of the morning, when she could almost feel her dreams being sucked out of her as her son nursed greedily. There were so many unknowns, they seemed to drown out all hope. And it was lost hope and loneliness that rose in her like swollen banks of misery.

When had life gone so wrong? Had it ever been right?

One day Jack would ask about his daddy, and she would have to think of something to tell him that would satisfy him. She was thankful she had managed to hide her pregnancy from Zack, especially after learning the truth. The difficult choice of carrying her baby to full term was overshadowed by the fact that the reason she had done so was not even reality. To learn that the baby she had carried for nine months wasn't the result of the love she had shared with Zack, but rather a despicable act of pitiful self-indulgence, a criminal act, really, disgusted her and became a source of overpowering anxiety.

As difficult as the situation was to absorb, every so often she would look down at baby Jack, glimpse a vague familiarity in his features, and find some small delight in his little smile. It seemed to hold a hint of hope that, somehow, they would be okay.

———

Zack stood outside the front entrance to Tom's childhood home. He hadn't seen Tom's parents since the funeral that spring and now it was almost Christmas. At the end of term, he'd wasted little time leaving the house he'd shared with Tom, driven by a desire to escape the memories of his friend's death. Last week, he had finally sorted through the few boxes he had hastily packed. Now he stood facing his former housemate's mother, holding a box containing a smattering of her son's belongings. He shifted from foot to foot. Returning them was proving more difficult than expected.

"Why don't you come in?" she offered.

"Actually, I'm on a tight schedule. I have a few errands to run, but thanks." It was less truth and more an excuse. He didn't want to sit and relive any memories of Tom by being bombarded with questions. *She's probably just being polite anyway.* Too much guilt had attached to him already, like some pestilent parasite, ever ready to inflict blame. He handed her the box.

After placing it on the hall bench, she turned back to the door. "Oh, just a minute. I almost forgot. I found a letter." She disappeared and returned a moment later holding a crumpled envelope. "Do you know anyone by the name of Rachael?"

The mention of her name came like a stab to his insides. He nodded.

"It was in the pocket of Tom's jeans. Could you please give it to her?" She held out the envelope.

"I haven't seen her in a while..." He searched for an excuse not to take it from her outstretched hand. Looking into her earnest face asking this small favour, he relented and took the letter.

Once in his car, Zack took a deep breath, slid the sealed envelope into the back pocket of his jeans, and drove away, his mind full of vacillating thoughts.

———

Katie placed the last of the Christmas cakes in the front window, which was already filled with numerous delightful creations. She gazed fondly from one intricate gâteau to the next like a little girl admiring toys in a department store display. There were tortes with handmade chocolate Christmas trees perched on top, others with delicately-depicted winter scenes and miniature chocolate figures set carefully in place, and still more with splendid, decorative icing and candied oranges cut in diamonds. The assortment made for a stunning display.

Madame Bonnard has certainly outdone herself. She had been working day and night to fill the many Christmas orders. Katie had been witness to the long hours of preparation, and in her late night studies, noticed that the light from the window of the boulangerie never seemed to go out. Now it was the morning of Christmas Eve, and soon her boss could breathe a sigh of relief.

A soft knock on the window pulled her from her musings, and Katie looked up to see Monsieur Rideaux, who passed by every day on his morning walk, smile and wave. She smiled and waved in return mouthing, "Joyeux Noël!"

By the time the bakery opened, customers were lined up outside, some coming to pick up Christmas orders, others hopeful of procuring a last-minute Christmas dessert, along with the regulars stopping by for their morning coffee and pastry. By mid-afternoon, quantities were dwindling. When the day drew to a close, and Madame Bonnard flipped the sign on the door to *Fermé*, the shelves were barren and the front window empty. It had been a tiring but profitable day.

"I'll stay to help you clean up," Katie said.

"Non, non! You go."

"Look at this place. I'm not going to let you tackle this alone. It's Christmas Eve."

It had been a struggle throughout the day to maintain any semblance of order, and the floors were in desperate need of mopping. Madame Bonnard relented and the two worked as a team. The baker chatted as rapidly as she moved, and Katie was in awe of her stamina and excitement. Tomorrow she would celebrate Christmas with her mother and sister in Versailles.

When the store was in order, Madame Bonnard motioned Katie over to her. She handed her an envelope and pressed a small box into her hand.

"Don't open it until tomorrow," she said with twinkling eyes.

Katie hugged her. "I have something for you, too."

Reaching beneath the counter, she pulled out a flat, rectangular parcel. "But I want you to open it now."

Madame tore at the festive paper. Delight washed over her features as she uncovered the contents to reveal a carefully-rendered pen and ink drawing of the bakery. The view was from Katie's balcony, and captured the little storefront perfectly.

"Oh! C'est très beau. Merci!" Madame Bonnard gathered her into a tearful hug.

———

Rachael listened to her mother's voice instructing the caller to leave a message then said, "Merry Christmas, Mom and Dad," and pressed the end button on the phone. Her parents were celebrating Christmas in Hawaii. They might get the message when they returned in two weeks.

Even now, they remained completely unaware of her situation. As far as they knew, she was still at university in the throes of completing last-minute assignments and exams. She had no idea how long she could keep up the charade, but at least they had stopped asking why she hadn't been home for a visit. It was wrong, but she hadn't been able to muster the courage to tell them.

Rachael sank down on the couch and glanced at her watch. Jack was tucked into bed, oblivious to the various shouted greetings and slamming doors that echoed throughout the hallway of the apartment complex. Occupants with visitors arriving to celebrate Christmas Eve, or bustling down the hallways loaded with gifts, should have added to the excitement and festivity of the season, but instead the hubbub only added another layer to Rachael's loneliness.

She pushed back her shoulders and drew the blanket up over her lap. *I won't feel sorry for myself.* She had done enough of that over the past months. Not that there was a shortage of things to feel down about, especially tonight, but somehow she had begun to move forward, not on her own strength—she hadn't the composition for that—but forward nonetheless.

Rachael had begun to change, and she smiled at her progress. The gentle love of the Saviour, whose birth she would celebrate tonight, had been the source of this transformation two short weeks earlier. She had let go, realizing she wasn't in control and never had been.

It had happened on a day she felt like giving up. She had run out of money. Her cupboard held nothing but a can of beans. Baby Jack's newborn pyjamas had grown tight around his chubby tummy and legs. Worse, he was sick with a fever and had been crying endlessly, day and night. She had done all she could. All her resources were spent; she was spent. She had lowered herself down to the cold kitchen floor, leaned against a cupboard, and let herself spill out familiar tears of despair. She hadn't prayed in years, didn't really even know how. But that day she groaned. *Please help me God. I don't know what to do. Please help us.*

Within an hour, a knock sounded at the door. Pushing herself up from the floor, she ran her hands over her damp face and walked over to answer it. A woman she didn't recognize stood in the hallway. Her sweet smile was a sharp contrast to Rachael's tear-stained face.

"Merry Christmas! I'm from Central Church. We just wanted to share God's love with you. Please accept this Christmas basket from us."

Rachael barely had the strength to take the oversized basket from the woman's outstretched arms and stare at it. The woman couldn't have known how substantial a gift she had given. From behind the closed door, through eyes blurred with tears, Rachael tore away the clear wrap. The basket was laden with food, baby clothes, diapers, supplies, and gift cards—one with enough to buy food for over a month.

But there was something else near the bottom: a small Bible.

With trembling fingers, Rachael flipped through the pages and randomly stopped to read from a book called Matthew, the sixth chapter.

Therefore I tell you, do not worry about your life, what you will eat or drink; or about your body, what you will wear. Is not life more than food, and the body more than clothes? Look at the birds of the air; they do not sow or reap or store away in barns, and yet your heavenly Father feeds them. Are you not much more valuable than they?

It was as though the words were meant for her. She needed no more convincing. For the second time, God had caught her attention. Both times he had sent her help just when she had lost all hope, once through a woman who had comforted her on the steps outside of the abortion clinic, and now a woman at her door. His seemed a gentle, pursuing love. Her self-sufficiency had failed, and her stubborn pride crumbled until all that remained were those simple words that stirred her soul and whispered into her heart.

That day she invited love in.

It was a healing love, a powerful love, a forgiving love. A love that swept in to awaken her soul and renew her fragmented heart. It was a love full of freedom and life, that lent courage and perfect peace. It was unfailing, constant, and beautiful, the only absolute truth she had ever known.

The intensity of complete desolation brought her to the outstretched arms of her Saviour. She smiled, feeling warmed by this enveloping love that tucked itself around her like the comfortable blanket now warming her lap. That same love had adjusted her heart and mind toward Jack, dissolved the hardened bits, and allowed her to love him despite the circumstances of his birth.

Right now, only the love of God enabled her to face Christmas alone.

Katie threw her backpack on the bed and checked the time. In an hour and a quarter, the Christmas Eve service she planned to attend would begin. She changed her outfit between bites of one of the croissants Madame Bonnard had saved for her. Ten minutes later, she was descending the stairs to the Metro.

Anticipation ran through her as she hurried along the sidewalk, past cafés and boutiques, hoping to arrive early enough to claim a seat at the traditional Christmas Mass held at Église St-Germain-des-Pres, the oldest church in Paris. She alighted at St-Germain-des-Pres. Floodlights lit the stone walls of the ancient church as its bells pealed through the evening air, inviting all who could hear to join the festivities.

Wavering shadows danced across Romanesque columns that rose to frame the centre aisle in the candlelit sanctuary. Mural paintings flanked the length of the nave, and stained-glass windows added even more beauty and solitude. A crèche was set up in the sanctuary, the nativity figures a reminder of the reason they gathered to celebrate.

Katie absorbed every detail of the breathtaking scene as she moved to a vacant wooden seat in the crowded church. Soft organ music drifted through the space like a familiar friend, adding to the sweet, serene atmosphere. Once settled, she closed her eyes and listened, sending a quiet prayer toward the vaulted ceiling, thinking especially of Rachael this Christmas Eve. *God, wherever she is, watch over her tonight, and help her see how much you love her. Amen.*

CHAPTER

Twenty

A KNOCK STARTLED RACHAEL AWAKE. THE TELEVISION, displaying coverage of the New Year's gathering in Times Square, had been muted. The ever-present hum from the refrigerator pervaded the tiny apartment, but otherwise everything was quiet. She blinked. Had someone actually knocked? The gentle tap came again. She glanced at her watch. Still early, but who would be knocking tonight?

Rachael stumbled to the door and peered through the peephole. Her eyes widened. Stepping back from the door, she pressed a hand to her chest to calm her racing heart. The knock came again. *Open the door.* Her frozen body refused to obey. After a stunned moment, she took a deep breath, raked her fingers through her hair in a desperate attempt to smooth it, and opened the door.

He was halfway down the hall but turned at the sound. The two stood staring at one another in a stiff silence that lasted seconds but seemed like minutes.

"I thought maybe you weren't home." He walked back toward her.

The voice she had so often missed came confident but cool.

"Zack... I wasn't expecting..."

"I know. I'm sorry. It's a bit late, but I—"

"How did you know where I was?"

"Justin told me where to find you. I thought maybe I had the wrong place."

What is he doing here? How could Justin have told him? Does he expect me to invite him in? The questions raced through Rachael's mind while he stood before her in the hallway. If she did ask him in, he would ask questions, and the prospect of that was too frightening.

"I needed to bring by this letter." He reached into his coat pocket. "Tom's mom found it and asked me to give it to you."

He held out an envelope.

Tom's name sent waves of revulsion shuddering through her. She pushed them back and reached out a trembling hand to take the letter. "Thanks."

Darn those green eyes. He's more beautiful than ever. She studied the letter in her hand to avoid Zack's searching gaze.

"Are you doing okay?"

"Yeah, fine." She looked up and forced a smile to hide that she was so overcome at seeing him again she was close to tears. "Doing really well." The letter shook in her hand and she stuffed it into the pocket of her sweater.

"How long have you lived here?"

"About three months." She stepped into the hall and closed the door, afraid that he would see a baby toy, or worse, hear Jack cry.

"You decided to move back to Cambridge?"

"Yeah, you know... closer to home, less expensive than Waterloo."

"True. Good plan."

"Not going to any New Year's parties?"

"No, my partying days are over."

"Mine, too." She smiled again to mask the pain, to push away the thought of last New Year's.

He smiled too, the first she'd seen in nine months, but the one she remembered so well. Her chest ached. She pictured him spending a quiet evening with some beautiful woman who was probably waiting for him in the car.

"Well, I guess I better go."

No, don't go! Everything inside her wanted to scream. *Stay a few more moments before I never see you again.* She nodded. "Thanks for making sure I got this." She held up the letter.

"No worries, Rach."

"Happy New Year," she called after him as he started down the hall.

"Happy New Year to you, too."

Rachael watched until he disappeared into the stairwell. When the echo of his footfalls faded, she went back inside. She rested her forehead on the closed door, willing her heart to beat normally. *Just breathe.* She swallowed away threatening tears, forcing them to remain tucked away in the deep hidden place she reserved only for Zack.

She ached from wanting something she could never have. Zack Wilson standing at her door had been like a dream she never wanted to end. She had wanted to talk to him, invite him in, be friends again—or more—but those days were over. Their lives had intersected once, but now they were two different people leading vastly different lives, never to merge again. The life she lived with Jack was far removed from the one they had shared.

Now, more than ever, she lamented the loss. She had expected this evening to be a difficult one, but Zack being so close, yet so far, was nothing short of misery.

Jack's muffled cry came from her bedroom, interrupting the nostalgia. She tugged her phone from her pocket to check the time. The wrinkled envelope fell to the floor. Rachael picked it up and tossed it onto the coffee table then hurried to the bedroom to nurse her baby boy.

Rachael kissed Jack and laid him on the sofa, speaking softly to him as she did. She had nursed and bathed him, and now his eyes blinked closed as she settled in beside him. Her gaze fell on the envelope on the coffee table. *Why would Tom write me a letter?* A shudder moved through her. She loathed the idea of touching it, let alone opening it. There was no telling what its contents might be, and she wasn't sure she cared to find out.

Lord, whatever it says, help me to trust you.

With a sigh, she leaned forward, grabbed the envelope, and ripped it open. Her hands shook as she pulled out the lined paper. The writing was messy, as though hurriedly written, but legible enough.

Dear Rachael,

I'm writing this before I do something I've thought about doing for years. I have no idea why I'm telling you, but I guess I thought it would be the decent thing to do and you do deserve to know the truth.

When I found out that you and Zack broke up, I hoped there might be a chance for me. I knew you didn't much like me, but I thought if I pretended we had sex you might go out with me. Writing it down makes me see how stupid that was and what a jerk I am. Your reaction was pretty clear. I knocked on the bathroom door, but when you didn't answer, I tried it, found it locked, and left.

All that to say, I never slept with you on New Year's Eve, or any other time.
I'm sorry I lied to you. I hope you won't hate me too much.

Tom

Rachael stared at the letter then re-read it to let the words soak in. Tears of released shame and grief wetted her cheeks. Months of tortured thoughts freed their grip on her soul as invisible chains were cut away.

With a full heart, she studied baby Jack, the magnitude of his little life overwhelming her. She reached to pick him up and pull him in close until his tiny, soft cheek rested against hers. She took in a deep breath and exhaled, feeling the months of strain draining from her life.

Suddenly, everything looked different.

Rachael spent the remainder of New Year's Eve cuddling Jack and thinking and praying long into the night. By morning, she knew with all certainty that she needed to tell Zack. Her thoughts had clarified and she saw the truth: he deserved to know. She had no idea what he would do or say, and fear and doubt still loomed over her. Whatever happened, she took comfort in knowing God would be with her through it all. That thought encouraged her to stop hiding the truth.

Justin would have Zack's number, and he would be more than willing to share it with her. She hated to think of the havoc this would cause in Zack's life. If he had a girlfriend, like she imagined he did, it would make the situation even more delicate. Though the whole idea was unnerving, her desire to cast off all secrecy was greater.

Twenty-One

KATIE WOKE ON NEW YEAR'S DAY TO SUNLIGHT SHINING through the lace curtains. She had slept in and now the sun had risen above the buildings that faced hers. She laced her fingers behind her head. Such a luxury was rare and made even more perfect by the fact that she had the day off. No school, no bakery, just a whole day to herself. Though she hadn't expected to sleep so late, the rest of the day was fully planned. She would spend time in prayer, go for a long run, put away her scant Christmas decorations, and clean her neglected apartment. After that, she planned to have a relaxing soak in the tub.

Just the thought of taking a bath brought back memories of last Christmas with Justin's sudden visit and the resulting bathtub dunking they had both received. She bit her lip. Still, after all this time, thoughts of him didn't come easy. He was the most thoughtful man she had ever met. But, like Aiden, he wasn't the one for her. Would there ever be *the* perfect one? A soul-mate to share every moment with, even a whole lifetime?

Maybe a leisurely day isn't such a good thing after all. The sheer lack of busyness was already creating havoc in her thought life.

As they so often did, her thoughts turned to Rachael. How had her friend spent New Year's? As young girls, they always called each other on Christmas Day to share about the gifts they had received and make plans to play together with their new toys. Katie had tried calling her after the service on Christmas Eve, but Rachael hadn't picked up. Even though they had exchanged a few brief texts on Christmas Day, it wasn't nearly the same as being together, or hearing Rachael's voice. The memories of all the time they had spent together while growing up made being far away difficult.

Since arriving in Paris, they had kept in touch through texts, but the messages had been brief and superficial. Katie worried that the distance was creating a rift in their friendship.

Last night, she couldn't sleep and lay awake praying for her friend. *I wish I was closer.* Although hurt by Rachael pushing her away, maybe it had been for the best. It was possible that Rachael needed space to grow without her.

How had Rachael's decision to end her pregnancy affected her? The repercussions could be difficult to deal with, especially at this time of year. She brushed aside the dark thoughts, swung her legs out of bed, and eased her body up. One last stretch, and she was ready to begin her perfect day.

————

Zack hadn't expected to be standing in front of Rachael's door again so soon, or ever again for that matter. But he'd wanted to return ever since he had seen her less than twenty-four hours before. It had taken everything in him to walk away. Pride alone had moved his feet down the hall and away from her. When she'd called him earlier that day to ask him to come back, he hadn't hesitated. He could only hope that she wanted to talk about something positive. She'd sounded nervous over the phone but insistent she wanted to meet with him in person.

Zack drew in a breath before knocking. His heart pounded under his coat and his palms were clammy. He rubbed them over his jeans before she could open the door and see him.

Suddenly she was there, smiling and asking him in. "Thanks for coming." She motioned for him to sit on the couch. "Would you like a drink?"

"Water would be good." He sank down on the edge of the sofa, taking in the tiny apartment.

Rachael joined him with two glasses. She handed him one and placed the other on the side table before taking a seat at the other end of the sofa.

"Nice place."

She laughed lightly and looked around the room.

"Better than a dorm room," he said, trying to break through the stifling awkwardness.

"True." She looked down at the hands she'd folded in her lap.

In the uncomfortable silence, Zack watched as Rachael took a tiny sip from her glass.

"Is this about the letter from Tom?"

A shadow crossed her face. "Partly," she said, lowering her drink.

He reached for her hand. She pulled hers away, as if protecting herself from him. "Thanks for coming," she said again, this time in a business-like manner, as if spouting the opening line of a shareholders meeting.

"No problem, Rach." Just like the night before, the familiar short form came before he could stop it. Thankfully, she didn't appear fazed.

"I know the way last year ended was hard and didn't make much sense," she began. "I hope what I'm going to tell you will help you understand a bit better."

"Okay..." He cocked his head. *Is she actually going to tell me why she dumped me, after all this time?*

She took a deep breath. "I never stopped loving you."

Her words struck him like a defibrillator to his heart. How long had he wondered why she had suddenly ended it between them? How many times had he asked himself how she could have fallen out of love with him so abruptly? Now she was telling him she had always loved him? Then why had she pushed him away? His hands clenched into fists on his knees.

"In February of last year I found out I was pregnant."

The improbable words pierced the thick air between them.

"I kept it from you by pretending I didn't care anymore."

Zack couldn't speak. He'd been tackled once, playing football, and taken a helmet to his chest. For several seconds he'd fought to draw in air, wondering if he would ever breathe again. He felt the same way now. Finally he managed to rasp out a single word. "Why?"

"I didn't want you to feel obligated... or mess up your life." She stared into her glass, swilling the water around. "I was going to have an abortion, but I couldn't bring myself to do it."

A deep cold gripped him, as if all the blood was draining from his limbs.

"I went ahead with the pregnancy, and in September gave birth to a baby boy."

His heart pounded beneath his shirt and his hands shook. He pressed them into his thighs to steady them while his lungs searched for air.

"Zack? Are you okay?"

He reached for his coat and stood. "I have to go." He strode to the door and flung it open, so hard it slammed against the doorstop.

Rachael followed him to the elevator, her throat thick with fear. If he left, it was possible she would never see him again. Jack might never be able to meet his father. *I've been so stupid.* If Zack took off and didn't come back, she would only have herself to blame. "I'm so sorry. I thought it was for the best."

The elevator door opened and Zack stepped in, punching the button to close the door.

"I didn't mean to hurt you."

The closing door shut out her words.

———

Zack slumped against the elevator wall. Fury coursed through his body. He pounded his fist on the wall behind him and cursed when a sharp pain shot through the side of his hand. How many months had he spent dealing with the pain and despair, never quite managing the loss? With a few words, she'd ripped his heart wide open again. What did she expect him to say? That everything she had put him through was okay? That keeping his son from him was perfectly acceptable? Was he supposed to pretend she'd never broken his heart? That she'd just done it again? He could never do that.

When the doors opened to the lobby, Zack stormed out of the building and yanked up his collar against the biting wind. Street lamps cast dingy pools of light onto the pavement, dimly highlighting the snow-dusted sidewalk. Discarded Christmas trees, ready for garbage pick-up, perched on top of snow banks at the edge of the road. Any lights that still adorned houses looked garish instead of festive. *So much for joy and peace.*

He wracked his mind for some shred of hope. Something to grab hold of to make sense of this madness. *How could she have been so deceitful?* All those dark months spent trying to make sense of what happened between them, the hollow longing… He stopped and pressed a palm to a street light pole, leaning forward slightly as he fought to steady his breathing. Adding to the stinging pain was all that he'd missed, all that Rachael had decided on his behalf. He'd never even been given the opportunity to choose whether or not he wanted to be part of his child's life.

He straightened and kicked the icy snowbank.

It was less than ideal that Rachael had become pregnant, but even if she had chosen not be with him, or didn't want him to interfere with her decisions, the least she could have done was be up front. Because of her, he hadn't known he had a son, hadn't been able to witness his arrival into the world. He'd been deprived of the first several months of his child's life, as well as any input into the family he would go to. *What kind of a person does that to someone?*

He jammed his hands into his pockets. His mind sifted through possible explanations for Rachael's behaviour. She'd told him she had never stopped loving him. Easy to say, but her actions certainly didn't back up her words. Zack drove his fingers through his hair. What else had she said? Something about thinking it was for the best, not wanting him to feel obligated or mess up his life. *She should have let me be the judge of that.*

The truth struck him like a slap across the face, and he stopped in the middle of the sidewalk.

She did it for me.

His mind reeled under that thought. Trying to stop missing Rachael, to forget she mattered, to stop feeling anything for just a while had been excruciating. But what had it been like for her trying to cope on her own? *If only I had known the truth.* Was it love that had driven her to try to spare him, although it meant being alone?

Zack sagged against the cold cement wall beside a darkened store window. Even if it was, could he find a way to let go of what she had done in the past so the two of them could figure out if they had any chance at a future?

The 3 am feedings were the hardest, waking Rachael out of deep sleep, but tonight she hadn't made it to bed yet. When Jack woke, she was still on the couch, going over in her mind what had happened with Zack. *What have I done? I should never have kept the truth from him.* In all the months prior to their breakup, she'd never seen him so angry. And could she blame him?

She'd been so sure telling him was the right thing to do. Now she was more confused than ever. Perhaps she should have just left it alone, left things the way they had been between them. That would have been so much easier. Only keeping the truth from him hadn't been easy either. It had been agony.

Speaking in a soft voice, she laid Jack in his crib and tucked the blanket around him. She ran her fingertips over his pink cheek until his eyelids flickered closed. Pulling the door shut behind her, she considered sleep herself, but her insides churned. Rachael plugged in the kettle to make a cup of tea and slumped on the couch to wait for the water to boil.

A faint knock sounded on the door. Had Zack come back? Rachael pushed to her feet, pushing back the hope that leapt in her chest. Pressing her hand to her stomach, she made her way to the door on weak legs and pulled it open.

Without waiting for an invitation, Zack stepped through the doorway. She resisted only a moment when he drew her to him, then sank into his embrace. He held her gently yet firmly, and when she gave in to tears he stroked the back of her hair.

Finally she pulled away and looked into his eyes. "You came back."

———————

Zack wiped at her tears with his thumb even as his own eyes filled.

"What made you come back?"

He moved his hands to her shoulders. "You."

Her eyebrows rose. "What do you mean?"

"I thought about you, how this situation would have looked from your perspective, and I started to see things differently. I realize that everything you did, and all you went through, you did because you cared. And all this time I've been feeling sorry for myself. I had no idea."

"How could you have? I was convinced it was for the best, but now I realize how wrong it was to keep the truth from you. Can you forgive me?"

He lifted her chin up with a finger. "You're amazing."

Rachael let out a choked sob as another tear slipped down her face. She swiped it away before his hands found hers. Several breaths passed between them and she thought he might kiss her. She inhaled and worked to steady her racing heart.

He stepped back. "I do forgive you. I would have wanted to be there for you, but I understand."

She leaned in and kissed his cheek.

He searched her eyes. "For the record, I never stopped loving you either."

KATIE SET THE TEA POT DOWN AND SETTLED IN THE CHAIR beside Jean, pulling a blanket up over her legs. The afternoon sun cast its warming glow on the buildings in front and though it wasn't the right time of year to properly enjoy the balcony, the two of them had decided it was worth a try. Katie poured tea into a cup and passed it to Jean, the steam filling his face. Jean had taken her shopping to a grocer and now they were sampling the Verveine tea she had discovered.

Katie blew on her hot drink. "Any New Year's resolutions?"

Jean shrugged. "Maybe open another café."

"Wow. No small plan."

He smiled. "And you? I bet you have a list."

"Very funny. As a matter of fact, I do."

"Okay. Let's hear them."

"I'll give you my top three, how about that?"

Jean threw his head back and laughed. "That must be some list."

"I want to do a bit of travelling while I'm here, you know, outside of Paris. Maybe a few weekend trips by train. My second resolution is to try to do a couple of extra paintings for the gallery to pay for travelling. And, who knows, maybe I'll even be able to afford a visit home. I miss my mom and Rachael."

"And what about Justin?"

His name came as an unexpected stab. Why did Jean have to be such a good listener?

"Kaitrin, a bit of advice, for what it's worth. Use the hurts in your life as springboards for success." He gazed at her, his dark eyes intense.

"Deep Jean, very deep."

He smiled but grew serious again. "Let me say this. My father told me before he died that life is a lot like a see-saw—it has ups and downs. You must choose whether you spend more time up or down. It takes a lot more effort to hold it down than to ride. Whatever you are facing, Kaitrin, have the courage to ride both the ups and downs, without regret, but with abandon. Do not second guess yourself, just enjoy the ride."

She couldn't have expressed her deepest fears herself, but in a few short words, Jean had handed her a word picture that addressed each one.

"How did you know?"

"I have done some listening," he said, a knowing smile spreading over his lips, "and made a few mistakes of my own."

———

"Rach, can I ask you where the baby is now?"

Rachael cocked her head, confused. "Where ..." Her chest squeezed. Zack thought she had given their son up. She swallowed and pointed to the bedroom. "He's right in there."

His eyes widened as he shifted his gaze to the closed door. "You kept him?"

She nodded.

"Can I see him?"

"Of course."

He jumped off the couch and pulled her up with him. "You kept him," he repeated, and whisked her into his arms and spun her around.

"What are you doing? You're crazy." She laughed along with him.

"Maybe, but I've been a dad for weeks already and didn't know it."

He gently lowered her to the ground, and she led him to the bedroom door. She turned the handle, opened the door, and gestured for him to follow. They crept to the side of the cradle where Rachael showed Zack his sleeping son. He reached into the crib and touched Jack's cheek.

"Meet your daddy, Jack," Rachael said softly.

It seemed to take a moment for the name to register. "Jack? I like it. Hello, Jack."

At the sound of their voices, Jack stirred and blinked open sleepy eyes.

"Hi, sweetie." Rachael bent down to pick him up. She gave him a quick squeeze before handing him to Zack. He gently took the baby and pressed him to his chest.

"Hi, little buddy. Nice to meet you," he whispered into his ear.

———————

Zack spent the rest of the day at Rachel's apartment. Her heart was full. In all her life, she couldn't remember ever feeling so happy. Zack didn't want to let go of their son. He kept gazing at Jack's light green eyes and rosy face, remarking on familiar traits.

"You'll spoil him," Rachael said, when he held him all through his morning nap.

"You think?" His eyes sparkled when he looked up to meet hers.

"Yes, he usually sleeps in his crib."

"Should I put him there?"

"No, it's okay. One time won't hurt."

It wasn't until Jack was tucked in for his afternoon nap that they returned their full attention to one another.

"I hope you didn't have any other plans today." She hated how uncertain she sounded.

"No, nothing. Just recovering from New Year's."

"So you went out after all?"

"You wanna know the truth?"

"I don't know. Do I?"

She dreaded hearing him say he was dating someone else. After all, it had been months since they had last seen each other. It was likely he had moved on. She wouldn't blame him if he had.

"Yes, I think so," he said, with a crooked smile. "I spent the night thinking about my incredibly brief visit with you and wondering why you didn't invite me in."

"You did not." She swatted his arm.

"Actually, I did. It was pretty rude of you." His face grew serious. "What made you change your mind?"

"You wanna know the truth?"

"I don't know. Do I?"

She had no idea how to begin. *Might as well jump right in.* Clasping her fingers together to keep them from trembling, she told him about Tom, the amnesia, and how she had finally remembered the conversation that had caused it.

Zack's face grew pale, his lips tightened, and anger flickered in his eyes. With some reluctance, she handed him Tom's letter. While he read, she folded and refolded Jack's receiving blanket, running her finger over the embroidered bunny pattern until Zack finished and folded the letter. He sat in silence for a long time, staring at the small square of paper, a deep frown pushing his eyebrows together. Finally, he set the letter on the coffee table.

"I can't believe you did this on your own, Rach. You shouldn't have. I can't imagine how——"

She pressed a finger to his mouth. There were a million words they could have said, but it wouldn't change anything. Perhaps, in time, those words would be spoken, but not now. Now she only wanted to enjoy that he was sitting here beside her. Zack grasped her hand and held it between his. His touch spoke more than all the words she had stopped him from saying, told her he understood, that she mattered to him. She exhaled.

"So, what made me change my mind? After I read that letter and found out the truth, I couldn't sleep last night. I realized I needed to tell you. I finally understood that it was the right thing to do. And I …" she contemplated their clasped hands, "I haven't been alone. That's something else I wanted to talk you about. I gave my heart to Jesus a few weeks ago. And he's been with me and with Jack. He's taken care of us. Because of him, my life has changed completely."

Zack stared at her blankly. "That's good, Rach. I'm glad you found something that helped you through this."

That wasn't exactly the response she'd been hoping for, but it was a start. Maybe, in time, he'd come to see the difference Jesus had made and want to know more about it. In the meantime, she would pray for him, and love him.

He squeezed her hand. "You're incredible, you know that? Having the baby alone, keeping Jack… thank you."

He pulled her close and kissed her, softly at first, then deeper as she responded. Too soon he pulled away and looked into her eyes. "For months I've felt dead inside, like nothing much mattered. I tried to forget about us, about you, but I couldn't."

"I'm sorry I…"

This time he placed his index finger over her mouth. "It doesn't matter now. Marry me, Rach. I love you. I want to be with you and Jack."

Everything in her wanted to cry out yes, but something stopped her. Something she had never needed to consider before, but that was now the most important thing in the world.

CHAPTER
Twenty-Three

FOR THE FIRST TIME, RACHAEL UNDERSTOOD KATIE'S hesitancy surrounding relationships. Zack had asked her to marry him a second time, and she still hadn't been able to give him an answer. The more time they spent together, the weaker her resolve. He was the father of her child... their child. They loved each other and were so compatible, and he was adorable with Jack. It made sense that they should be together. He was even joining her and Jack for church each week. But there was one thing that stood in the way: Zack didn't love God.

Rachael had begun attending a women's Bible study at a church downtown. They talked over coffee and snacks and prayed together while the children were cared for in the nursery. It was a much-needed break for Rachael, and the ladies were kind and welcoming. That was a relief because she had so many questions, and they were patient in answering them. By the third week, Rachael had confided in one of the women. She told her story and asked for advice concerning Zack. The woman simply listened, and instead of giving advice, she encouraged Rachael to pray.

Rachael didn't feel as though she was any sort of expert at prayer, but the woman said it was just like talking to a friend.

"Most importantly, just like any friendship, don't do all the talking. Take time to listen."

Rachael had been doing a lot of talking. The idea of listening was interesting. She always thought praying was just asking for what you wanted and waiting for God to respond. At the Bible study she learned about the Holy Spirit and his guidance. Then she remembered the night she had prayed about Zack and how she felt certain she should tell him the truth. Since then, she had been praying the Holy Spirit would again provide direction regarding Zack. She wasn't sure how long he would wait for her, or if he would even ask her to marry him again.

During the work week Zack stayed at his place in Toronto, but every weekend he visited her and Jack. It seemed reasonable for Rachael to offer him the couch. That way he could stay in town longer than just one day. The three of them went on all sorts of outings together, and after Jack was settled for the night, she and Zack would make dinner together and linger over a glass of wine. They had long conversations filling in the gaps of the past few months. Rachael found it difficult to tell Zack much of what she had struggled through. She hated to see the sadness in his eyes when she described those hard months without him, and felt guilty for all she had put him through.

Looking down at Zack's head resting on her lap as she ran her fingers through his hair, she felt so comfortable and content and marvelled at how her love for him had grown even fuller over the past four weeks.

He looked up at her and smiled. "What are you thinking?"

"About how much I love you, and how glad I am that you're here. And you? What are you thinking?"

"Pretty much the same, as well as how glad I am that you kept Jack."

She nodded. The thought of what might have been flashed through her mind. Even this moment right now might never have happened if there was no Jack.

"I've wanted to ask you how you came to your decision to keep him." He sat up and reached for her hand.

She had held off telling him but knew he would eventually ask. These weekend visits had been so magical she hadn't wanted to ruin a single moment. But he was asking now, and she owed him the full explanation.

"It was an awful time. I'd pushed you away, and Katie too, so except for Justin, I was alone. And I was so confused. The worst part was thinking about how I would manage a baby with no money and no place to live. It felt so impossible that I decided an abortion was the only choice I had."

Zack shifted to face her but didn't speak.

"I thought that if I terminated the pregnancy, at least I'd have a chance at life. So I booked it and even went to the appointment, thinking that it would end my problem." A tear slid down her face, and she winced when she considered how she had thought of Jack as a problem. "But once I got into the room, I felt sick. I ended up passing out, and after that I couldn't go through with it. So I left."

"Thank God you did." He wiped at his eyes.

"It's so easy to say that now, but at the time I hadn't a clue what I was doing. It's a miracle I walked out of that office still pregnant."

Zack ran his thumb over the top of her hand.

"I sat down on the steps outside the clinic to consider my options but started to cry. After a while a woman, a complete stranger, came along and put her arm around me. I think she was praying for me, but she didn't say anything. Afterwards I felt better and more certain I'd made the right decision. As hard as it was, from that moment on, I decided to keep the baby."

"Wow… and you never considered adoption?"

"No, I guess it was all or nothing. If I was going to go through all that, I was going to keep the baby."

"I have so much respect for you, Rach. I don't know how you managed."

"That had a lot to do with God."

"What do you mean?"

"I'm certain he guided everything. The lady who sat with me, the one I told you about who brought the gift basket, even me fainting in the office. And then what happened with you."

"Me? How?"

"After you brought the letter from Tom, I prayed and realized I had to tell you. I can't believe all that was a coincidence." She looked at his thoughtful eyes. "I'm so thankful you came back."

"So am I." He leaned over and kissed her softly, sliding his hand to the back of her neck. His touch sent a shiver of warmth rushing through her body. He kissed her more fully, and she reciprocated. After a few breathless seconds, Rachael pulled away. They had shared so much intimacy before, it would be easy to let it happen again.

"Is something wrong?" He leaned back to look at her.

"No, it's just that…" How could she explain her relationship to God with him and how it had changed her principles? Now seemed like the worst timing. Or was it?

"What is it?" His brow furrowed and she rushed to reassure him.

"I met God, Zack. After everything that happened, I gave my life over to him."

"What does that mean?"

"It means that I'm not the boss of my own life anymore. I love Jesus and want to try to do things his way more than mine. It's why I go to church, not out of duty or to follow rules, but because I love him." Were those enough words delivered just right to make him understand? More than anything right now, she needed him to understand.

"I'm glad that helped you get through all this, but you're the one who chose. You're such a strong person." He kissed her on the nose. Her heart ached with both longing for him and a yearning for him to understand. Without the latter, she feared she would never be able to spend her life with him.

The following weekend, when Zack arrived, he suggested she have some alone time and he would stay with the baby. He looked different. His eyes seemed brighter, his demeanour lighter than usual. He always insisted on buying the week's groceries, and as much as she wanted to refuse, she swallowed her pride and let him. After grabbing a few necessities, Rachael stopped in at her favourite coffee bar and ordered two coffees to go.

Arriving home, she swung open the apartment door to see Zack asleep on the couch with Jack nestled on his chest. The two of them were snoring, and she wasn't sure who looked more adorable. Zack's chest rose and fell and she imagined herself nestled there, his arm folded around her shoulder. Armed with the tray of coffees in one hand and grocery bags in the other, she stepped softly across the floor to the kitchen. As beautiful as these weekend visits were, they were hard on her heart.

At the rustling sound, Zack's eyes blinked open. His drowsy smile stirred her insides. She set the bags on the counter and moved to the side of the couch. She bent to kiss Jack's sweaty forehead and reached to squeeze Zack's outstretched hand. His eyes looked greener than usual and the twinkle in them made her shaky.

"You really will spoil him, you know." She tried to remain serious, but Zack's pouting lip made it impossible to keep a straight face. She handed him a coffee and returned to the kitchen to unload. Zack placed Jack on the sofa and tucked a pillow beside him. He joined her in the kitchen and began emptying a bag while she put away.

"I had an interesting conversation this week." He passed her a bag of carrots.

"Oh yeah?" She pulled open the fridge door.

"I went out for a beer with a guy from work, and he started telling me his story about how he met God."

Rachael's pulse pounded in her ears. She stopped moving.

"It was pretty amazing. He said God healed him from depression and that he now follows Jesus. He says it's changed everything for him."

She pushed the fridge door shut and turned to face Zack who was holding out a box of crackers.

"What he said made sense to me, and it sounded a lot like what you told me. Then he asked if I wanted to pray with him there at the bar." He gave up and set the crackers on the counter instead.

"Did you?" She was breathless.

"Yeah."

He said it so matter-of-factly.

"The weird thing is I felt different. I can't really explain it, except that I've felt peaceful and happy ever since."

Rachael felt like hollering with joy but swallowed instead. "I can understand that."

"So, I wanted to say that you should go ahead and take all the time you need on this marriage thing. I'm not going anywhere. I'll wait for you, Rach."

He turned to reach into another bag, but she grasped his elbow and pulled him around to face her. "Yes."

"What?"

"My answer... it's yes."

He blinked as though registering the information. "You mean you'll marry me?"

She nodded and smiled.

He laughed and tugged his hands from hers. He plunged his hand into his front pocket then bent down on one knee. "I've kept this handy just in case." He gazed up at her with twinkling eyes and a beautiful grin, then held up a small felt box and opened the lid. "Rach, I would like nothing more in the world than for you to be my wife."

"And I'd like nothing more than for you to be my husband."

Zack removed the ring from the box, slid it on to her finger, and kissed the top of her hand. He stood and moved in close. "I love you," he whispered. Then he cupped her face in his hands and pressed his lips fully to hers. Breathless and overcome with joy, she let herself be swept away into the arms of love.

CHAPTER
Twenty-Four

KATIE READ THE NAME AND ADDRESS AT THE TOP CORNER of the envelope. Rachael. Her chest squeezed. She missed her friend so much. Grasping one corner, she ripped open the envelope and pulled out an invitation. She gasped. Rachael and Zack were getting married. From their sporadic texts, Katie knew Zack was back in Rachael's life, but she hadn't predicted a wedding so soon. She read the date, just two months from now, and sighed with pleasure. A May wedding. *Looks like I'll be travelling sooner than I thought.* If she could sell one more painting, she'd have enough for the airfare and would be able to check off two of her resolutions at once. She tacked the invitation on her corkboard, adding it to the small collection of memorabilia she'd gathered over the past few months.

She didn't waste any time but set straight to work on her newest painting. It was to be an abstract of the Eiffel Tower by night beneath the stars, just as she had experienced it with Jean. Katie planned to make prints and postcards and hoped they would be popular with the tourists who visited the gallery. If she was lucky, she'd have a little spending money for her trip too. Though she had a lot of work ahead of her, May couldn't come soon enough.

———

Mindful of Toronto traffic on a Friday afternoon, Katie drove the rental car from Pearson International Airport directly to the University of Waterloo campus to avoid the gridlock. She contemplated getting a coffee but decided against having caffeine so late in the afternoon. Instead, she headed straight for the university parking lot.

Opening the car door felt like reopening a part of her life that had been left behind years before. She stepped out onto the asphalt and memories of her first year at U of W flooded back. It didn't help that it was spring, the time of year that now held such bittersweet memories. She lifted her chin. This spring was different, and a joyous occasion had brought her back here.

The deserted chapel at St. Jerome's University, located within the University of Waterloo, was quaint and sparsely decorated. Katie lowered herself onto a padded chair at the end of a long row, grateful for a few moments to collect her thoughts and emotions. The clock on the wall above the exit door told her she had less than half an hour to wait. She took a deep breath and let her body slide down far enough to rest her head on the back of the chair. When she closed her eyes, her mind wandered to the last time she had stood on this campus. Less than a week after final exams, she had packed up a year's worth of schoolbooks and memories and left for Paris.

Rachael's face was still so clear in her mind. The undeniable look of disillusionment and even abandonment she'd tried to hide. The two girls had stood looking at each other, words insufficient and useless, wanting to surrender to fear and loss but choosing to act like grown-ups instead. In the silence of failing words, when there should have been so much to say, they merely uttered an awkward goodbye, gave a clumsy farewell hug that fell far short of their years of friendship, and parted. Katie had wondered if that was the beginning of the end of their childhood bond.

But her fears hadn't been realized. If Rachael was anything, she was faithful. Their texts and occasional phone calls had kept them in tune with each other's lives, a little, anyway, but the arrival of the wedding invitation had been both a shock and an unexpected delight.

Katie sat in the chapel, marvelling at the changes a year had brought and life's unexpected ironies. Tomorrow her lifelong friend would get married. She sighed. A seemingly impossible situation had somehow turned itself around to become something beautiful.

Katie forced herself to push away the only shadow that hung over the past year and the wedding celebration. Every time she thought of Rachael's decision to terminate her pregnancy, sadness rose in her. Had Rachael ever told Zack? Katie vowed not to bring it up. It had been Rachael's decision, and she needed to respect that. If Rachael wanted to talk about it, she would have to be the one to bring it up. Katie needed to allow her friend the freedom to move on.

She smiled, remembering Jean's advice, so much the same, that she needed to allow herself to move on. His wise words echoed in her thoughts now. "Use the hurts in your life as springboards for success."

Just as his light-hearted demeanor helped her to be less serious when in his company, so she hoped his advice would do the same. Jean had become a confidante and kindred spirit, and in the silence of the chapel, she thanked God for sending him into her life.

The heavy door bumped closed behind Justin. It hadn't occurred to him to enter quietly, but suddenly he became infinitely aware of the silent room and the woman who straightened in a chair at the front of the chapel and turned to look back at him. Justin had a sudden urge to flee but found his feet fused to the floor.

A smile crossed her lips. "Do you always sneak up on people like that?"

Always the one to gently smooth out an awkward situation. He'd missed that. He wished he could appear like Katie, open, natural, and acting like they were old friends, but he didn't have it in him.

Suddenly, she was standing up, sliding out of the row, walking toward him—still strikingly beautiful, just as she had left him one year ago. Reality soaked in during the seconds it took her to reach him. *I should have known she'd be here.* A mixture of irritation and disbelief, tempered by good manners, stirred within him.

She reached out and they shared an awkward hug. The stab of pain that shot through him at the sight of her, the feel of her, scared him. He couldn't fall for her again, he wouldn't. Somehow he would safeguard his heart. He stepped back. "I wasn't sneaking..." but wouldn't let himself say the rest. As his words trailed off, he made no attempt to mask over the sentiment they should have held. A fleeting sense of triumph rose in him when an apologetic look crossed her features and she dropped her gaze to the floor between them.

That was it then. He would hold her at arms' length—would protect himself out of necessity and the need to survive. It had been a long year of forgetting. Like a chain-smoker breaking the habit, he had deliberately forced himself to go on without her, to keep busy, to not indulge in thoughts of her. And it had worked. He had quit her and had no inclination to set himself back a year by opening up, lighting up, or inhaling any breaths of her whatsoever.

Sure, he'd wondered what he would do if, or when, he ever saw her again. Now, with a sense of relief and regained strength, he knew. Thankfully, he would never have to wonder again. The moment had been dealt with. Katie was a vice from his past, and there she would remain.

"How is Paris?" he asked, stiffly.

"Very good, thank you." Her voice was flat, controlled—she was following his lead.

"Learning a lot?"

"Yes. It's been a fantastic experience."

"How long are you here for?" As soon as he said the words, he wished he could snatch them back. He sounded too interested and needed to bring the conversation back to a friendly, polite exchange.

"I have to return next week."

"And then what? How long will you stay in Paris?" He frowned. There they were again, questions that came before he could filter them.

"Indefinitely." She blinked, as though she'd surprised herself with that answer.

"You must really like it there."

"I do. I was given a scholarship to continue. How about you? How's the job going?"

"Good, good. Challenging."

"That's good." She rubbed her hands along the front of her jeans. "How was graduation?"

"Okay. It felt great to be done, but it was tough the way the year ended."

She nodded. "I heard about Tom. I couldn't believe it. You must have been shocked."

"Yeah. We were all so busy finishing up and getting ready to move on, we didn't see it coming, which made us all feel guilty. Especially Zack." He shook his head. "Seems like such a waste. He had his whole life ahead of him, you know? It was a real wake-up call."

Katie's face softened. "I'm sure it was."

"Sometimes we're so preoccupied with our own lives, we don't even notice other people or what they're dealing with, you know? We don't bother to stop for one minute and ask, I mean really ask, how someone is doing. What is wrong with us?"

The question hung in the air, until he answered it himself. "Too self-absorbed, I guess."

Heat rushed into his chest. How had he let the conversation get so personal so fast? He glanced at his phone. "I guess the others will be here any minute."

"Yeah, I guess so."

He looked up. The sadness in her bright blue eyes made it almost impossible to stay detached. Justin put the phone away and shoved his hands into his pockets.

"What role do you have in the wedding?"

"Best man."

He didn't bother to ask her. He'd known it the moment he saw her there, and her short laugh confirmed it. "Do you think we've been set up?" Her cheeks had turned pink.

"It sure looks that way."

She sat back down in the row of chairs and he took a seat beside her. Her perfume—the scent he remembered so well—drifted on the air. The aroma was sweet, beautiful, just as she had been to him. "So you and Zack became good friends?"

"Yeah, but it was more Rachael and I who spent time together. With you leaving and the break-up and all, it was a really tough time." He hoped it didn't sound as though he was talking about their relationship. "She was going through a lot, and by default, we became close."

"I'm glad you were there for her."

"I guess you've heard about the way they got back together and the baby and everything…"

"Some, but not much about the baby. She kept that part to herself."

"Well, we ended up spending a lot of time with each other. Zack asked me to be best man, knowing all Rachael and I had gone through together, and since then we've become good friends too."

"I had no idea," Katie said, clasping and unclasping her fingers in her lap.

"What do you mean?"

"That you and Rachael were spending so much time together and that you knew about the baby."

"No? She told me you guys were keeping in touch."

"Yeah, but she never mentioned you."

"Really?" He frowned slightly. "She never ceases to surprise me. Always carrying around a secret or keeping things to herself."

"Thanks for being there for her," she said, resting a hand on his arm.

Beneath her touch, his muscles tightened, as if fighting with his heart not to surrender while guarding the fragile remnants still intact.

———

They sat in stiff silence. *He's changed.* Or had he just changed toward her? Katie longed to hear one of his jokes, see the playfulness she remembered in those warm brown eyes, feel as though he still cared for her just a little. But what could she expect? They had gone their separate ways over a year ago and hadn't seen each other since. He seemed irritated by her presence, but at least he was being civil. Could she really blame him for giving her the cold shoulder?

She spoke into the silence. "To be honest, I didn't expect to see you here."

"I wasn't sure you'd come either. Rachael told me a while back you were staying on in Paris, so I guess I assumed you wouldn't be at the wedding."

"So, you were able to help her deal with the baby then?" She couldn't help asking, overpowered by the need to know but resolved not to broach the subject with Rachael. Finding out from Justin would make it easier to avoid the subject with her friend.

"Yeah. It wasn't easy. She had a pretty tough go. But it looks like those days are over now. It all worked out for them."

Katie sighed. Someone else knew there had been a life. Someone else had been able to help Rachael through the abortion while she had been so far away. *Thank you, God, for sending Justin to help Rachael when she so desperately needed a friend.* It didn't take away the sadness and responsibility she still carried over the life that had been taken from her friend's womb, but it was a small miracle that Rachael hadn't faced the past few months alone.

Voices in the corridor and the shriek of a child shattered the stillness of the chapel. The doors swung open, and Katie's life-long friend stood there with a baby perched on her hip.

"Katie!" Rachael rushed toward her. She hugged Katie around the chubby baby. What was going on? "Auntie Katie, meet Jack Justin Wilson." Rachael laughed at Katie's dumbfounded expression and thrust the child into her arms.

"Rachael, you…?"

Her friend didn't let her finish. "Yep. He was born September the eighteenth, and I can't imagine life without him."

Is this really happening? She can't be serious. Katie couldn't draw a breath. "Excuse me." She handed the baby back then turned and strode out the side door of the chapel.

The door banged shut behind her. Katie stood on the pathway and pressed her fingers to her temples. She inhaled, attempting to calm herself.

The door swung open behind her. "Kat. What's the matter?"

She exhaled and turned to face Rachael. "What's the *matter*? Do you honestly have no idea?"

"I thought you'd be happy."

Katie straightened, weighing her words. "Do you have the slightest clue how I felt all this time, believing you'd had an abortion?"

"I thought it would be an amazing surprise when you came to visit."

"Yeah, I'm surprised, all right."

"But you're mad."

"Yes, I'm really mad. Didn't it cross your mind that I might care about you and the baby?"

"I know you did. That's why I thought this would be so great for you."

"Great? Seems pretty selfish if you ask me." Katie was shaking. She clenched both hands into fists. "I've been sick with worry for the last year, not to mention how sad I felt thinking that you'd... " She swiped at the angry tears trickling down her cheeks with her fingertips.

"But I didn't." Rachael's voice quivered.

"And I'm glad about that, but you also didn't let me in on that fact. I'm your best friend, or at least I thought I was. How could you keep this from me?"

Rachael's eyes filled too, and she blinked. "I'm sorry."

Katie wouldn't let her off the hook that easy. "That doesn't make up for what you put me through."

Rachael sagged against the side of the brick building. "You're right. I've been so selfish. I never thought about how much this might be affecting you. For so long I was confused. I came close to having the abortion, but I couldn't go through with it. I wanted to tell you, but in person, not over the phone."

Katie's forehead wrinkled. "Is that why your texts and calls were so short, and so few and far between? Sometimes you didn't even answer."

"For a while I think I was depressed. I was working a lot and was so tired. I didn't want to talk about it while I was figuring out what to do, because I was confused enough already."

"And after you decided not to go through with it?"

"After I was scared and incredibly stressed. I didn't know what I was going to do, how I'd even manage if I kept the baby. It was a really dark time for me."

Katie made an attempt to push aside the bitterness and see the situation from Rachael's perspective. She tried to imagine what she would have done, but she wasn't Rachael and the two of them were nothing alike. Was it really fair to impose her morals on Rachael? It was tempting to think the decision would have been easy, but she'd never had to make it herself.

"I'm sorry." Rachael reached out a trembling hand but stopped just short of touching Katie's shoulder. "I guess I was so caught up in my own stuff that I didn't stop to think about how you'd feel." She lowered her hand. "I don't know what else to say except that I'm sorry."

Justin poked his head out the side door. "Sorry to interrupt, but they're ready to begin the rehearsal."

Katie nodded. "We'd better go in."

Justin held the door and Rachael followed her inside. For now, Katie would push aside her feelings and do her best to be the maid of honour.

CHAPTER
Twenty-Five

AFTER THINKING RACHAEL'S ABORTION WAS FACT, AND turning it over in her mind for months, learning otherwise proved difficult for Katie to absorb. Holding baby Jack during the rehearsal dinner seemed surreal, and she thanked God for both his life and the joy emanating from Rachael. Seeing her interact with Zack, their reciprocal love and respect, and the laughter and intimacy they shared was, to Katie, a welcome relief. Like the thawing of an ice floe in spring, the hard, frozen bits of the months before melted away. Even so, Katie couldn't shake the feeling of betrayal.

Later that evening, with Jack tucked in for the night, Katie settled onto the couch at Rachael's apartment. She'd pushed aside her feelings for the evening but now expected that she and Rachael could finish their earlier conversation. Hopefully Katie could come to a place of forgiveness, if not complete understanding.

"Are your parents going to be there tomorrow?" Katie deferred diving in right away.

"My dad is for sure, but my mom…" She handed Katie a cup of tea. "I didn't tell my parents about Jack either, not until a few weeks after he was born. My mom's still pretty upset with me about that, and about dropping out of school. I don't think she's coming."

Katie wrapped her hands around the mug. "That's too bad." *Although I kind of get it.* Not telling Katie was one thing, but keeping their grandson from her parents? She didn't really blame Rachael's mom for being so upset. And what about Zack? When had Rachael told him? Had he been as angry as the rest of them over her silence? Why all the secrecy, anyway? She shifted on the couch. *God help me to let go of this anger. I want to forgive. I want my friend back.*

As if sensing where Katie's thoughts had gone, Rachael didn't try to defend herself for her decision to keep Jack a secret. She just settled in a worn recliner and popped the lid on a can of soda. "And your mom's still in England?"

"Yes. I haven't seen her in months."

"She phoned to congratulate us on the wedding and apologize for not being able to get away and attend, which was really nice of her. How's your grandma doing?"

"Not very well. I'm planning to visit the weekend before summer term, because Mom can't leave her."

"Now that she's rented out your house, you'll be forced to stay with us when you're here."

"Sure. I can be your babysitter."

"What about your dad? Do you ever think about him?"

Rachael hadn't asked about her dad in years.

"Sometimes, but not as much as you'd think. It's something I try not to think about, because if I do, well, it's just too hard."

"Do you remember what he looks like?"

Katie shook her head. "I have a photo in my Bible of us hiking on a trail somewhere. I'm on his shoulders. It's taken from far away and pretty blurry, but better than nothing." She tightened her grip on the mug of tea. "I pray for him sometimes. I wish I knew more about him, or had a letter or something of his, but I don't know much except what my mom's told me, and she's not very interested in talking about him." She took a sip of her tea and stared into the mug.

"Sorry I brought it up."

"No, it's okay. Most of the time I can let it go. It's not worth dwelling on. But if I can't talk to you about it, who can I?"

"True. On that note, I have a few other things I need to say to you." Rachael pulled her legs up onto the chair. "First, I'm sorry I didn't tell you about Jack, that I kept it from you."

"Why did you?"

"For a long time I didn't know what to do. I felt so trapped. I knew that if I had the baby, I would have to do it on my own, and that really scared me. I couldn't tell my mom, and I refused to tell Zack, so except for you, Justin was the only other person who knew I was pregnant."

For a few seconds Rachael stared into her cup of tea, as if gathering her thoughts. Then she looked up and met Katie's gaze. "It killed me to keep it a secret, to keep it from Zack. I was so stupid and proud." She laughed in that sad way only possible when reflecting on past misery.

"Justin was amazing. He really helped me through a lot of stuff. He was just there, you know. He didn't tell me what I should do—he simply listened. I don't know what I would have done if I hadn't had him to talk to."

Katie felt a stab of guilt. How many times had she unwittingly shown her disapproval instead of doing nothing but listening and being there?

"I struggled so much with what to do, it started to drive me crazy. I couldn't think straight anymore. I thought that if I could just have it dealt with and put it all behind me, I could go on with my life and pretend it never happened, you know?"

Katie leaned forward and squeezed Rachael's hand as her friend wiped a stray tear from her cheek.

"I walked into that clinic terrified… I mean I was literally shaking. But I was determined to do it and move on. Everyone makes mistakes, but I had the opportunity to fix this one. If I did, at least I'd have a chance at life." She reached for a tissue and blew her nose. "I doubt you can understand…"

Katie smiled, hoping to assure Rachael no judgement was being passed, that this time she was there to simply listen.

"As soon as I saw the women in the waiting room, I started to think about how often it happens, and how many "mistakes" people get rid of. I tried to stuff it and just do what I came there for. And then, in the exam room, I passed out. When I came to, something hit me. I can't explain it, but I had to get out of there. I just couldn't do it. It didn't matter if keeping the baby was going to be hard, I just couldn't…"

She twisted the tissue between her fingers. "I ran out of the clinic, so there I was, standing on the sidewalk, wondering what I was going to do. I sat on the steps and started to cry. Right then and there. Just let it all go. People walked by and looked at me, but I didn't care. Then the weirdest thing happened. This lady sat down beside me. A total stranger sat down right there with me. She put her arm around me and held my hand. At the time, I didn't think much of it; I was too much of a wreck. If I saw her today, I wouldn't even recognize her. But just the feel of her hand…"

Rachael swallowed. "The way she showed love to me without saying a word—a complete stranger. An amazing thing happened—I know you'll get this—suddenly I felt better. This feeling of total relief, peace almost, came over me. For the first time in my life, I felt comforted and loved, even though at the time I couldn't have told you why or by whom."

Katie wiped a stray tear from her own cheek and reached for the tissue box.

"When I got back to my apartment later, I knew something big had happened, but I was too afraid to face it. I carried it around for months, what happened that day. I was so stubborn, so sure I was going to do it on my own. But there was something else…"

Rachael went on to tell her of Tom-Cat's visit to their dorm room and his subsequent letter. "When Tom told me those things, I was so upset I passed out and gave myself a concussion. I couldn't remember his visit until after Jack was born. When my memory came back, I had just given birth. I was a total disaster. It really messed me up."

Katie got off the couch and moved to sit beside Rachael. She wrapped her arms around her friend and let her cry. After a long while, Rachael pulled back and dabbed at her eyes.

Katie rubbed her shoulder. "If you keep this up, you'll have red eyes in all your pictures."

They laughed through tears, and Katie could see why Rachael had needed to explain. A confession held inside so long can deaden a person's feelings like a cruel, numbing anesthetic. Rachael needed to talk until there was no more to tell.

Her friend produced a small piece of paper and handed it to Katie. She unfolded the note and read the scrawled words. Repulsion raged in her, as though a fire had been lit in her insides. She read Tom-Cat's signature at the bottom of the page and stared at the clumsy handwriting. Her hand shook as the words fought to sort themselves in her mind.

"Oh Rach." She handed the letter back, tears welling again.

"I can only tell you that losing my memory was a blessing. If I had known, I would have gone ahead with the abortion for sure. One night, after a really rough day of constant crying from both Jack and me, I was at a complete loss. That's when I cried out to God and, not long after, a woman showed up at my door and gave me a basket full of stuff—all the things I needed. I thought about the kind woman at the clinic and realized that God had tried to get my attention, twice.

He sent those women to show me how much he loves me. I really had nothing left to lose. I don't know how much more obvious God needed to make it, but I sat there on the floor and prayed like never before. I asked God to forgive me for my sins, show me what to do, and help me through the mess. And guess what?"

Katie smiled. "You felt peace?"

"Yes! And I felt forgiven. Instead of being sad, I was filled with joy. Exactly how you described to me you felt. I still didn't know how I was going to get by, but I wasn't worried about it anymore."

"And why couldn't you tell me any of this, at least in an email?"

"I almost did, so many times, but I wanted you to see for yourself, to explain it to you in person. It was too important to me. An email wouldn't do. I thought that with your scholarship ending you'd be coming back soon and I could tell you everything. Plus, I wanted to see the look on your face when I told you and when you saw Jack." Rachael wiped the last tear from her cheek. "Can you forgive me?"

"If you will forgive me for not being here for you."

Rachael nodded. "Of course I do. I never expected you to give up your life for me; I was happy for you that you were able to go to Paris and follow your dreams."

Katie hugged her before moving back to the couch. "So, what happened with Zack? How did you finally tell him?"

"It sounds strange, but I have Tom-Cat to thank. If he hadn't written that letter, Zack and I might never have met up again. Tom's mother gave the letter to Zack to give to me."

Warmth flowed through Katie. Her friend's life was unfolding beautiful- ly, like a flower that had waited for spring, waited through the winter storms, through relentless rain, waited for the warming sun. Katie marvelled at the good- ness of God and acknowledged that only He could turn those months of dark- ness to light.

"By the end of our first day together, Zack asked me to marry him. I was so caught off guard—I couldn't believe he had asked me. That old fear came rushing back that he was just feeling sorry for me and doing the right thing."

"But you said yes."

"Not right away. I asked him if I could let him know. I had to make sure he meant it and that he wasn't just rushing into it because he thought he *should*. And there's something else. Remember you always said that you never wanted to marry a man who didn't share your beliefs?"

"Yes." Her chest ached at the thought of the two men she had ended relationships with over that, even though it had been the right thing to do.

"Strangely enough, that was echoing in my head. I couldn't shake it. Every weekend after work, Zack drove from Toronto to spend time with me and Jack. After a month, I started to allow myself to believe that he was serious and really wanted this. So, I told him how I felt about God."

"How did that go?"

"I told him about the lady who had sat with me on the steps and the other one who had come to my apartment—perfectly timed—and how I finally asked Jesus into my life. I could see he didn't understand right then, but when he came to visit a week later, something was different with him. He explained how he had prayed with a workmate, that he had met God."

Rachael pulled another tissue from the box. "That's when I understood I could finally accept his proposal. Next thing I knew, he'd gotten down on one knee and pulled this from his pocket." She held out the ring Katie had noticed but not yet examined.

"Oh Rach, it's beautiful. It's a miracle how all this worked out; I'm so happy for you."

"And I can't tell you how happy I am that you could be here for this."

"I wouldn't miss this day for the world."

"God is good, Kat. When I look at my life, I'm overwhelmed. It's more than I deserve, and way more than I could have ever thought to ask for or imagine."

Twenty-Six

KATIE STUDIED HER REFLECTION IN THE MIRROR. DID SHE look as nervous as she felt? She patted the dark shadows under her eyes and sighed. Tears, jet lag, and lack of sleep had left their mark. After their lengthy talk, she and Rachael had shared a midnight snack, even though they knew they should go to bed. Not knowing when they would enjoy time like that together again, they were reluctant for it to end, but they finally turned in for the night.

Instead of sleep, Katie lay on the couch listening to the unfamiliar sounds that resonated from Rachael's one bedroom apartment: the hum of the fridge, the rhythmic ticking of the kitchen clock, and Jack's little squeaks and grunts. Apprehension about the day ahead seemed to build with each passing hour. By 5:30 am, when the birds were just beginning to stir, Katie gave up on sleep, switched the side table light on, and flicked open her Bible. Even that, like sleep, had been a futile attempt; she found it impossible to concentrate, reading words but not absorbing a single one.

She told herself it was just nerves for Rachael and tried not to admit how anxious she was about standing up as maid of honour with Justin as best man. Rachael had thought it would be okay, but in reality, it was nothing short of awkward.

Last night, she had asked Rachael what made her think to partner them at the wedding. Her answer had been candid, a little too matter-of-fact.

"I took a chance. Apart from Zack and my son, you two are my favourite people in the world. Not to mention that you are meant to be together. You can't blame me for wanting to help that along a little, can you?"

She held up a hand before Katie could respond. "I kinda hoped that once you saw each other again you'd figure it out, but I knew you both well enough to believe that if you weren't going to get it together, you'd at least be civil. Right?"

Katie sighed. It wasn't the night to try and explain to Rachael that she didn't agree that she and Justin were supposed to be together. Nor was it appropriate to tell Rachael that the moment she had set eyes on Justin again, the familiar nervousness had returned, and she'd had to force herself to fend off feelings she didn't wish to rekindle.

No, she would keep that from Rachael, her own small secret. She didn't need Rachael passing on anything to Justin. Rachael had made it all too clear that she thought Justin still had feelings for Katie, and Katie did not want to do anything to get his hopes up.

So, she would conceal her feelings, covering them up just as the much-needed foundation applied under her tired eyes would conceal the dark, puffy shadows, and no one would be the wiser. She would simply do what she had come to do: enjoy her friend's special day and get out as quickly as possible when it was done.

———

Katie pulled her wrap over her bare shoulders as she climbed out of the car onto the sidewalk in front of St. Jerome's. Spring seemed delayed here. Already the tulips were blooming in Paris, but in southern Ontario, a chill lingered and patchy remnants of slow-melting snow could be seen among the trees.

Katie waited for Rachael, reaching for her friend's bouquet as she slid from the back seat. The two girls walked into the foyer of the chapel. From there they could see into the small sanctuary, which was filled with fifty close friends and relatives, some talking in hushed tones, others perusing the wedding program.

Rachael faced Katie. "Thank you for being here."

Katie straightened Rachael's veil and squeezed her friend's hand before passing back her bouquet. "You know I wouldn't miss it."

"Oh my goodness." Rachael pressed a hand to her chest. "I'm so nervous."

"Don't be; just enjoy every moment. You look beautiful."

"Thanks to the eye drops." She offered Katie a wry grin.

The music signalling Katie to start down the aisle began. She took a deep breath, sent a reassuring smile to Rachael, and stepped into the sanctuary. She dutifully smiled at the guests as she passed the rows, careful to avoid casting her eyes in the direction of Justin, who stood planted beside Zack at the front.

The ceremony was beautiful. Katie spent half of it dabbing at her eyes. It was plain to see how in love Zack and Rachael were. As they murmured their vows to one another, they appeared lost in their own world instead of making their marriage promises before a crowd of gathered witnesses.

Throughout the ceremony, Katie avoided eye contact with Justin, even though she felt his gaze on her. *I wish I could have enjoyed this moment with him, but that's not possible.* Preoccupied with thoughts of how she would get through the rest of the day, she forced herself to focus on the ceremony and not think ahead to the photos and reception. *One step at a time.* Right now, all she wanted to do was share fully in her best friend's beautiful moment.

———————

Even though he willed himself not to stare, Justin couldn't take his eyes off Katie as she walked down the aisle. She looked incredible, her dress hugging her figure and making her eyes appear even bluer than usual. For a moment, he let himself imagine she was walking down the aisle to him. He was thankful when Rachael appeared at the back of the chapel and he found an excuse to look elsewhere.

After the ceremony, Katie linked her arm through his so they could walk out of the sanctuary together. Her gentle touch was light and perfect. When they reached the foyer and she stepped discreetly away from him, he fought the disappointment. A residual tingling warmth remained where her arm had been.

———————

The reception was held at a nearby hall, and after the dinner and speeches, a quartet played while the guests swayed to the music on a makeshift dance floor or conversed in small groups. Katie sank onto a chair, slipped off her heels, and rubbed her hand over the side of her face. Justin excused himself from a group of university friends and walked toward where she sat with her chin resting on her hand, watching Rachael and Zack as they made the rounds talking to their guests.

"Mind if I join you?"

She hesitated before holding her hand out to the seat beside her. "No, not at all."

He pulled out the chair and sat. "Tired?"

"Yes, very."

"Feeling the time change?"

"I guess so. Rach and I were up pretty late as well."

"It was a great day."

Katie nodded.

The music slowed. Together they watched as Zack led Rachael to the miniature dance floor. As they swayed together, Zack spoke into Rachael's ear. Whatever he said made her laugh. Justin smiled. Rachael's head fit neatly under Zack's chin, as though they'd been made for each other.

Before he could talk himself out of it, he turned to Katie. "Hey, do you wanna dance?"

She studied the hands she'd clasped in her lap, and Justin thought she might decline, but then she looked up at him and smiled. "Sure, let's go."

He offered her his hand and led her to the dance floor. The feel of her slim waist beneath his fingers made it difficult for him to think straight, and he struggled to find the words to make casual conversation.

Zack and Rachael danced past them, both smiling a little too widely in their direction. Rachael reached out and gave Katie's arm a squeeze before being whisked away.

"They make a great couple," Justin said, using the distraction to his favour.

"They sure do. I've never seen her so happy."

"Me neither. It was a tough year for her."

"You know that better than anyone."

The song ended too soon, and Katie released his hand. Justin followed her back to the table where she reached for her glass of water.

"Thanks for the dance." She took a sip before sitting down.

Justin settled on the chair beside her. "Hey Katie. Can I ask you... are you happy?"

"Of course. How could I not be happy for them?"

"No, I mean are *you* happy?" He leaned forward and rested his forearms on his thighs.

A server came to refill her water glass and she took a small sip, as if buying time to answer.

"Yes, I am, actually."

He searched her face then leaned back, nodding his head with resigned acceptance. "I'm glad for you." He squeezed her hand before standing up and walking away.

―――――

Katie needed time to regain her composure. For several minutes, she experienced the heady effects of Justin's deep, brown eyes and his gentle touch. She hadn't expected his forthright question and had taken a moment to figure out how to be honest without disclosing the whole truth. She swallowed back the words she longed to say—the words that would have answered the question he was really asking. She couldn't let him know how he made her feel, that just being beside him made her want to forget everything she'd ever said about not being able to get involved with him because of the difference in their beliefs. *He could love me the way I need to be loved. He would be an amazing man to spend my life with.*

Before he turned away, a weak smile had crossed his face. The temptation to stop him, to run after him, to give in and tell him what he wanted to hear, was fierce. It took every ounce of her will to remain rooted to the seat until the danger of going after him had passed. The familiar feel of his warm hand on hers, however fleeting, had sent tingles up her arm. She wished she could have prolonged the moment, but deep down she knew she had done the right thing. Anything else would have been utterly selfish.

Why did the right thing have to be the hardest thing? And how was it that, after all this time, just a few moments with Justin brought back such powerful feelings? *So much for discipline.* Maybe she was wrong and he *could* grow into a relationship with God, even if they were dating. Maybe she would see him one more time before leaving and say some small thing to let him know that she wasn't as cold as she appeared.

Or maybe it would be better if she just didn't see him again at all.

PART

Two

CHAPTER
Twenty-Seven

KATIE MANOEUVRED HER CAR INTO THE DRIVEWAY BESIDE the thatched-roofed cottage she had become the owner of three weeks earlier. The house of her dreams had been waiting for her along the banks of the river in the village of Sonning On Thames, and, after a short amount of negotiating, she'd managed to procure the quaint, eighty-year-old cottage.

She smiled, remembering the moment she'd seen it for the first time, the *For Sale* sign jutting out from the hedged-in front garden. Roses climbed a trellis arching over the wooden front door—their soft pink beautifully complementing the cream-coloured stucco walls. Leaded window panes gave the front of the cottage a whimsical smile. From their ledges hung carefully-tended window boxes with a fascinating profusion of flowers in a wondrous array of colour and variety. Annual and perennial plants and shrubs of seemingly every sort crept along pathways and peeped out of every patch of garden bed.

The back garden was still more beautiful. Koi swam among lilies and played under a fountain's spray in a rock-edged pond. An irregular path led away from the pond, gracefully weaving under mature trees and through the secluded garden, each bend and curve offering a new and marvelous vista, culminating at the river's edge. The property was absolutely idyllic and made even more perfect by the thatched roof. She could barely believe it was hers. It was truly a dream come true.

Ten years of apartment living had made the move to England even more delightful. Not that she had minded living in the city—she loved Paris and kept an apartment there for her needed trips—but this property was the culmination of what felt like years of effort. It still amazed her how much people were willing to pay for her art, but she was grateful that they were as it enabled her to find this incredible place to live. The move also allowed her to be closer to her mother, who had remained in England and had been living in Bournemouth these past years.

Katie climbed out of the car and gathered her basket of groceries before heading up the stone path. After ducking to miss a newly-opened rose, she unlocked the front door and bent to pick up the mail from a pile below the letter slot. She stepped in and set her groceries on the hall bench so she could sort through the mound while pushing closed the old, wooden door that creaked willfully in response.

Among the ordinary pile of mail was a card from Rachael. She ripped open the envelope, revealing one of her own printed cards of a painting called *Jongleur* or Juggler, in English, a piece permanently exhibited at the Pompidou Centre in Paris. Warmth spread through her chest. Rachael remained her biggest fan.

Tucked inside the card she found Jack's latest school picture. Rachael had written on the back, *Jack: 10 years old*. It had been over a year since the three of them had visited her in Paris, and in that time he had changed so much. Katie smiled at his confident, boyish grin. He had Zack's light hair and green eyes, but Rachael's face shape and dimples. The photo was a stark reminder of how quickly time passed.

The grandfather clock in the hall told her she had two hours before she would meet with her agent Peter Morneau for a drink at the Bull, a nearby pub in Sonning. Time enough for a cup of tea in the conservatory and some quiet time with her heavenly Father.

———

Peter held a chair out for Katie and she sat down and waited for him to settle onto the seat across the table from her.

"Before I forget, this came to my office." Peter reached into his suit coat and handed Katie a letter. "It's an invitation to attend the opening of a new arts centre in Cambridge, Ontario. Isn't that your hometown?"

She nodded and scanned the letter with interest.

"Unfortunately, it overlaps the opening of your exhibit at the Artcurial."

Katie frowned. She had looked forward to showing at the Artcurial in Paris since their invitation months prior. She couldn't miss the opening night reception.

"Exactly overlaps?"

"Well, the opening at Artcurial is on the first of September and the Cambridge gallery opens the evening of the second."

"That will work. I'll go to the opening then take the first flight from Paris the next morning."

"Would you make it?"

"The flight is only about seven and a half hours."

"That's pushing it."

"You're forgetting the time change; Cambridge is six hours behind Paris."

"Oh, right. I take it you'd like me to accept the invitation for you?"

"Yes, please. That will give me a chance to visit friends, too."

He took out his phone. "I'll take care of it."

They worked well together. Peter was a no-nonsense sort of fellow who thrived on a challenge and made things happen. Katie likened his life to a tornado, a whirlwind with him in the middle, still and calm. How he juggled his clients and their patrons was no small task, but he did it with seeming ease, making each one feel important. Just yesterday he had flown from Paris to London, where he spent the day visiting contacts on her behalf. Although he and his wife lived in Paris, they both travelled a great deal with their work and kept a residence in the south of France that they enjoyed over long weekends and holidays. He had offered it to Katie numerous times as a get-away, but she had yet to take him up on it.

She sighed. If her life got any busier, she would certainly have to consider it.

Opening night at Artcurial was a success, with fellow artists, critics, and other notable ambassadors in the art community in attendance. Katie was starting to become accustomed to evenings like these. The crowd waiting to be spoken to, the what-were-you thinking-when-you-painted-this questions, the smile that made her cheeks ache, the thank-you-all-for-coming speech, and finally the talk from Peter praising her talent, during which her face still warmed, after all this time. Through it all, she worked to treat each person with respect, as if they were the only one that mattered to her.

The best part was the unfailing support of her friends. Among them was Jean who, over the years, had attended as many events as his schedule allowed, this one being no exception. A constant encouragement, and familiar with her discomfort with being in the spotlight, he seemed to keep a pulse on her and would deliberately slide in at the most appropriate moments, such as when she'd been caught too long in a conversation with a critic or was looking weary over a lengthy line-up of people waiting to speak with her. A quick word or well-timed joke from him, and once more the evening would be running smoothly.

Then there was Madame Bonnard, who had become like a grandmother to Katie. Now retired, she managed to attend nearly every opening and never tired of bragging about Katie to as many as would listen. It didn't matter to her that Katie needed little touting these days. Even a small print, the size of the original she had sketched for Madame Bonnard, fetched far more than Katie would have ever dreamed.

Well into the third hour of the Artcurial festivities, Katie excused herself and headed for the ladies room. She managed to reach it after only two diversions, one from an art critic, the other a professor. Once inside, she took a deep breath, said a silent prayer, and quickly refreshed her lipstick.

She purposely took the long route back, meandering down a short hall leading to a nearby room. An enchanting photograph of a field of haystacks with children playing under an immense sky hung on the wall just outside the door, above a ledge holding a stack of leaflets. Katie reached for one of the brochures to find out the photographer's name. Her breath caught in her throat. Her gaze darted back to the photograph and then to the title card stuck inconspicuously on the wall beside it. Sure enough, it too read: Justin Burke.

Entranced, she crept into the room, soaking in the framed images. His work was everywhere. Beautiful, sensitive storytelling without words. She brought a hand to her mouth. So he had done it. He had followed his dream.

Most of his work dealt with human subjects in nature, captured seemingly unaware. His timing was impeccable. The candid shots were taken from everywhere in the world and depicted ordinary people in everyday life. A farmer dwarfed in the middle of his field peering into the upturned hood of his tractor. A humorous one of a toddler eating a pomegranate, blood red juice dripping everywhere amid a crazy grin. A haunting one of a child in some war-ravaged country, digging among a refuse pile, rags hanging off an emaciated body.

Katie turned a corner, stepping into an area entitled "Earlier Works". She saw it immediately. A duplicate of the photo she had long since put away.

Contemplating the enlarged version of her much younger self, her throat tightened as the memories came flooding back. Like an old song brings long-forgotten recollections, this photo summoned powerful remembrances.

"There you are; they want to toast the artist."

Peter was slightly more ruffled and flushed in the face than usual. Though she recognized that, to the casual observer, he would appear jovial, in control, and at the top of his game.

"I'll be right there."

He shot her an imploring look before scanning the room, obviously wondering what Katie found so interesting. "Nice work." He stopped short in front of one of the photographs.

"They are, aren't they?"

Peter's head tilted slightly as he examined the picture. "Is that you?"

She planted her hands on her hips. "I wish you would look as interested in my paintings."

He ignored the dig. "It is. I don't believe it. Do you know this guy?"

"I used to, a long time ago."

"Wow. That's amazing." Her agent leaned forward to look at the card. "Eyes of an Angel. Hmm." He swivelled to face her.

"Don't look at me like that." Heat crept up Katie's neck. "Like I said, it was a long time ago."

Another lifetime, in fact.

————

Katie kicked off her heels and sank onto the sofa in her room at the Sheraton Hotel at the Charles de Gaulle International airport. For a few moments, she remained in a collapsed position, attempting to unwind, but a strange restlessness gripped her. She sat up and perched on the edge of the cushion to massage her aching feet.

After a few moments, she rose and moved to the window. The hotel overlooked the runway, and from a rain-streaked window, Katie watched a British Airways plane taxi to the runway. She drew in a deep breath and slowly exhaled as the lights on the plane flashed rhythmically, reflecting off the pavement. In only a handful of hours she would take a 747 back to Toronto.

She bent down and pulled the leaflet she had taken from Justin's exhibit out of her bag. Her eyes settled on the section, "Artist's Story". With great interest, she read about Justin's training, his purpose, and his goals. They all dealt with helping the world's less fortunate. The statement detailed how he spent a great deal of his time in third world countries, using his background in engineering to help develop better water systems and his lens to tell stories that gave others a voice in the world. Her chest tightened at the quote, "God hasn't forgotten about them… we have."

Katie blinked. What did that mean? Was Justin a believer now? The brochure trembled in her fingers and she set it on the side table. Pride and loss mingled together and her chest ached.

Exhausted, she climbed into bed. Given that it was one in the morning, she thought she would fall asleep immediately, but her mind was too full and cognizant of the fact that in a mere five hours her alarm would sound. Instead, she lay awake, staring into the dark and listening to the dull, unfamiliar sounds of the hotel.

Just as sleep began to envelop her thoughts, a pressing need to pray struck her. To her surprise, Aiden's name was whispered through her being. Was she dreaming? Katie attempted to settle back to sleep, but again it came, this time more forcibly.

Pray for Aiden.

She sat up and fumbled for the light. What a ludicrous thought after all these years.

Is this really you? Sometimes it was difficult to discern between the leading of the Holy Spirit and her own subconscious memories and desires.

Pray for Aiden.

By the third time she was certain. She needed to pray—was being called to do so.

The message that pressed itself into her spirit was urgent. It came in persistent yet powerful waves, an insistence that she pray for help and protection. She didn't know from what or why, only that it was inexplicably necessary. So Katie prayed into the early hours of the morning, uttering inaudible words that reached through the span of heaven and into her Saviour's ears, unleashing heaven's help.

CHAPTER
Twenty-Eight

HIGHWAY 401 WAS SLICK FROM THE SUDDEN DROP IN temperature and freezing rain. Aiden had worked late at the clinic and stayed downtown to enjoy an end-of-the-week drink with a fellow physician, hoping to miss the worst of the commuter traffic. Given the road conditions, he was sorry he hadn't taken the SUV this morning instead of his Porsche. Its low-profile tires were less than ideal for the slippery roads. Those drinks he'd had on an empty stomach weren't helping. They may have put him just over the legal limit, and he slowed down.

He didn't make a habit of driving under the influence, but he'd promised his mother he would arrive at a decent hour for a family dinner, since the whole family was gathering for a birthday celebration for his sister. Besides, he'd only had three beers and would be fully sober by the time it took to drive from Toronto to Cambridge. He made a careful lane change. At this rate he would arrive home by eight and, although that might mean missing dinner, it was decent-enough timing.

But the conditions were worse than he thought. He counted three vehicles in the ditch within a ten-kilometre stretch of road. The truck drivers took no notice and barrelled past the slower traffic. Brake lights flashed ahead and Aiden veered onto an off ramp onto back roads. This route took a little longer, but if there was an accident on the highway as he suspected, he'd be better off taking an alternate route.

The icy surface of the off ramp proved a challenge, but Aiden managed to manoeuvre the vehicle to the right side. Once on a narrow side road, parallel to the jammed-up highway, going straight was much less daunting. *As long as I don't have to stop quickly.*

As he hit a sharper-than-expected turn, sudden headlights came into view, shining on the glassy pavement on his side of the road. A split second too late, he turned the steering wheel in an attempt to veer his car away from the oncoming vehicle. The ice offered no deliverance. The last thing he saw before the crushing pain was the blurred face of the woman behind the wheel of the minivan. The last thing he heard was the deafening sound of crushing metal drowning out his scream.

Suffocating blackness moved in like a dense fog. Everything grew still.

All too soon, there were no more breaths left to take. Cold moved through him, enveloping the pain.

Then he felt nothing.

————

Katie whispered pleading words into the night. At a time when she should have been asleep, she remained in a place of intercession, her utterances rising into the darkness.

————

Aiden could see his crumpled car, the van in the ditch, the woman inside slumped over the steering wheel, and the children. Children!

Then he saw himself.

A man was rushing toward his car while a woman, his wife, maybe, ran to the van. The man wrenched open Aiden's door. He leaned over Aiden and, without moving his body, began CPR.

Aiden watched in confused fascination.

The light that came next was intense, bright, and unimaginably beautiful. Music swirled through the air around him. Aiden had never heard it before, but was instantly aware he had longed for its sound his whole life.

A figure stood beside him. Aiden knew him, although they had never met. They walked as friends journeying along a deserted road. Was the man an angel? His guardian angel? But something else lurked in peripheral shadows as he and the angel strode toward the light. Something dark, threatening. Terrifying.

Pain jolted his body. Someone was screaming. A child? A woman? A siren split the night air. Red lights flashed. A hand that didn't seem attached to his body reached out to touch the agonizing source of his suffering. A warm wetness spread over his fingers.

"Don't let him move," a voice yelled.

Still, blissful blackness overtook him again.

————

Although she couldn't see or hear it, a deep awareness that an invisible battle was being fought as she prayed filled Katie. A battle as real and more powerful than those waged by human hands. Her hands were clasped tightly as she interceded on Aiden's behalf, waging war on her knees with the help of heaven's armies. She whispered into the dark until the first light came and the intensity and unease in her spirit finally subsided.

————

After being briefly diverted to Montreal due to the ice storm, Katie landed at Pearson International Airport in Toronto six hours after her expected arrival. She was travel weary, and sighed as she came down the escalator to meet a lengthy customs line-up. Three quarters of an hour later, she retrieved her bags from the luggage carousel and headed for the arrivals gate. Rachael called to her from the partition and the two friends met and hugged.

"Rough night?" Rachael relieved Katie of one of her bags.

"The worst. I can't stand delays. Especially when I was sitting and waiting for news on my flight and couldn't go to a hotel for a decent sleep."

"Well, it's good in a way. I wouldn't have chanced the freezing rain. There were a ton of accidents. The 401 westbound was actually closed for a few hours."

"Wow, so it was really bad?"

"Definitely. But smooth sailing now that the salt trucks have been out."

They weaved their way through the crowded terminal building.

"How's Jack?"

Rachael's face lit up. "Growing like a weed and very excited about your visit."

"Me too. I can't wait to see him."

"We'd better hurry. Your opening is at seven, isn't it?"

"Yep." Katie glanced at her watch. "Two and a half hours. I guess we better keep moving."

"Yes we better, crazy woman. You'll have to tell me all about last night's opening while we drive."

They pushed through the crowd, piled the cases into Rachael's car, and set off for Cambridge. They were still catching up on one another's news when they pulled off the 401 onto Highway 24. Their hometown had grown over the past ten years, and every time Katie returned, there was something new to see. Even so, it still had a way of feeling like a small town. It seemed so long ago that she had called this place home.

At 5:30, Rachael turned into the Wilsons' driveway. Jack must have been watching out the window, because he came running outside in stocking feet.

"Jack, get your…"

But his mother's admonitions were lost as he flung his arms around Katie and welcomed her home with a huge bear hug.

For the second morning in a row, Katie walked Jack to school, stopping in at a local coffee shop after she'd dropped him off. When she had lived in Cambridge, she'd rarely taken the time to sit and enjoy a coffee, preferring to order at the drive-through. But now, with the luxury of time, she sat down in one of the few available seats. A well-read *Cambridge Times* lay on the table.

She chuckled as she read the front page headline: "Artist Returns Home". The article included a picture of one of her paintings, and she scanned the first few paragraphs. As she went to turn the page, another headline caught her eye. Its header, in smaller font near the bottom of the page, read, "Cambridge Man Kills Three".

Katie's eyes widened as she read. *Following a fatal head-on collision Friday evening, former Cambridge resident, Dr. Aiden Ford, remains in critical condition in Cambridge Memorial Hospital.*

Her heart thudded in her chest. Aiden! She pored over the words, blood pounding in her ears.

Ford's vehicle crossed the centre line and struck an oncoming van on Hwy. 97 near Freelton. Dead are Amy Scott and her two children, three-year-old Bethany and five-year-old Josiah. Police say alcohol may have been a contributing factor. Charges are pending.

A shiver swept through Katie's body. "No." She pressed a hand to her mouth.

The barely-touched coffee turned in her stomach. She rose and fumbled in her coat pocket for her cell phone while forcing open the coffee shop's glass door. Outside, the icy wind whipped her full in the face and she backed around the corner of the building to wait for the taxi.

———————

Katie followed the signs for the intensive care unit at Cambridge Memorial Hospital. Turning down the last hallway, she spotted Mrs. Ford sitting alone in a waiting area. From a distance, Aiden's mother had changed little, but as she drew closer, Katie could see that her face looked pale, pinched, and drawn. Her deeply-circled eyes stared at nothing and she sat motionless as though sleeping while fully awake.

Katie stopped a few feet away. She was entering into a delicate situation. Her courage wavered. Should she go? Something inside gave her strength, and she forced herself forward until she stood in front of Aiden's mom.

She swallowed with difficulty and touched the woman lightly on the shoulder. "Mrs. Ford?"

It took a moment for the words to register. Aiden's mother glanced sideways, not directly at Katie. Perhaps she was expecting a doctor or nurse with additional news, but seemed exhausted at the prospect. Hers was the frame of a devastated woman.

"Mrs. Ford?" Katie tried again.

The woman slowly swung her gaze up to meet Katie's.

"I know it's been a while, but I…"

"Katie Banks? Why, it's been years." Mrs. Ford pulled herself off the vinyl chair and stood.

"Yes, it has. I, uh, I just heard and I, well I hope you don't mind me being here."

"Not at all. It's nice to see you. Thank you for coming."

She spoke haltingly, as though forming words required more effort than she had strength for. Katie wrapped her arms around Aiden's mom, hoping the gesture would impart at least a small measure of comfort.

They found a place among the worn seats.

"You must be in town for the opening of the arts centre. I read about it in the paper last week."

"Yes, I came in on Saturday."

"Congratulations. What an honour for you."

Barbara Ford's small talk was altruistic but strained. Katie rested a hand on her arm. "How's Aiden doing?"

His mother took a deep breath and the tension deepened in her face. "He's been in a coma for almost three days." Each word appeared to cause her physical pain. "He suffered trauma to the brain. Three of his ribs are broken and they operated on his collapsed lung. His knee was shattered and there are several smaller fractures. So, overall, not very well."

"I'm so sorry."

"Thank you." Mrs. Ford twisted a damp tissue in her hand. "It probably wouldn't have been so bad, but for some reason he wasn't wearing his seat belt." She contemplated Katie, as if she might be able to offer an explanation.

When Katie didn't, Aiden's mother shifted in her seat. "How much did you read?" She rubbed the side of her hand across her forehead. "It was bad, you know. I had no idea what had happened. The police just called and said Aiden had been in an accident and that we should go to the hospital."

She stopped and drew in a shaky breath. "The man who arrived first on the scene said Aiden had no vital signs. He managed to give him CPR and that brought him back until the paramedics came. They worked all night to keep him alive."

Katie reached for Mrs. Ford's hand as a tear slid down the older woman's cheek.

"They brought the mother and her children to the hospital in separate ambulances. I didn't realize they were part of the same accident." She swallowed, as if attempting to push back the flood of sudden tears. "I heard a child crying and calling for her mommy from the stretcher. The mother and one of her children were pronounced dead on arrival. The other child died a few hours later. I didn't know it was my baby that... I didn't know..." A guttural sound preceded the full sobs that shook her body.

There was nothing Katie could say to that. She softly rubbed Mrs. Ford's back.

"Now Aiden won't wake up," his mother whispered.

"What does his doctor say?"

"The longer he's in a coma, the less likely he is to come out of it. I asked what his chances were and he told me that, considering the trauma, only twenty to thirty percent. Apparently the fluid buildup isn't responding to medication."

Katie bit her lower lip. *Father, give me words of comfort.* "I'm so sorry," she repeated. What else was there to say?

"I'm trying to stay positive. I keep hoping..." Mrs. Ford attempted a watery smile. "Anyway..." she cleared her throat, "how long are you staying?"

"Just a week. I'm leaving Friday for New York, then on to Miami to see some clients. I'll head home on the twentieth."

"You've done so well with your art."

"Thank you. I've been fortunate." Katie tucked a strand of hair behind her ear. "Would you mind if I went in to see him?"

"You can, but the doctor asked that we don't speak to him too much. They don't want his brain over-stimulated right now."

"Will you be okay here?"

"Yes, I'm just waiting for Aiden's dad to arrive. Aiden's in room 110, just down the hallway on the left."

"I'll see you in a few minutes." Summoning every bit of inner strength she had, Katie rose and started down the hall.

————

For years, Katie had tried to put away memories of Aiden. Now, seeing him lying in the hospital bed, she barely recognized her first love. How unnerving it was to be in a room with him after all this time and witness him in this condition.

She lowered herself onto the chair at his bedside and scrutinized his pale, expressionless face. Faint smile lines rimmed his eyes—lines she'd never had the chance to see form. Katie reached out and softly placed trembling fingertips on his cheek, just below the bandage wrapped around his head, closed her eyes, and began the very thing that she had come to do—pray.

————

For the next three days, Katie came and prayed over Aiden. On the third day, the doctor spoke with his parents about surgery. The medication had been ineffective, and they couldn't wait any longer. Nurses checked him constantly, and family members took turns sitting in Aiden's room. The doctor's prognosis was grim.

Katie was due to leave the next morning. Before going back to her room to catch a few hours of sleep then head to the airport, she spent a few final moments alone in the room with Aiden, lifting silent prayers asking that God's will would be done in his life.

————

Miami in October was beautiful. Warm, sunny—a perfect retreat. By Tuesday afternoon, the work portion of Katie's trip was complete, and apart from a casual dinner with a gallery curator at her favourite restaurant by the beach, she could enjoy a few moments to herself. After a tiring day of visiting three clients, a luncheon interview with a reporter from the *Miami Herald*, and another interview with a local art magazine, she rushed back to her hotel room to change for a run along the beach before sunset. The doorman greeted her as she breezed through the lobby to the elevator. Her cell phone went off just as the doors slid open.

After stepping inside, she pressed the button for the fourth floor with one hand while fumbling through her oversized purse for her phone with the other. It rang numerous times before she located it. *Whoever it is really wants to speak with me.* The elevator reached her floor and Katie held the doors open as she pressed the device to her ear.

"Kate?"

She frowned, not recognizing the husky voice. Her mind raced to remember anyone ever calling her Kate.

"Yes, this is Katie."

"Hey Kate, it's Aiden."

Katie slumped against the panel of buttons to keep from collapsing to the floor.

CHAPTER
Twenty-Nine

HAD SHE HEARD CORRECTLY?

"Pardon?" The question came out raspy and Katie cleared her throat.

"It's me, Kate; it's Aiden."

For a moment she couldn't speak. She'd let go of the doors, but her bag blocked the opening. The doors tried to close but opened back up again several times before her brain registered that she needed to step out. She staggered into the hallway.

"Kate? You still there?"

"Yes. Aiden. You're okay?"

"Well, I wouldn't go that far."

"But you... you woke up! When?"

"On Saturday afternoon."

"So they didn't have to operate?" She struggled to comprehend what she was hearing.

"No, I regained consciousness just before they planned to take me in. Thankfully they didn't have to."

"What about the swelling?"

"Going down every day. The doctors have no explanation."

Thank you, Lord. "So there's no permanent damage?"

"It appears that way. So far, so good, anyway."

"Wow. That's absolutely amazing." Tension, like an unplugged valve, drained from her limbs.

"I heard you were here."

"Yeah, I was. I read about the accident in the paper while I was in town visiting Rachael."

"Thanks for coming, Kate. Totally unexpected."

She'd always loved the way he said her name. "I know. Pretty weird, right? Your old girlfriend showing up after all these years." She attempted a chuckle.

"Why did you?"

His voice had thickened, likely with fatigue. She weighed her words carefully, not wanting to agitate him. "I had my reasons."

"Care to share them with me?"

"Maybe another time." She propped a shoulder against the wall. Was she actually talking to Aiden after all this time? "How did you get my number?"

"I had my people call your people."

She managed a shaky grin. However battered his body might be, his sense of humour was still intact. "Impressive."

"Thanks. When are you in town again?"

"I don't know. I'm not back that often."

"Let me rephrase that; when *can* you be back in town? I'd really like to see you."

She moved the phone away from her mouth and took a deep breath. *Give me wisdom, Lord.*

"Kate? Would you consider coming back for a visit? A real one this time?"

"I… I'm not sure."

"Okay," he said slowly.

"Listen. I was about to go for a run." *I need time to think about this.* "Can I call you later?"

"I'm not supposed to be on the phone. My brother lent me his cell. If the nurses find out…"

"You never did like to obey the rules, did you?"

At the beautiful sound of his laugh, the years seemed to fall away.

"Ouch. I guess I shouldn't be doing much of that."

"Your ribs?"

"Yeah. That's one nice thing about being unconscious, no pain."

"Why don't you call me tomorrow?"

"Tonight. I may not be alive tomorrow."

Katie frowned. "That's not funny."

"Sorry. Tonight. Please?"

"Okay. I'm out for dinner, but try me around ten."

It wasn't until they said goodbye that she realized her hand was trembling. In fact, her entire body was shaking. Katie pushed away from the wall and started down the hall, a prayer already forming in her mind.

This time, she wasn't going to make any decisions before discussing it with God.

———————

It had been a tiring day. Aiden needed to rebuild his stamina, but for now it took everything he had just to breathe. That second conversation with Katie had been exhausting, and he'd slept for four hours after hanging up. The nurses would not be impressed if they knew he had made two calls. It had been worth it though. He had successfully talked Katie into coming back to Cambridge before flying home to Paris.

The nurses were being strict about visitors. They'd told him that, just before dinner, a man had asked to see him. Aiden was sleeping at the time, and since the man wasn't family, they decided not to let him visit. *I wonder who that was?* Aiden thought about it for a few seconds before drifting back to sleep.

———————

Walking toward the hospital entrance, Katie passed a mixed crowd of patients and visitors, smoking as they hovered under the building's canopy in the chill of the fall morning. As she neared them, one man held his cigarette away from his body and moved to open the door. Even inside the lobby, Katie caught the faint smell of stale cigarette smoke filtering into the seating area where patients visited with friends, one on crutches, one in a wheelchair, all in dull blue hospital gowns.

She rode the elevator to the third floor. Standing outside the door of Aiden's room, Katie paused. *Lord, please give me the words to say.* She entered the room. Aiden slept on the narrow mattress, his head slightly inclined. Katie stopped at the foot of his bed. Her throat tightened. In less than a week, he looked so much better. Colour had seeped back into his face, and all but one of the many tubes that had been hooked up to who-knows-where were gone. The only outward sign of the ordeal was the bandage still wrapped around his head.

"Thank you, Lord, for keeping him alive," she whispered. She rounded the bed and pulled up a chair.

Aiden's eyes flickered open as she settled in. "Hey, you came."

"Yeah. Sorry, I didn't mean to wake you."

"I'm glad you did." He smiled weakly and attempted to straighten up, but winced and sank down again.

"Let me help." Katie moved to the side of his bed and adjusted the pillows behind his back. "Those ribs still giving you trouble, huh?"

"Yeah. They hurt worse than my head now."

"I hear they take a while." Her heart thumped at a ridiculous rate in her chest. How unreal it was to be with him.

"So the doc says."

Katie gripped the bed rail with both hands. "Welcome back."

"Thanks. I should be saying that to you. I hear you came to see me three days in a row last week. Who would've thought?"

Katie glanced out the window. Were her cheeks as red as they felt? "It was the last thing I expected." She said it quietly, almost to herself.

"Is that right?"

"Well, it's pretty strange, don't you think? After years with no interaction, your former girlfriend comes to visit you in hospital?"

"It's not like you were the only one; they were lined up, apparently."

"I noticed." She laughed with him and the muscles in her back and shoulders relaxed a little.

"Why *did* you come, Kate?" His eyes fixed on hers.

"I came for the opening of an arts centre. They invited me and—"

"That's not what I meant. Why did you come *here*?"

She paused. "I came to pray for you."

His eyebrows lifted. "Really?"

"Yes, really."

He pursed his lips. "Well, looks like it worked."

Was he joking? "It does, doesn't it?"

"It was pretty great of you to do something like that. Thanks for caring."

"What makes you think I care?" She let go of the rail with one hand and flicked her fingers lightly against his.

"You wouldn't come and pray if you didn't."

She ignored his smug smile. "Would you believe me if I told you I was asked to pray?"

His brow furrowed. "What do you mean? Who asked you?"

Aware that it might sound ridiculous, she decided to dive in and tell Aiden the story. She had learned that, where God was concerned, things often appeared unconventional. He wasn't limited to a human way of thinking or doing things, and when he wanted to do something, often unexpected and even miraculous things happened. She began with how she had felt a strong urging to pray. She hadn't been given specifics, but felt she had to do it.

"When I read the article, I realized that I must have been praying for you from the time of the accident all through that night."

"Are you telling me you were praying thousands of miles away in the middle of my accident?"

"It was about 7:45 in the evening your time, 1:45 am in Paris."

"Wow." His blue eyes grew wide. "That's incredible."

"I thought so too." She let go of the railing and leaned back in the chair. "I could hardly believe it when I read about the accident, but as soon as I did, it made sense why I felt I had to pray."

A nurse in a pale green uniform entered the room and strode to the side of his bed. "How are you feeling today, Dr. Ford?" She gave Katie a quick, no-nonsense smile.

"Pretty good, thanks."

"You have company?"

"Yes, I do. Meet... my sister."

Katie shot Aiden a warning look as the nurse studied the monitor showing his vitals.

The nurse nodded and left the room as suddenly as she had appeared.

"That's Gina. She's a barrel of laughs."

Katie wagged a finger at him. "Sister, huh?"

"Cousin? Auntie?"

"I think you're experiencing more effects from that knock to the head than you think."

He shrugged. "You just got here. I didn't want you to get kicked out before I had a chance to spend time with you."

"Oh, I almost forgot." Katie reached into the bag she'd dropped at her feet when she sat down. On the way to the hospital, she had stopped to buy treats for Aiden. "You used to like these." She placed the items on the side table.

A smile warmed his face. "Vanilla yogurt and berries. Good memory."

"I thought you might like a break from hospital food."

"Thanks. I haven't eaten much, but this is great."

"Do you want me to find you a bowl?"

"Not right now. I'd rather you just sit here. I want to know what you've been doing all this time besides becoming famous."

She settled back on the chair. "I've been away for almost ten years."

"Paris. I heard."

"You did?"

"My mom mentioned it. She always liked you, so she's been following your career."

His cheeks flushed a little, but Katie ignored it. "She's right. After my first year of university, I went there to study and liked it so much I decided to stay. After I graduated, I found an agent and began showing in galleries. It went well, and now I'm living in England. Decided to buy my retirement home early."

"Congratulations, but aren't there a few things you want to do before you retire?"

"Like what?"

"Most people get married first, have kids, grow old..."

She glanced down at her bare finger. "Why wait when you find the perfect place?"

"But not the perfect person."

That stung, but she forced a smile. "Being an artist can be pretty solitary work."

"That fits then. You always were a bit of a hermit." He winked, a playful grin pulling at the sides of his lips.

"Thanks for the assessment, *Doctor* Ford. How did you manage to make it through med-school anyway? You always were a bit of a... social butterfly."

"Very funny."

"Sorry. I just remember how much you liked to, uh, have fun."

"Party, you mean?"

Katie let that slide by as she tugged her chair closer to the bed. "Not that I ever doubted you had the ability. You were always an intelligent guy."

"Thanks for the assessment." He laughed and her heart lightened. "I guess anything's possible when you put your mind to it."

"True. Good for you. Do you work in this hospital?"

"No, I have my own clinic in Toronto. I specialize in sports medicine. I do a lot of work with professional athletes, and I'm the team doctor for the Maple Leafs."

"So basically you're famous too."

"Absolutely." He raised himself up on his elbows. "Aren't you going to ask me about my status?"

She swallowed. "No. That's not a question I normally ask."

"Maybe you should start," he said, his eyes fixed on hers.

She examined the hands she had clasped in her lap. The implication was loud and clear.

————————

Katie stayed all afternoon. Although weak, Aiden seemed in high spirits, and was enthusiastic about his recovery. When the doctor came into the room as dinner-time approached, he checked the monitor and pressed his stethoscope to Aiden's chest. "I hope your visitor isn't tiring you out too much."

"Doc Thompson, this is Katie Banks, an old ... friend of mine."

"Nice to meet you, Dr. Thompson." Katie slid to the front of her chair. "No worries, I was just leaving." She reached for her bag.

"A few more minutes wouldn't hurt, would they, Doc?" Aiden flashed the physician his most charming smile.

"I don't suppose they would," the doctor said slowly, glancing from Aiden to Katie. "By the looks of things, they might actually do quite the opposite."

"Thanks, Doc."

"Sure. But keep it short." He hung the stethoscope back around his neck.

"We will." Katie looked pointedly at Aiden.

"I'll stop by later," Dr. Thompson said as he left the room.

"Where were we?" Aiden dug his elbow into the pillow and shifted a little to face Katie.

"I don't remember."

"I think I was asking you what your goals are for the next five years."

She rolled her eyes, trying to ignore his teasing expression. "I don't think you were, but if you are now, they are to relax a little more, enjoy my new home. Maybe not do quite as much travelling for my work."

"That's disappointing. England is a long way from Canada."

Which is probably a good thing. "What about you, besides getting better?"

"Date the girl of my dreams, get married, have kids, you know, the usual."

Nurse Gina poked her head in the door. "Dr. Ford, there's a gentleman here to see you. Are you up for another guest?"

"Sure. Has he passed the family-only rule?"

"I'm sure your *sister* won't mind."

Katie bit her lip. The nurse was clearly on to them. "You go ahead. I need to head out anyway."

Aiden lifted a hand. "No, stay. Please."

The nurse disappeared and a moment later a middle-aged man in a Toronto Blue Jays ball cap stepped into the room. Katie smiled at the newcomer. His eyes were kind but carried an echo of sadness. *Is he upset about Aiden's accident?* She turned to Aiden, expecting an introduction, but from his confused expression, he didn't know the man.

"I'm Dennis Scott." The man removed the cap and clutched it in both hands. "I hope you don't mind that I've come."

Scott. How do I know that name? The truth struck Katie with the force of a lightning bolt and she pressed a hand to her stomach.

"Not at all, but are you sure you have the right room?"

"You *are* Dr. Aiden Ford?"

"I am. But I'm afraid I don't know who you are."

Katie studied him. Had the concussion affected his memory?

"I know you don't. We've never met, but I thought you would know the name."

"Scott, you said?"

The man nodded.

"I'm afraid I don't."

The man closed his eyes. When he opened them again, the sadness had deepened. "My wife and children were in the other vehicle."

Katie's chest tightened until she could hardly draw a breath. How could this man have come here? She swung her gaze back to Aiden, who cocked his head and stared at the man. Shock rippled through her. Had no one told him what had happened?

The man's shoulders bowed, as though he carried a load too heavy for any human to bear. "I just came to tell you that I forgive you. That's all." He pulled the ball cap back onto his head before turning and shuffling out of the room.

CHAPTER
Thirty

A THICK SILENCE HUNG IN THE AIR.

Katie shifted uneasily, her focus on the bag on her knees. Did he really not know about the other car? Should she tell him?

"Kate?"

Why hadn't his parents told him? It wasn't her place…

"Kate. Look at me." All traces of humour were gone from Aiden's voice now. She swallowed and raised her head.

"Do you know what happened?"

A deep pain gripped Katie's stomach. She nodded.

He lay back on the pillow and stared up at the ceiling, as if debating whether or not he wanted to know.

How could she tell him? He was still vulnerable. If he learned the full story, the emotional pain, heaped on top of the physical pain, could be too much in his condition. She fumbled with the handle of her bag. "I'll go get the doctor."

"No."

She inched to the front of the chair. "Really Aiden, I think it would be best if you talked to—"

"You." He turned his head on the pillow. "I need to hear it from you." The words came out heavy, wooden, as though he'd resigned himself to whatever she was about to say.

Katie gripped the rail and started to rise. "Your parents are in the café. I can go grab them and…"

He grasped her hand and she sank back down. Heat rose in her chest. Why hadn't anyone told him? How could they have put her in this terrible position? The palm of her free hand was damp and she rubbed it on her pants. The fact that they hadn't told him yet must mean that they were trying to make sure he was fully in the clear before talking to him about it. So how could she?

His face crumpled. "Just tell me, Kate. I have to know."

Her stomach twisted. If only she could take away all his pain and protect him, find a way to fix everything, some remedy to turn back time and make it so none of this had ever happened. Instead, she sat helpless and unprepared. How could she possibly tell him in a way that wouldn't break him?

He blew out a breath. "He mentioned children," he said quietly. "What happened to them?"

Katie opened her mouth, but no words came. Her mind struggled to form an explanation. She squeezed his hand. "There were two children. They didn't make it."

His eyes closed. "And the woman?"

"Their mother. She died as well."

Aiden turned his head away from her. If only there was some way to make this easier.

"It was an accident, Aiden, a terrible accident. One of many that night. The roads were so bad. Even my flight was delayed. You can't blame—"

"Please stop." He pulled his hand from hers and rolled over.

"I'm sorry." Words had never seemed so insufficient. Pain squeezed her heart. She touched Aiden's shoulder and his muscles tightened beneath her fingers. Katie settled back in the chair.

"Go home, Kate."

She shook her head. "I can't leave you, not now."

"It was a mistake…"

"Of course it was. I know that."

"I meant asking you to come back. I appreciate that you did, but now I need you to go."

"You don't have to push me away. If you're sad, be sad. It doesn't bother me."

"Things have changed. Why would you want to stick around?"

"Why not?"

"Kate, let's be real here." He turned back to face her. "If what you're saying is true, I could be sent to prison. You want to be associated with that?"

"I came back, didn't I?"

His face darkened. "Because you felt sorry for me."

"Of course I felt sorry for you. Who wouldn't? But I also wanted you to know something of God's love. That's why I came back."

"Don't." His eyes flickered with anger.

God, show me how to reach him. She gripped the bed rail again. "You wanted to be real. Well, this is as real as it gets."

"I don't want to hear it." The words came out harsh, bitter. He flung an arm over his eyes. "There's nothing for you here, so please, just go."

She stayed in her chair.

Eventually, the room grew dark and he fell asleep.

———

At some point in the night Aiden awoke from a fitful sleep, sweating, his heart pounding in his chest, the ghosts of his dreams following him into wakefulness. The room was dark, only a crack of light came from under the door. He sensed someone in the room, heard the faint sound of breathing, and reached for the string close to his head to turn on the light. Katie slept, her knees curled up under her on the chair beside his bed. He pulled the cord and the room went black again.

———

"Morning!" The orderly rattled into the room with the breakfast cart, startling Katie awake.

"Good morning." Katie injected as much cheerfulness into the greeting as she could, although she watched Aiden warily as she rubbed a kink in her neck.

The orderly plunked Aiden's breakfast tray down on the table beside him and left the room, his whistling echoing down the hallway.

Aiden focused his attention on the runny eggs on his plate. "You're still here?"

"Uh huh." Would nonchalant work? She stretched her arms over her head and yawned.

"They let you stay the night?" He picked up a fork and poked at a limp piece of bacon.

"No one said a word."

"You hungry?"

"No, go ahead, I'll get something downstairs. Any requests?"

"Same one as last night. For you to leave."

The words pelted her like bits of gravel, but she lifted her chin. "I'm not going anywhere."

"You're outstaying your welcome."

"There's a first time for everything."

Katie wasn't normally this stubborn, but the occasion demanded it. Somehow she knew Aiden didn't want her to leave. And although he wasn't able to admit it, he needed a friend more than ever.

More than that, he needed God.

"Suit yourself." He dropped the fork and picked up a piece of toast.

Katie stood. "I'm going to grab a tea. I'll be right back."

A grunt was his only response.

She walked out of the room. On impulse, she hit the elevator button for the fourth floor so she could pass by the chapel. Despite the rumble from her stomach, something drew her inside. The small room, lined with chairs, was empty. Katie slid onto one and bowed her head.

Lord, help Aiden. This is such a difficult time for him. Speak to his spirit. Show him your love. Let him know you. Let him receive your love.

After several minutes, peace flowed through her, driving out the fear and anxiety. She stood and left the chapel, feeling as though a great burden had been lifted from her. She made a quick trip to the coffee shop and returned to Aiden's room with a cup of tea in each hand and two breakfast sandwiches. Given the way he'd been looking at it, Aiden's breakfast had likely been taken away untouched. She wheeled the tray over to his bed and set the sandwich in front of him.

"Stop being so nice."

Katie ignored him. She crossed the room to the window and pulled open the curtains. "It's a nice day out there."

He squinted in the brightness as the sun spilled into the room and across his bed.

"I didn't ask for your help, Pollyanna."

She leaned back against the window ledge. "Yeah, you made that pretty clear."

"When did you become so stubborn?"

"When did you?"

"Listen, I don't know what you think you're doing, but I'm not interested in your charity."

"I call it helping a friend."

"How much more plain can I be, Kate? I don't want your help." His anger hung in the room after the sound of his voice died away.

She waved a hand through the air, as though brushing away his words as one would an annoying cobweb. "If I promise not to help, can I stay?"

"You're driving me nuts."

"I'll just hang out, tell dumb jokes, read to you when you get tired of ignoring me. I'll sneak in whatever junk food you feel like, and scratch the itch on your toe you can't reach because it hurts too much to bend, and..."

"Okay." He flung both arms in the air. "You win, but no dumb jokes."

The smallest hint of a smile played around his lips. It disappeared quickly, but still, it was a small victory. ·

Katie would take it.

———

Three days passed. Katie spent most of the time sitting on the chair beside Aiden's bed, pacing the halls when he had other company, and fielding increasingly urgent texts from Peter about when she might be returning to England. On the morning of the third day, the police came to speak with Aiden and write up a report. Her back pressed to the wall outside his room, Katie overheard Dr. Thompson ask the officer for more time before they formally pressed charges. Aiden was exhausted after their questioning and slept much of the day.

Katie sat and watched him. So much had transpired over such a short time. The day she had returned from Miami, she met the boy she had once known, who now seemed trapped in a man's body. Apart from the injuries and laugh lines, he had hardly changed. Now, on the morning of the fourth day since her arrival, she was witnessing the growing pains imposed on a man forced to face harsh truths about his life. No matter how much he thought he could steer his way into his own destiny, he was learning that life was not his to control. In a single breath, everything had changed.

And not just for him.

———

When Aiden opened his eyes, Katie dozed on the chair next to his bed, the same spot she had spent the better portion of the past few days. The sun shone through the window and fell on her, illuminating her blonde hair. How was it possible she was still there? Aiden held his breath as her eyes squinted open and she straightened and met his gaze. Her smile did it every time.

Stay strong. He clenched his fists under the blanket. "Can you do me a favour?"

She stretched like a cat and an old familiar longing slammed into him. *Knock it off. Nothing can ever happen between you and her, your life is way too messed up now.*

A mischievous glint entered her eyes, and his resolve weakened. "Let me get this straight—are you asking for my help?"

He scowled. "If it's too much trouble, I can ask someone else."

She sobered immediately. "Of course it's not too much trouble. What do you need?"

He contemplated her for a moment. Would she think he was crazy? Aiden lifted his chin. It would be better if she did, maybe then she'd go and leave him in peace. "Would you find out Dennis Scott's phone number?"

Katie blinked, but when she spoke, her voice was carefully controlled. "Sure. Anything else?"

He hesitated, and a sheepish smile curled at the corner of his mouth. As long as she was here, might as well take her up on her offer of assistance. "A coffee, if you're going that way."

"I'm going that way." She uncurled herself and stood up. "Be right back."

He watched her leave, his chest tight. He'd missed that smile, and the graceful way she moved, like a dancer. She drove him crazy. She was so obstinate, yet incredibly patient and kind. It made no sense. The last thing he wanted was for her to go, but after he'd found out what he had done... How could she still want to be around him, knowing who he was? Yet somehow she did. Her presence was both comforting and unnerving.

He despised her seeing him this way, so physically and emotionally wrecked. The worst part was that, from the moment she had walked into the room, all his old feelings had crashed through him again. Feelings he had no right to have. Feelings he had clearly never fully released.

That first morning, those feelings had given him hope, something to look forward to, and a reason to get better. She was more beautiful than he remembered, more beautiful than any woman since her, but it was more than physical attraction. He hadn't a clue how to put words to it. Maybe it was who she had become in the years since they had parted, the way she carried herself, or her quiet confidence. Or was it the way she looked at him with her sweet smile?

The sadness returned, like night swallowing day. His feelings couldn't be entertained. It wouldn't be fair. Everything was different now. Complicated. Since hearing the outcome of the accident, one thought had consumed him—it should have been him who died in the collision.

Thirty-One

"YOUR COFFEE, MONSIEUR."

Katie whisked into the room and handed him the paper cup. "And your phone number." She produced the sticky note with Dennis Scott's number written across it. Her fingers trembled slightly as she held it out.

"Thanks." He snatched the paper and tossed it onto the table beside the bed.

"Dr. Thompson said you should try and get some fresh air tomorrow. I thought we could go joy-riding down the hall in one of those wheelchairs."

"No thanks."

"Aren't you going stir-crazy sitting here? I know I would be." She worked at controlling her voice to make it sound casually optimistic instead of pleading.

"Well, you're not me."

"True enough, but it might do you some good. It's been a long week."

"Look." Aiden clutched the blanket on his bed so tightly his knuckles went white. "In case you haven't noticed, I'm not exactly at the top of my game. My future isn't looking overly bright, and I'm not ready to swallow my pride and let you help my invalid body into a wheelchair and have you push me around. It may sound like great fun to you, but I'll pass."

Love suffers long and is kind, it bears all things, believes all things, hopes all things, endures all things.

The verse from I Corinthians filled her head, perfectly timed to crush the angry retort that had risen in her throat.

"No problem. I'll just wait until you *are* ready."

"Do you ever give up?"

"I don't make a habit of it."

"You always were a control freak."

Her head jerked. She was *not* a control freak. How dare he accuse of her that when all she had done was try to be a good friend?

"It's true. Miss Goody-goody in high school, always doing the right thing, never letting your hair down..."

"And you were always reckless and irresponsible."

For a second, he looked as though he had been slapped in the face. Then, like a soldier knocked down in battle, he quickly regained himself and snatched up his weapons.

"Admit it, Kate, that's what you liked about me. It was exciting."

She clenched her teeth so hard they ached.

"Don't pretend you don't remember."

Heat roared into her chest, flushing her face. Of all the arrogant jerks... "What happened between you and me was a temporary lapse of judgement on my part. It never was and it never will be anything more."

"Suit yourself." He lifted the coffee cup in her direction.

"Besides, it never meant a thing to you anyway." She spat out the words, giving in to the perfectly-aged bitterness. "You did what any eighteen-year-old boy would have done in that situation. It wouldn't have mattered who it was."

"So you *do* remember," he said simply.

Katie caught her breath and flicked her hair over her shoulder. "I'm leaving now. I have things I need to do."

She jerked her coat off the back of the chair and stalked out of the room before she could say anything that she might regret.

The following day, the sun shone brilliantly in a cloudless sky, warming the room and lighting the autumn trees outside Aiden's room in a glorious array of colour. It was Sunday afternoon and Katie still hadn't returned. If he'd had the strength, Aiden would have paced the small strip between his bed and the door. What if Katie never came back?

He had drifted in and out of sleep all night. He'd faced a few ugly truths about himself, two of which Katie had thrown in his face in the heat of anger. *You're a fool, Aiden Ford.* She was probably at church this very moment praying for his soul.

The worst part was, she'd been right. Much of his conduct over the years *could* be deemed irresponsible. He had avoided taking responsibility for his actions whenever possible. But the accident made that impossible. His negligent behaviour had taken the lives of three people, and his own life lay in shambles, crumbling beneath him, all due to his poor choices.

No wonder Katie was gone. Although he had purposely pushed her away, as soon as she had left, a sinking sense of loss filled the smug space inside. She may have been right about a few things, but there was one thing she was seriously wrong about. What they had shared had mattered to him a great deal. He had tried for years to get over her. And now he knew he never had.

His fists clenched at his sides. She was better off without him. If she never returned, it would be for the best. What kind of a future was there for the two of them? Even as the question passed through his head, the answer came to him. Katie was a part of him. He had never really let her go, and all these years later, he'd come to see that would never change. Whether he ended up alone, disabled, or in jail, she would always inhabit his thoughts. Amid those dark reflections, he held onto the slim hope that she would return. If she did, he would treat her the way she deserved to be treated, like the incredible person she was.

"Katie! Where have you been?" Rachael nearly screeched the words, and Katie held the phone away from her ear. "I texted you five times, left a bunch of voice mail messages. What's going on?"

Katie sighed and pressed the device to her ear again. *Where do I begin?* "You wouldn't believe me if I told you."

"Yeah, well, try. I was worried about you. You never take that long to answer my messages, and your cell is normally always on."

"Sorry. Everything is…" She caught herself before she could lie and say fine.

"What is it? Are you okay?"

"I went to see Aiden."

"You did what?"

"I visited him in the hospital last week."

"Oh Katie. What made you do that?"

"It's a long story." She hated the long pause on the other end. Visiting Aiden sounded ludicrous now, even to her.

"Why did you get involved, Kat?"

"I uh, I…" Why *had* she gotten involved? Her presence in his room had only caused both of them pain.

"Are you at home?"

Katie hesitated. "No."

"Where are you then?"

"I'm at the Hilton in Cambridge."

"I thought you were going home after the Miami trip."

"I was, but Aiden called me."

Rachel's long exhalation of breath hissed in Katie's ear. To Rachael, she probably sounded like a high school girl controlled by her latest crush. "I heard he came out of the coma. How is he?"

"Surprisingly okay. He's weak and has a lot of injuries, and he's having a hard time dealing with, you know, everything that happened."

"Why are you doing this?"

"He needs a friend."

"I'm sure he has friends. You shouldn't be the one to help him." Rachael sighed again. "Don't go there, Kat. It was bad enough the first time. He's not worth it. You two are a total mismatch. Always have been. Don't try to resurrect something that was never meant to be in the first place."

"I'm not. I'm just helping him. Trying, anyway."

"Let someone else. You know what will happen if you keep going back."

"What will happen?"

Rachael's silence spoke volumes. "Look, there's no hope for the two of you, if that's where you're going with this."

Katie couldn't blame Rachael for her reaction. She'd even expected it. It was why she had avoided her friend's texts and calls.

"I saw round one. Trust me, you don't need this. And you don't need to get involved in someone else's mess. And it *is* a mess."

That's true. Still… Katie twirled a strand of hair around one finger.

"Are you still there?"

"Yeah."

"Sorry for getting so worked up. I just don't want to see you get hurt again."

"I know."

"Besides, I've heard stories. Let's just say he hasn't settled down."

"You can't believe everything you hear."

"I know that. But you haven't been around in a long time—you don't know what's been going on. I tried so hard to keep it from you while you were here, leaving the TV off in case you saw the news. I knew what your reaction would be. How did you hear about it anyway?"

"I read it in the paper."

"Can I just say again, that even if he gets better, there's no hope for the two of you? He's not a nice guy. He may even end up with a prison sentence. Don't be a martyr for him. He doesn't deserve your kindness, and he certainly doesn't deserve you. You know what they say: only fools rush in."

Rachael's words hung in the air, pricking Katie's skin like drops of freezing rain.

"I appreciate what you're saying, but right now I feel like I'm supposed to be here. Besides, I'm not rushing in."

"If you say so. At least stop hiding out at a hotel and come stay with us while you're here."

"Thanks, but I'm keeping pretty odd hours. I don't want to disrupt you guys."

"You won't."

"No, really, I appreciate it, but I think I'm better here."

"Can we at least meet for a coffee?"

"Sure. I'll be in town a little while longer. Sort of taking it day by day, but let's touch base tomorrow and set something up."

"Great. I'll check back in with you. Make sure you answer your phone this time."

Katie tossed her cell phone into her purse and sank down on the edge of the bed. Rachael's words reverberated through her head.

Why am I doing this?

That morning, she had sat in the balcony at her former church, listening as the pastor spoke about God's unrelenting love for all people. He talked about God knowing us humans so well, seeing all our ugliness but loving us in spite of it all. He had spoken about how God never gives up on us, and is always beckoning us to himself.

For Katie, it had been a sweet reassurance, a reminder that God loved her, and especially that God loved Aiden and hadn't given up on him. That offered a measure of relief that she took as a sign that she should go back and see Aiden. But now, hearing how convinced Rachael was that she shouldn't be spending time with him, Katie wavered.

She thought about the angry words they had exchanged and how unchanged he seemed. Maybe Rachael was right. Maybe she was wasting her time and would be better off going home. Perhaps it would be wiser to let someone else help him. But even as she thought it, she felt a possessive tug at her heart.

An unsettling thought struck her. Had she heard correctly that night? Had God really asked her to pray for Aiden? Yes, she was sure of it, remembering the urgency she had felt in her spirit. But what about now? Had she run ahead? God hadn't asked her to go to the hospital, had he? Or to return? Or even to stay?

"Lord, only in your way. I only want to go the way you want me to," she whispered into the silence of her hotel room. She waited for some sort of confirmation.

Love suffers long and is kind, it bears all things, believes all things, hopes all things, endures all things.

That verse, playing through her mind, convinced her of one thing. She needed to return to the hospital.

———

Mr. Scott stood in the doorway, clutching his ball cap, until Aiden invited him in. Aiden had called to request that he return, aware that they were now inextricably connected, both of their lives altered drastically by the same tragic event and both straining under its effects. Aiden had no reference point or insight into what that might be like for this husband and father, but hoped that somehow he could say something that would help. Seeing him there, that suddenly seemed an insurmountable task.

"Thanks for coming, Mr. Scott," Aiden said, struggling to find the right words.

Mr. Scott nodded.

"When you visited, I found what you said troubling. You said you forgave me, but at the time I didn't know what you were forgiving me for. I hadn't even asked for your forgiveness."

"My forgiving didn't depend on your asking."

"How is that possible?"

Mr. Scott smiled a sad smile. "It didn't have anything to do with you, really."

Aiden frowned. "I don't understand."

"I know."

"Seems a little backward, don't you think?"

"Yes, but I've known a great deal of forgiveness in my life."

"Lucky for me."

"It doesn't make dealing with what happened any easier, but it does make it possible for me not to be bitter."

"I'd rather you be bitter. I deserve it."

"Thankfully, we don't always get what we deserve."

Aiden mulled that over. Could the man really forgive him for what he had done? He lifted both hands, palms up. "I'm sorry. I took away your family. I can never make what I did okay. I mean, I can never reverse it. I know there's nothing I can say that will come close to making it better."

"You don't need to say anything. Like I said before, I forgive you."

"I don't understand how you could. You should hate me."

"I guess you're right." Mr. Scott lifted his shoulders. "But somehow I think God wants you to know what mercy feels like."

Aiden shook his head and looked away. Mercy felt like a gift far too costly to accept.

Katie came back late Sunday afternoon. Aiden had been trying to read a book but looked up at the sound of a tentative knock on his door.

"Can I come in?"

Relief poured through him. "I thought you left town."

"I thought about it." She crossed her arms. "But I have this friend who needs a friend right now, so I decided to stick around."

"He must be glad you did."

"Oh, he is." She strolled into the room. "He actually enjoys my company, even though you'd never know it."

"I'm sure he does. Who wouldn't?"

A smile of understanding passed between them.

Aiden blew out a breath. "Hey, look, I'm sorry for how I behaved. It was pretty awful."

"It's okay. You've got a lot going on right now." She lowered her purse from her shoulder and hooked it over the back of the chair. "How was today?"

"It was interesting."

"I saw Dr. Thompson on my way in. He said you had visitors."

"The police came. They aren't pressing charges."

"Really? That's amazing!"

"My blood alcohol level was within the legal limit, and they said weather was the main factor. There were over two hundred accidents in the area that night due to the ice storm, plus they said Dennis Scott isn't pressing charges, so I guess I'm a free man." *Or not going to jail, anyway.*

"That's great, Aiden."

He drummed his fingers on the tray table.

"Still hard, huh?"

"Big time."

"That makes sense. You've been through so much, it's going to take time to process it all, but it's still such good news."

"It doesn't change what happened."

"No, it doesn't." Katie settled onto the chair.

"At first I only knew there was an accident but couldn't remember any details. Now I can't get the details out of my mind. They're always there, haunting me."

"It was a major tragedy, Aiden. It'll take awhile to come to terms with it, and you might even need counseling. At some point, you'll have to forgive yourself."

"I can never do that."

"Dennis Scott forgave you."

"Yeah. He came back today and told me again."

"So you're free and forgiven."

She was so bright and optimistic. He wished he could catch some of her enthusiasm. "I don't feel like either. I feel like a monster."

"Hey, it will get better." She reached over and squeezed his arm. "Time has a way of softening the edges."

Aiden held out his hand and she placed hers in his. He squeezed gently, not wanting to let go. Running his thumb over the top of her hand, he traced her delicate fingers, enjoying the softness of her skin. They sat that way for a few moments, until Katie pulled away, her cheeks pink.

His fingers still tingled and everything in him longed to reach for her again. *Give it time, Aiden.* "How about that walk you promised?"

Katie jumped up. "I'll go get the chair."

CHAPTER
Thirty-Two

KATIE PUSHED AIDEN'S WHEELCHAIR DOWN THE CORRIDOR, bumping into a hospital food cart and the elevator doors that closed against the sides of the chair before they got inside. By that time, they were laughing so hard it took a moment for Katie to notice that the elevator was close to full capacity. The people forming the throng of bodies inside attempted a feeble amount of squashing together until the couple finally squeezed in just as the door made its second attempt at closing.

The crowd in the industrial-sized lift was quiet, and in the sudden stillness before the descent, the two couldn't help resume the laughter they had managed to contain upon entry. Nine deadly-serious faces looked at them, two in the far back corner cracked a smile, and one old man shook his head.

After they had exited the lift, Katie wheeled Aiden outside to a quiet spot at the edge of a courtyard to enjoy the late-day sun. Canada geese flew overhead in a V-shaped pattern, their calls echoing off the hospital's brick walls, while other birds twittered among the shrubs and trees dotted about the garden enclosure.

Katie parked the wheelchair beside a bench and bent to secure the wheel brakes before sitting down next to Aiden. The courtyard was a sun-trap, blocking the autumn wind and making the afternoon feel several degrees warmer. The remnants of the late-fall garden and the leftover colours on the trees made for a glorious display. Katie was encouraged when Aiden tipped his face to the sky, letting the sun fall full on his face. He began to take a deep breath but winced. His ribs would take time to heal.

He reached for her hand. "I know you've stayed longer than you'd planned, but is there any way you'd consider staying a bit longer? I'd really like to spend more time with you."

The world spun around Katie, and she stiffened. His eyes were intent, searching hers. She lowered her gaze and breathed a silent prayer for strength.

His thumb lifted her chin. "Did you hear me? Please look at me, Kate." Aiden's voice was husky and soft.

She met his gaze. Hope was etched into his eyes, mixed with stubborn resolve. "Yes, I heard you."

"Let me be with you."

Katie swallowed. Part of her did want to stay with him, to throw all reason aside and be hopeful with him, to hang onto this moment and never let go. But she would be holding onto a prefabricated idea of him, a make-believe man she had once loved but had learned not to. She couldn't let herself travel to that place again. There was too much pain. Too much at stake. That was one path she couldn't take a second time.

Rachael's words echoed in the back of her mind. *There's no hope for the two of you.*

"I can't." She tried to pull her hand from his, but he tightened his grip.

Her mind whirled with thoughts of his betrayal years ago, the cost of what she had given away, and the countless tears she had shed over what he had never understood was too precious to measure.

"What is it, Kate? Don't worry, I'm well on my way to a full recovery, physically anyway. The rest will take some time, but I'll be okay, if that's what you're concerned about."

She frowned. "Of course not."

"Then what is it?"

There were no words to explain that the intimacy between them all those years ago had forever changed her. That she had lived with regret as her constant companion and bondage to the past as an accomplice. She would not let him stroll back into her life and leave his numbing effect on her for another ten years.

"I'm not the same person I was twelve years ago. We can't just turn back the clock."

"Why not?"

"Because you hurt me." The words slipped out before she could stop them.

His brow furrowed. "You're the one who broke it off, Kate."

"You're the one who cheated."

Realization swept over his face followed by a staggering look of defeat, as if a dart had punctured him and he was suddenly deflating.

"Is that why you called it quits with no warning?" He dropped her hand, as though her skin burned his.

"No." She clasped her fingers in her lap. "I didn't know at the time. If I had, things would have been very different with us." Tears welled. Katie tried to hold them back, but a dam inside her had burst. All the years of holding up walls she had built to keep out the hurt fell away, crumbling in one torrent of tears that now ran freely, tumbling off her nose, cheeks, and lips.

Aiden's arms wrapped tightly around her as her body heaved and shook. He held her until her weeping subsided. Then he leaned in and kissed first her forehead, her nose, and then her mouth, drying the residue of her tears with his lips.

At last, the simple words came softly in her ear. "I'm so sorry, Kate."

———————

The clouds came in uninvited that day, first puffy white and then grey and bulbous. Soon only grey covered the brilliant blue in a menacing layer that blocked the sun altogether. The late autumn days had been a beautiful spectacle, and Katie and Aiden soaked in their fading glory, enjoying the courtyard amid the hospital grounds for the third day in a row.

The first day, the sun had warmed Aiden's pale cheeks and brightened the dark circles beneath his eyes, the bright blue a reflection of the rich, brilliant sky overhead. The second day, he again leaned back in the wheelchair and closed his eyes, fully inviting the sun's warmth to radiate on his face. The third, Katie had successfully wheeled his chair outside and now sat on the bench beside Aiden. They felt the sudden change in light and temperature as the sunny courtyard grew dim and cool.

Katie pulled the sleeves to her sweater down. She hadn't slept all night, tossing and turning before giving up altogether and sitting up to read her Bible until first light came. So much confusion swirled around her situation that she needed clarity. Knowing there was only one place to find it, she had read her Bible and prayed. Afterwards, she returned to the hospital to face the man she hadn't offered any answers to the previous afternoon—the one beside her now, who had extended love that remained unreciprocated.

She gazed at his face, still and peaceful in repose. Was he asleep?

Without opening his eyes, he murmured, "I'm so sorry."

She shifted to face him on the bench. "For what?"

"For who I was, what I did. I loved you then, and I love you now. I realize I never stopped."

Years of regret and longing filled Katie, choking her until all she could manage was an incoherent sound.

He straightened and took her hand. "The biggest mistake I ever made was letting you go. I've spent all those years since regretting it. It's like you are a part of me I can't let go."

The words made Katie's chest ache. They were both beautiful and sad, so many wasted years. To her, he seemed so brave and so weak—whether that was the effect of the accident, the medication, emotions, she couldn't tell. Her heart was full hearing his words, and the mass of hurt she had carried like a burdensome weight—a constant reminder of his indiscretion—fell away. She squeezed his hand.

"I never understood. I never really knew what happened," Aiden said.

"I know. I'm sorry too. I should have talked to you, explained everything I was thinking and feeling."

He searched her eyes. "I think you tried, but I thought I had my life so completely figured out, I couldn't hear anything anyone else had to say about it. I thought I had it all. But now I see, I really have nothing."

"What do you mean?"

"Look at me Kate." He waved his free hand in front of himself. "I've made a mess of my life. I've chased my goals, I got all I thought I wanted, but lying in that hospital bed made me see those pursuits were so empty... *I'm* empty. I guess I got what I deserve." He laughed bitterly.

"Don't say that."

"It's true. I did whatever I wanted, took as much as I could get. I didn't worry about what I was doing to anyone else, as long as I got what I needed." He rubbed his temple with his fingers. "And now I've taken too much."

What could she say to that? Neither of them spoke for a few minutes. Finally, Aiden lifted his head. "I need to know the truth."

His fingers tightened around hers as though he was afraid she might leave. Drops of moisture dotted his forehead. Her eyes narrowed.

"The truth?"

"What you believe, and why."

He let go of her and gripped both wheelchair armrests.

She contemplated him. Could this be the same person who had refused to listen to her even mention God a few years, a few days, earlier? *God, give me the words to say to him, and help him to hear.* She crossed one leg over the other, her boot swinging in the air. "I believe that Jesus is the Son of God and that he came to earth to die for our sins. If you believe in Jesus when you die, you'll be with him in heaven for all eternity."

She paused to assess his reaction. There was no scorn on his face, only interest. "The Bible says that everyone who calls on the name of the Lord will be saved."

"What does that mean?"

"That if you trust in Jesus, believe that he died for your sins and give your life to him, you will be with him in eternity, forever. Life here is really just the beginning."

"But I've made some big mistakes…"

"We all have regrets, things we would do over if we could, but that's the beauty of it. There's nothing you can do, or not do, to be good enough. You can't work your way into heaven because Jesus has already paid the price for us. John 3:16 says that God loved the world so much that he gave his only Son so that anyone who believes in him can have eternal life. You only need to accept it, agree you are a sinner, and ask for forgiveness. It's that simple. It's God's grace. He loves you, Aiden, and wants to set you free."

There was so much more she wanted to add. Things like, *it's what I tried to tell you years ago,* or *I've prayed for you for so long,* but she let that be enough. *God, soften his heart. Let my words sink in.*

"How do you know for sure?"

"I know because of how I felt that first day I received Jesus, a peace, joy, and love like I've never known. And because of so many everyday miracles, like you waking up, and even this moment." His eyes flickered and her chest squeezed. A battle was waging inside him. "I know because of how I feel inside, and even more, because of how God has changed me."

"Yeah, I can see it in your eyes. I noticed it that first day too, when you told me you'd found Jesus, but back then I hated it, maybe because I was afraid of it. I guess I had every right to, since it took you away from me."

She couldn't refute the charge, although it sent pain darting through her. God *had* asked her to let him go, and even though she had never shared that with Aiden, he'd obviously grasped the reason.

"I know. Breaking it off with you was the most difficult thing I've ever had to do. But I needed to put God first."

Before he could respond, a drop of rain struck her forehead. The downpour came seconds later. Katie struggled to turn the wheelchair and manoeuvre it along the sidewalk. By the time they reached the hospital entrance, puddles had formed along the uneven pavement, and the two of them were thoroughly drenched.

Katie sipped on hot tea while Aiden slept. She watched him, hoping he hadn't caught a chill from the soaking and worried she had somehow been negligent of his needs.

It was dark when Aiden finally woke.

"I guess the fresh air knocked me out." He stared out the window at the dark sky.

"I was concerned about you."

"You were?" His eyebrows rose.

"Dr. Thompson came by while you were asleep. He checked in on you and calmed my nerves a little after the scolding Gina gave me for keeping you out in the rain."

"Did she really?" Aiden chuckled softly.

"Yeah. You missed a visit from your parents and dinner. I saved you some of my sub." She handed it to him. "You must be hungry."

"Starving. What time is it?"

"Seven. Are you comfortable? Do you need anything else?"

"Yes and yes. I need you."

Her cheeks warmed. "Very funny."

"And I need to finish our conversation." His eyes twinkled. "I'm serious on both counts, but we can just finish our previous conversation for now."

His smile made her insides stir.

"Okay, where were we?"

"I was wondering if you meant what you said."

"Which part?"

"That breaking up with me was the most difficult thing you've ever had to do."

"Yes. I meant it."

"Did you ever wonder if it was as difficult for me, knowing that I had betrayed you?"

"Aiden, don't—"

"Did you?"

Her shoulders slumped. "It doesn't matter now. It was a long time ago."

"I think it does. It mattered a couple of days ago."

"I shouldn't have said anything. What's done is done."

"Can you forgive me for it?"

"Of course I can."

He rested a hand on her knee. "Don't say that because you feel you have to."

Katie covered his hand with hers and said the words she had always known she'd needed to but never thought possible. "I forgive you, Aiden. I really do."

He let out his breath in a rush, as if he'd been holding it. Katie pressed a hand to her chest. Speaking the words had freed her, had allowed her to let go of the hurt and make room for another feeling to take its place. She loved Aiden, had always loved him. It was as though the deep pain he'd inflicted had sealed that love inside a tightly-capped bottle. Now forgiveness had loosened the lid, and the neatly-sealed contents were spilling out.

Katie pushed back her shoulders. She wouldn't give her heart permission to move into this place with Aiden. Forgiveness would be enough. Love had to remain an unwrapped present. She'd waited this long to find a man who shared her faith, she couldn't sacrifice that now. Her gaze met his. He was watching her, a strange glimmer of peace mixed with regret in his eyes.

"You're right. You aren't the same person you were back then. You seem much happier, more content."

"I am, mostly anyway," she said, feeling anything but content at that moment as she struggled to settle the confused desires of her heart.

"And I am the opposite."

"You don't have to be."

Aiden drummed his fingers on the bedrail. "I see now that your faith didn't really take you away from me." He sat up. "It rescued you, and I wanted so badly to keep you from it. I didn't want to accept it and worked hard to believe it didn't exist."

"The *it* being God?"

Aiden nodded. "I want what you have, Kate. But how can I be sure?"

"You can pray. I can pray with you if you want me to."

Aiden's fingers stilled on the rail and she clasped them in hers. Katie prayed. A strong sensation came over her, like they were the only two people on earth. As if, in this little lime-green hospital room, time stood still for just a few moments.

All was silent except for her words, followed by Aiden's whispered prayer of faith. Aiden spoke to God, confessing that he believed Jesus was the Son of God who died on the cross for his sins, telling him he was sorry, asking him to forgive him for it all, and surrendering his life to God.

From the tangle of conflicted emotions inside Katie, one rose above them all, flooding her entire being: joy.

After her Tuesday morning coffee with Rachael, Katie returned to the hospital. When she walked into the room, Aiden stood, his back to her, balanced on a pair of crutches. He clearly hadn't heard her come in, because when Katie shrieked in glee, Aiden nearly lost his balance. She had to rush to stabilize him.

"Surprise!" he said, teetering on the verge of collapse.

"Surprise, yourself." She laughed and steadied him with her hands on his waist. When she let him go, she dug her hands into her hips. "What are you up to? Has the doctor authorized this escapade?"

"Hey." He offered her a mock frown. "I'm killing myself to amaze you here. A little encouragement, a bravo, a wow, would be nice."

She brought her hands together slowly and deliberately, her clap oozing with sarcasm.

He shook his head. "Tough crowd." He moved in closer while balancing on the wooden supports. Keeping the crutches firmly under his arms, he waited until she met his gaze. "I love you, Kate."

His lips touched hers, tentatively at first. When she didn't pull away, he kissed her with trembling abandon. After thirty seconds, Katie summoned the strength to step back and catch her breath. In his eyes, she saw a kindness and depth of love she hadn't known years before. They radiated peaceful joy and confidence and reflected true love. Not just for her, but for the God who had redeemed him. There was no reason to hold back anymore. That was all the permission she needed to fully embrace his offer of love.

Aiden gripped a crutch with one hand and pulled Katie to him with the other, embracing her in a way that melted away the wasted years spent apart.

"Marry me, Kate," he whispered into her ear.

CHAPTER
Thirty-Three

KATIE ARRIVED AT THE HOSPITAL EARLY THE FOLLOWING morning, planning to surprise Aiden with a full breakfast of bacon and eggs, packed up in a thermal container. The storm that had blown through the day before had brought in a cold front. *A walk down by the river with Aiden would be perfect.* Katie entered the huge building and rode the elevator to the third floor. Dr. Thompson had said there was a chance Aiden would be strong enough to leave the hospital by the end of the week, and that ample fresh air would do him good.

Katie rounded the corner, swept through the doorway of Aiden's room, and stopped short. His bed was empty. She checked the time. 8 am. *That's strange.* Morning showers didn't begin until after nine when breakfast had been cleared away, and no tests were performed until the doctor arrived. She sighed and lowered the cooler to the ground as a young nurse she didn't recognize strode into the room, sheets in hand.

"Can I help you?" she asked, moving toward the bed.

"Yes, I'm just wondering where Aiden is this morning."

"Are you family?"

"Uh, no. I'm his... fiancée."

The nurse set the sheets on the bed and contemplated her, biting her lip as if weighing what to say. "I'm sorry. He passed away last night. I'm sure the family will contact you with the details."

Katie blinked. The words wouldn't register.

"There must be some mistake. I'm looking for Dr. Aiden Ford."

The nurse tugged the patient name tag from the end of the bed and showed it to her. "I'm afraid there's no mistake. Dr. Ford passed in his sleep."

The room whirled around her, and Katie grasped the bed rail. It was a lie. It had to be. Aiden playing a joke on her, trying to get her to laugh. There was no way it could be true. Only a few hours before he had held her in his arms and told her how much he loved her. He had asked her to marry him and she had—

"No." The primeval, guttural cry forced itself out from somewhere deep inside. Pain slammed through her until she felt she would either cave in or burst wide open.

"No..." she whispered, letting go of the rail and backing against the wall as she lifted her hands to her face.

The nurse touched her shoulder. When Katie jerked away, the woman left the clean sheets at the foot of the bed and hurried from the room, leaving Katie to mourn alone. After a few minutes, she stumbled across the room and dropped onto the chair beside Aiden's bed.

She had no idea how much time passed before Dr. Thompson poked his head into the room. "Miss Banks?"

Gripping the arms of the chair, she stared at the doctor, not bothering to wipe the tears from her wet face. "What happened?" Her voice came out a moan.

"I'm sorry. I'm afraid Aiden had a brain aneurysm that burst in the night. He died immediately."

His words flew around in her mind like birds, swooping and soaring and out of reach. "How could that happen? He was fine. I saw him yesterday. I said good night..."

"It's just one of those things that can happen to anyone. We don't know for sure if the accident brought it on, or if it was merely coincidental." Weariness lined his face. How many times a day did he have to give news like that to people he barely knew? "Will you be okay? Do you want me to call someone to pick you up?"

His lips were moving, but Katie couldn't register the words.

"Miss Banks? Can I call someone to come get you?"

The concern in his voice broke through the fog. She pulled her knees to her chest and wrapped shaking arms around them. "No. I'm okay. I'll just... can I have a few more minutes?"

"Of course. Please call if you need anything."

"Thank you, Dr. Thompson, for everything."

"I'm sorry," he said, pulling the door closed behind him.

Katie sat for several more minutes, trying to muster the strength to stand. Finally she rose and, on trembling legs, made her way to the side of the bed she had watched Aiden fall asleep in hours earlier. She ran her hand along the sheet he had slept under and over the pillow, still indented from his head. She pictured him there, smiling at her, telling jokes, and getting better.

He had been getting better.

She pressed a fist against her mouth. Unable to stay there another minute, in the room where his presence could still be felt, she fled. She didn't stop running until she stood overlooking the river. Katie hadn't answered the question Aiden had asked her the day before. She'd told him she needed time to think about it.

"So you'll tell me tomorrow?" His eyes had probed hers.

"Yes." She'd squeezed his hand. "I promise. I'll tell you tomorrow."

And now she needed one more day with him, an hour, even, so that she could tell him that yes, she wanted to spend the rest of her life with him.

———

Katie's paint brushes were strangers to her, food had become unfamiliar. The calls her phone took ended in messages she failed to retrieve. Part of her had died with Aiden, and what remained was consumed by misery. Her heart was weary with aching, and she had serious questions for God she didn't have the strength to ask.

Sobs came in relentless waves, only now instead of merely tears, an eroding bitterness chiseled away at her soul. Bit by bit, chunks of her faith were chipped away, and she didn't give a single fallen piece a second glance.

Five days had passed since Aiden's funeral. Afterwards, Katie had taken the first plane back to London. Since arriving home, she hadn't left the house. Every day was the same. From her bed, she saw the sun attempt to reach her past the drawn curtains, was aware of it setting each night, and when darkness came, she was thankful for the relief sleep brought.

Tears were her only companions. They welled up from every hidden place inside her and from every hurt she had ever suffered. The grief was incapacitating.

It collaborated with the immense loss she had suffered the day her daddy left. The feeling of complete abandonment, coupled with her inability to control life's harshness, was overwhelming. She doubted she would ever recover and cared little to try.

One bitter day followed the next, with Katie trying to shut out the world and numb the pain for a while. At some point it occurred to her that if she would pour her heart out to God in her despair, perhaps she would gain some comfort. Instead, she denied herself any consolation and closed herself off to her Saviour since, in her despair, she believed even he had abandoned her.

Within her heart, she eventually turned on God, screamed at him for being so unfair, questioned why, if he really loved her, he would repeatedly tear away the ones she loved. Had she been such a horrible person that she deserved this endless supply of sorrow?

Late in the afternoon of the fifth day, a knock sounded at the door. Katie ignored it, turning in her bed and yanking the covers up around her shoulders. Again it came and she pulled the pillow over her head. The third knock was louder and more persistent, until she finally yelled for whoever it was to go away.

"Kaitrin? Are you there?"

Jean. She contemplated not answering, but he had travelled from Paris… She climbed out of bed stiffly and staggered to the door. She opened it a crack, the light piercing her eyes. Squinting through the opening, she saw Jean standing on the front step, concern etching his features.

"I heard what happened."

Katie pulled the door open just far enough for him to enter. After stepping in, he bent to pick up the stack of mail piled on her hall floor and placed it on the wooden table inside the door. She closed the door behind him.

The man who had become like a brother to her over the years wrapped his arms around her. He said nothing for a long time, just held her and let her sob into his chest, stroking her hair. Eventually she pulled away and he held her at arms' length to study her. "Want to talk about it?"

She didn't. Not one single bit. Katie was exhausted. She'd cried until it felt as though there were no tears left and still more came. Now she was spent. What good would talking do? She pulled her robe tightly around her and turned in the direction of the conservatory. He followed her and took the seat next to her at the small glass table.

"I am sorry, Kaitrin."

She hadn't the strength for a response. Not even enough reserves to be polite. He studied her. From the look on his face, she must look frightful. She hadn't brushed her hair in days, hadn't even bothered to wash her face, and who knew what days of tears had made her eyes look like. Half-heartedly, she swiped at a strand of hair and tucked it behind one ear.

He touched her arm. "Are you hungry? Can I fix some tea?"

She gazed out the window, her eyes still working to adjust after so many days spent in her dark room.

"How did you find out?" she asked, her raspy voice barely above a whisper.

"Rachael called me. She's been very worried about you. She said you left without saying good-bye and have not answered your phone."

The mention of Rachael's name summoned a bit of reality, and a stab of guilt shot through Katie. She'd been selfishly oblivious to life outside her closed-off world. Katie hadn't even let her own mother know she was back in the country, or shared with her anything that had happened with Aiden. Of course her loved ones would be concerned. Just before Aiden's funeral service had begun, Rachael slid into the pew beside Katie and held her hand throughout. Since then, Katie had lost count of how many times her cell had rung. Rachael had obviously been trying to reach her.

She slumped against the back of her chair as Jean clattered about in the kitchen. He wouldn't know where a thing was. With a heavy exhalation of breath, Katie pushed to her feet and went to help. She found him opening cupboards and finding his way better than she'd thought. When she reached for the tea cups, he pointed to a kitchen stool. "I have got this. Sit." With no energy to argue, she complied and took a spot at the breakfast counter. When had walking become such an effort? Watching Jean in her kitchen, pulling things out of her fridge, helped her. The mere activity of another human being in her space changed the atmosphere and lifted her spirits. He worked in silence, appearing to understand that just being there was enough. Katie was grateful; she wasn't up for small talk.

He fixed her a sandwich with bread he'd found who-knows-where and homemade jam she had made from raspberries grown in her garden at a time when life seemed simple and good. The sight of the pretty glass jar made her want to cry again, but this time she swallowed back the tears, weary of the pain and, for the first time in days, mindful of the possibility of fighting it.

Jean placed a plate and teacup in front of her before pulling up the other stool to sit across from her. Under his critical eye, she felt compelled to bite into her sandwich. She forced herself to chew. Though sweetened with the jam, the bread was bland to her taste. A deep ache inside her stomach filled the place where her appetite should have been. She nudged the plate aside and ran a finger over the delicate handle of her teacup.

"There was no warning," she said. Even to her own ears, her voice sounded hollow from disuse and cynicism. "One day we were laughing, making plans, figuring out what it meant to be together after all these years..."

She stared at the hand-painted pansies on her cup and laughed bitterly. "He asked me to marry him. Can you imagine? What a joke." She wiped at the angry tears that fell quicker than she could reach them.

"Why is it a joke?"

She gaped at him. "Can't you see? My first love was thrust back into my life without my initiating it."

She couldn't find the strength to explain these tormenting emotions. There was no way to explain to Jean that the Holy Spirit had urged her to pray for Aiden. And that she had happened to read about his accident in the paper. Forces outside of her had guided her back to him. And now her faith had been rocked to its core. Everything she knew to be true about God was somehow askew, her spirit broken, until she was left wondering whether she ever really knew the one she called Lord. Grief had pulled a dark cloak around her, making it difficult to breathe, let alone explain. Instead she simply said, "And now he's been torn away from me again."

––––––––

Jean spent two days attempting to cheer Katie up. She appreciated his company, but she knew the restaurant business was ruthless. He had sacrificed enough already, and he needed to get back to work.

Standing at the door to wish him well before he left, she acknowledged the small improvement she had made in just forty-eight hours. In that time, Jean had managed to tempt her with his cooking which, under different circumstances, would have been delightful. He had also broken into her solitude and provided her with a small ray of hope, a life raft willing to carry her to a happier place.

"Are you sure you don't want to come back to Paris for a while? You have many friends there. It might be good for you."

"No, I'll be okay. Honest."

"You're sure? It is very quiet around here."

"I'm sure."

He gave her a hug then tweaked her nose. "Keep in touch, okay? Do not make me come all the way back here again. Call if you need anything, and answer your phone."

"I will. Thanks for being such a good friend."

"Call me next time you are in Paris, and we'll meet at our usual place."

"Café Pierre?"

He smiled and saluted her goodbye before climbing into the rental car. No sooner had she waved him off and stepped back through the front door than her phone began ringing. *Jean must have charged it.* She picked it up and saw Peter's name. She accepted the call.

"Hi, Peter." Katie made her way out onto the cobbled patio.

"Finally! I've been trying to reach you. I heard what happened. I'm so sorry."

"Thanks. Did Rachael tell you?" She lowered herself to sit on a cushioned iron chair.

"Yes, she was worried and couldn't reach you, so she called me."

"I'm sorry about that."

"No need to be. I know you've been through a lot. Are you doing okay?"

"Better than I was. Jean just left. He came to visit for a couple of days."

"So what are your plans?"

She tightened her grip on the phone. *Back to business.* "I've decided to take a break, Peter. A leave of absence, if you will."

"Katie, you've been away from work for three weeks. I've been holding off clients the best I can and have made excuses for your missed appointments. Any more time away will be detrimental."

She closed her eyes. "I'm grateful that you've taken care of everything. You always do."

"You need your work—it will help take your mind off things. Besides, you can't walk away now. You've got a good thing going."

He was right. Painting had always helped her. But this time she didn't want to use it as a distraction. As painful as it was, she didn't want to bury herself in her work and forget.

"I'll understand if you want to break our contract."

"No, of course not. How long are you thinking?"

"I'm really not sure at this point."

"Can you give me a rough estimate?"

"I don't know... six months?"

"Wow." His long sigh made her cringe.

"I'm sorry, Peter. If anything changes, you'll be the first to know."

Katie disconnected the call and rose to her feet with a groan. Leaving the phone on the chair, she wandered into the back garden. A climbing rose stuck out of a trellis and she tucked it back behind the wood before bending to pull a spreading weed. Drifting through the garden pathways, some bordered with hedges, others cascading with fading flowers, she chose a path that led to the river.

The Thames was a merry sight with boats cruising along at spaced intervals and ducks bobbing on the wakes of the passing vessels. She sank onto a grassy knoll and sat cross-legged, watching the activity. The distraction, after days of being consumed by her own grief, was welcome. Two white swans circled in the water at her feet.

Kicking off her sandals, Katie slid to the water's edge and dipped in her toes. A sudden memory rose, of a spring day when she was four or five years old and running barefoot along a trail by the riverbank. Birds sang in full chorus and her father, who was with her, had given her permission to wade in the river. When she jumped into the coolness, water rushed between her toes. Katie laughed and ran, leaping and dancing, not caring that the wetness was saturating her dress, listening to the song in her heart. The song had long since been forgotten—a song she doubted would ever play again.

She sighed as a row of ducks arrived and paddled close to the shore, watching her expectantly.

"I have nothing for you today." She spoke almost to herself as the memory faded. The feathered crowd soon dispersed, leaving her alone once more.

The same questions that had plagued her thoughts so often since Aiden's death repeated in her mind. Why had God brought her heart to this place only to tear it all away? Why would he ask that much of her? Didn't she deserve hope and a future? It seemed an absurdly repeating theme in her life, and try as she might to push the years of loss aside, they remained like an obstinate stain refusing to be rubbed out.

"Why won't you allow me a shred of happiness?" she cried out toward the sky, anger and bitter sorrow spilling out unbridled. Even as she uttered the words, shivers rippled through her. How dare she speak to God that way? Would he strike her down for being so disrespectful? Would he disown her? She collapsed back on the grass. No more tears fell from her eyes. Had her heart become too bitter, too furious, too hardened? Her emotions frightened her as they tumbled over her without restraint. Though her eyes were closed, her mind failed to formulate a prayer.

When at last she dragged herself home, Katie went to bed, fell into a fitful sleep, and dreamed of Aiden. She was sitting at his bedside in the hospital, as she had for so many hours during his recovery. He woke up, smiled at her, and said, "The good part is I'll see you again."

His smile had become one of radiant joy that shone from within.

"Don't cry, Kate. It's not really goodbye, just so long."

Even in her dream, she couldn't form an answer, didn't trust her emotions not to betray her. She was the one dying inside and would gladly take his place if she could.

He squeezed her hand and warmth travelled up her arm. "I used to ask myself why I met you all those years ago. Now I know—God knew what he was doing, didn't he, Kate? You were part of the plan for my life." He laughed and it sounded like far-off music.

A choking sound came from her throat, part laugh, part cry. He wiped a single tear from her cheek. "Don't cry for me, Kate. I'm happier than I've ever been."

———

Winter came softly, almost unwillingly, the same way Katie's heart had come to terms with Aiden's death. The snow layered the ground, covering any remnants of green, as if to protect it for another season. In the same way, God's love came to Katie, covering and protecting her. Even though she still didn't understand why God had allowed Aiden's death, she eventually stopped grappling with him and tentatively handed over her grief.

It was in the wake of her sorrow that Katie's heart was rekindled, and a kind of thaw began that, bit by bit, melted her frozen insides. That which had been frozen was likewise preserved, and out of these reserves Katie began to truly live.

Looking back, she marvelled that she had made it through. Much like a destructive fire in a pine forest, seemingly consuming every good and living thing in its fury, her life had appeared to be destroyed. But somehow, in the smoldering, ravaged remains and amid the glowing embers, life had been miraculously preserved. Just as tiny seeds fall from the pine cones during intense heat to bravely plant themselves in the blanched and blackened soil, forming a new forest, Katie had been in the midst of the fire. She had known something of its ruin, and now experienced the beauty of the seeds of her life beginning to grow again.

CHAPTER
Thirty-Four

KATIE READJUSTED HER EAR BUDS. SHE WAS LISTENING TO a Ted Talk while preparing for a run. She double knotted her laces, stood to tuck her phone and water bottle into her running belt, and swung open the door. In the front yard of the townhouse, she paused a moment to stretch, then started out.

The heat of the day had subsided as the late-afternoon sun dipped behind the trees. A faint breeze provided welcome relief from the residual warmth. Katie headed down the hill toward the shaded river trail. Today was the first time she had gone on a proper run in a year.

She had spent the past twelve months in Africa teaching art to the children at Hope Orphanages in Zambia. The only running she had done was playing soccer with the children. The hours spent bumping along the dusty roads in an antiquated Jeep, walking to church miles from the orphanage among a throng of enthusiastic youngsters, showing the children how to paint and draw, singing songs and dancing with little hands in hers, scrubbing school clothes in tin tubs, and serving Ugali out of the same had taught her so much. Living amid the poverty around her had brought her face-to-face with her own poverty. In doing so, she came face-to-face with the very heart of God. It was there, through the heartaches she witnessed, that her own pain began to pale. In Africa, she learned to laugh again and, in serving those in need around her, her heart had been made pliable to love again.

The African Christians' joy was contagious. At first, Katie had wondered how they could be so happy. Living with sickness, disease, and poverty, it seemed they had little to celebrate. But a few weeks among them had helped her to see that she was the impoverished one who lived amid the sickness of too much. They knew Christ in a way she had never needed to. Not until then, at least.

She watched women hand over their babies when they could no longer take care of them from the sickness of HIV. She saw siblings say goodbye as a sister or brother passed away from complications of malnutrition. Aged grandmothers carried infants strapped to their withered bodies, their own children having died prematurely. But, somehow, they found joy in the midst of abject poverty. They lived simply, yet resourcefully, and depended on God for everything.

Living with the African people, sharing their heartaches and caring for the orphans, put things into perspective. There, her own pain and grief didn't seem so all-consuming. There, she realized that she had needed the Lord more than ever when she'd lost Aiden, but had pushed his comfort away. At some point, self-pity and anger gave way to healing love, and she was able to place her loss in a sweet and sacred place: the tender arms of the one who died to save.

Who was she to question the God of the universe? To ask why she and Aiden hadn't been given more time? Somehow she sensed that God had understood. He understood her silence, her weakness, her questioning heart, and even the way she'd felt disappointed with him when her hopes and dreams hadn't come to fruition. Her prayers had felt like wrestling with God as she struggled to understand why. Other times she was too exhausted to form prayers at all.

Katie relearned that her life, her plans, and her dreams weren't fully hers to control. She had thought she knew this implicitly, that she had forfeited all control years ago when she had received Christ, but this realization brought her to the place of letting go of her life as she had imagined it. Soon after, she gained the capacity to trust the Lord again.

When at a loss for a consoling word to a grieving mother ravaged by the brevity of a child's life, or when consumed by weariness at the end of a long day, Katie found comfort in verses like Joshua 1:5, "... I will never leave you nor forsake you." God was with her, and she came to an intimate understanding of that truth. He hadn't forsaken her in her desperate need, she was the one who had turned away.

Katie smiled as memories of the children ran through her mind. She missed the feel of their arms around her neck as they rode on her back, how they brushed and braided her hair at every opportunity, and the way they sang and danced with abandon, inviting her to join them every time. Leaving them was so difficult, returning to England almost impossible. Life in Africa had been so poor, yet so rich. Once home, Katie was fueled with a passion that carried her along—the drive to help others in need. She understood this need firsthand, not only because she had lived it alongside the people, but because she had experienced her own poverty, need, and longing for God to fill the empty places inside her.

All this Katie thought of while she ran beside the Grand River. Between the trees that lined the trail, she could see the back of Cambridge Memorial Hospital. Thoughts of Aiden flooded in. The memories brought strong, warm remembrances now instead of entirely heartrending ones.

She pictured Aiden as she pushed him in the wheelchair and bumped into the elevator, saw him tripping over himself on the crutches, imagined his fun-loving smile. She thanked God that he'd made a way for Aiden to be with him and considered how far she'd come. She prayed for continued hope for whatever her future held and thanked him for this moment where she could run and feel alive and free.

Three days earlier, she had arrived in town to attend an opening for an art program in Toronto for underprivileged children. Tomorrow she would give an address to the graduating arts students at the University of Waterloo. The day after that, she was scheduled as a guest speaker at a Christian women's event.

Since Katie's paintings were now bought by galleries and collectors worldwide, life had the potential to be hectic. But a year in Africa had fixed that. Despite the invitations, Katie had determined she would maintain balance in her life. That included passing on much of her time and earnings to the children in Africa, whom she promised to visit every year.

Coming to the end of the trail, the place she had ended up the day she had learned of Aiden's death, Katie paused to look out over the river.

Lord, thank you for the healing in my life. You've brought me a long way from when I was last here.

Before continuing the rest of the way, she bent to pull up the sock that had shifted under her heel. As she did, another runner veered around the corner and bumped into her, sending her sprawling. The sun shone in her eyes, and Katie held one hand to her forehead so she could focus on the person who had crashed into her. The dark hair and unmistakable curls that fell across his forehead sent a flood of warmth through her as he scrambled to help her.

"I'm so sor—"

"Justin?"

His eyes widened. "Katie?" He thrust out his hand to assist her to her feet. Before she could grasp it, he pulled back his hand and dropped to the ground beside her.

"You're bleeding." He leaned closer to her knee to assess the damage. Katie couldn't take her eyes off him.

When she didn't speak, he sat back on his haunches. "Are you all right? I didn't see you there."

"I'm okay." She looked down at her knee then back up at his gentle, brown eyes. She felt light, strangely numb to the pain of the fall. "Some things never change."

His eyebrows rose.

"I see you still have the same old habit of sneaking up on people."

A smile crossed his lips as she repeated the long-ago line and her stomach fluttered.

"Here, let me help you." He jumped to his feet and clasped her hand to pull her up. "We can go to the river to clean you up."

"I'm fine. It's not that bad, really." But as she stood, the blood that had mostly pooled on her knee trickled down her leg. He led her to the water's edge. Once there, she watched, as if in a far-off dream, as he gently splashed water on her leg, washing off the blood. Then he took the edge of his T-shirt and pressed it on the cut.

"You'll ruin your shirt."

"It's not a problem. It'll wash out. Too bad I wasn't on a long run or I'd have my water pouch, and I always have Band-aids in it."

"I'm fine, honest." *Seriously Katie, can't you think of anything else to say?*

"Can I walk you home?"

She nodded and Justin took her hand again as they climbed back up the riverbank to the trail.

"Talk about bumping into someone after all these years." He chuckled as they reached flat ground. Before going on, he stopped to examine the cut. "Are you sure you're all right?"

"I'm sure."

If he looked at her one more time with those beautiful, concerned eyes, she might lose all restraint and kiss him. *You're gawking.* Katie cleared her throat and glanced away. He was even more handsome than she remembered. The thin, boyish frame had been replaced with a lean, muscular one. It was apparent that he worked out from the strong, shapely arm he had offered her. She was still enjoying the warmth where his hand had held hers.

"Where are you staying?"

"The home I grew up in. Are you sure you want to walk me? It's twenty minutes from here."

"Absolutely. It's the least I can do after ruining your run. You still have a place here?"

"Yeah, when my mom moved back to England, she kept it as a rental property. Now we use it ourselves when we come back to visit."

"Is that very often?"

"For me not as much, but my mom uses it quite a bit. What about you? What brings you to Cambridge?"

"I live here now."

"You do?"

"Yeah. I bought a place in the Gaslight District."

"Huh. I wouldn't have expected that."

He lifted his broad shoulders. "I lectured a few times at U of W's School of Architecture in town. I liked it here, so I decided to buy a condo. I use it as home base when I'm not travelling."

"School of Architecture? You took engineering."

"Yeah, but several of the non-profit projects I initiated lined up with their course material."

"Oh, that's good. Do you live alone?" She held her breath as she waited for the answer.

"No, it's me and Jerome."

She cocked her head.

"He's the perfect roommate. I'll have to introduce you to him sometime. I usually bring him with me for a run, but his paw is sore right now."

Relief coursed through her and she laughed. "Jerome is your dog?"

"Yeah, an Alaskan malamute. Got his name from St. Jerome's University. He's a great running companion."

Katie fought to control her emotions. Justin appeared as kind as ever, but the boyish arrogance had left him, replaced with a refined confidence and gentleness of spirit. He hadn't lost his spunk though, and nearing the end of the walk back, had the audacity to suggest she be more careful the next time she decided to stop in the middle of a trail.

By the time they turned onto her street, she was in trouble. Justin was still the gentleman she remembered, but the qualities she'd admired in him when they were young had only improved. *How is he still single?* Then it hit her. Maybe he wasn't. Just because he wasn't wearing a ring didn't mean there wasn't a girlfriend, a fiancée even, though he hadn't mentioned anyone of significance.

They reached her childhood home, and Justin walked her up to the tiny porch.

Katie stopped at the door and faced him. "Thanks for walking me back."

"Hey, it was the least I could do. I'm sorry I bowled you over on the trail. Can I make it up to you by taking you out tonight?"

The question caught her off guard. Should she go out with him? He'd changed, but that didn't mean his beliefs were any different. It could be a terrible mistake, opening that door she'd firmly closed years ago. When he smiled at her though, her resolve crumbled. "Yeah, I'd like that." Every nerve in her being tingled at the thought of spending more time with him. Was dinner just a friendly gesture or something more? She brushed the thought aside. Justin was an old friend. The two of them would go out for dinner, reminisce about old times and get caught up on each other's lives, and then part ways.

Katie didn't have the courage to analyze what the sadness she felt at that thought could possibly mean.

CHAPTER

Thirty-Five

THE DOORBELL SOUNDED A FEW MINUTES AFTER SEVEN. Katie was still brushing her hair when she heard it. She hadn't felt this uptight about her appearance in a long while, and took one last glance in the bathroom mirror before running down the stairs to answer the door.

When she swung it open, Justin stood on the porch, the wild flowers he clutched in one hand dangling limply from their stems. Her heart skipped a beat at the captivated expression on his face as he took a first glance at her. He held out the flowers. "For you."

"Where did you get these?"

"On my way back from dropping you off. I tried to save them, but I think they were upset about being picked."

She laughed. "They're still lovely. Thank you. Hang on a minute while I put them in water."

"How's the knee?" he called from the doorway.

"Fine. It only took 25 stitches," she called over the running water.

"Is that all? I thought at least twice that many."

She stuck the flowers into a vase and walked back to the doorway. "As it turns out, one Band-aid did the trick."

Justin grinned. His tailored shirt was tucked into belted dress pants, setting off his trim physique. She caught her breath as she reached for her purse on the hall table.

Moments later, they pulled up outside the Mill Restaurant. Justin jumped out first and jogged around the front of his Land Rover, beating the valet to open the passenger door for Katie. He handed off his keys, and they climbed the stairs to the restaurant overlooking the Grand River dam.

A female server in a crisp white shirt and black dress pants came and filled their glasses with water while delivering the evening's specials. "Could I get you something to drink?" Justin began to order a bottle of wine, then stopped mid-sentence. He shifted his gaze to Katie. "Make that sparkling grape juice, please, if you have it." He reached over and touched the back of her hand. "That is, if you still feel the same way about alcohol."

"Actually, a few years in Paris changed that a bit, but grape juice would be perfect."

The server came back with the bottle, making a polite gesture of opening the sparkling juice as though it were a regular bottle of wine before pouring it into their fluted glasses. "In all the years I lived here, I never ate at this restaurant." Katie perused the menu.

"Never? I'm glad I picked it then."

"It's so beautiful overlooking the river."

The server returned and asked if they were ready to order.

"Do you know what you want, Katie?"

Good question. She cleared her throat. "Not yet. What are you having?"

"How about chateaubriand for two?"

"Perfect." She closed the menu and handed it to the server.

Though she'd never had the opportunity, it had always seemed romantic to share an intimate meal prepared for two. When the chef came directly to their table to slice the meat and arrange it on individual plates, she found it even more delightful than she had imagined. Sharing it with Justin felt surreal.

In the glow of a flickering candle, they wasted no time catching up on the last fourteen years, filling in the gaps about their lives and answering each another's questions. Ever since their paths had crossed that afternoon, she had wanted to tell him about seeing his photographs at the Artcurial the night of her opening. It was over coffee that she shared the story.

"You're kidding." He leaned back in his chair. "I remember that exhibit well. I was out of town shooting for *Time* Magazine and was disappointed I had to miss it."

"I didn't know you did commercial work."

"I don't usually, but *Time* was interested in a project I was involved with in Africa."

Katie straightened. "Where in Africa?"

"Zimbabwe at the time, but I've travelled all over the continent."

"Really? What took you there?"

"I felt like that's where God wanted me to go."

He said it so simply that, if she hadn't known Justin Burke years prior, the statement might not have seemed terribly significant. But she had known him, and his words both amazed her and set her already-attentive heart on high alert.

"What do you do there?"

"I find ways to channel water sources to the more remote villages."

"And use your engineering training as well as do what you love, taking pictures. I remember reading that in the brochure at your exhibit. That's so amazing."

But what was even more amazing for Katie was that it seemed they shared the same passion for Africa. Her mind spun with the new information. Then, remembering his quote, she said, "A wise person once said, 'God hasn't forgotten about them, we have.'"

"I completely agree."

"You should. You're the wise man. It was in your brochure."

The server came to their table and refilled their coffee cups. When she was gone, Katie wrapped her fingers around the warm mug. "I've spent some time in Zambia."

He'd lifted his mug halfway to his mouth but set it down again without drinking. "Really? What were you doing there?"

"Have you ever heard of Hope Orphanage?"

His eyes widened. "I sure have. I've even visited the one in Zambia—twice. I know the woman who runs the orphanage quite well."

"Grace? Are you kidding?" Katie set down her mug too, afraid she might spill her coffee if she didn't. "I don't believe this. I spent the past year there."

"Lord in heaven, you are amazing..." Justin whispered.

Katie propped her elbows on the table and clasped her hands together to keep them from trembling. "You've changed your mind about God, haven't you?"

"I have. Quite some time ago, and it's made all the difference in my life."

As he spoke, Katie's heart soared.

———————

Even though they had eaten slowly and lingered over dessert and coffee, time passed too quickly. Justin took her arm as they left the restaurant. "Shall we take a walk by the river?"

"Yes, let's." Katie felt a little breathless. If ever there was an occasion where she wanted to slow time it was now.

The pathway from the restaurant led directly to the same trail where they had run into each other earlier that day. They paused side-by-side to share the view of the water flowing over the dam. The night air was slightly cool, and Justin removed his jacket and placed it over Katie's bare shoulders, reminding her of the night, so long ago, when he had first walked her home. The pleasant scent of his cologne drifted from the fabric and she breathed it in.

Justin grasped her arms lightly. "I have to say, you look beautiful. I wanted to tell you that when you opened the door tonight. Actually, I almost said it when I first saw you on the trail today."

The breeze blew a strand of hair across her face, and she pushed it back behind her ear.

"On the trail? All sweaty and scraped up?"

He grinned. "You were beautiful. You always were, but even more so now."

He let go of her and slid an arm around her shoulders. Her insides rippled, escalating the excitement that had barely let up since seeing him again. It seemed the most natural thing to slip her arm around his waist in response. They remained that way a few moments more, taking in the view.

Another memory surfaced, of the night they had stood side-by-side on the deck at Zack's party. Now, the feel of his arm resting on her shoulders sent a warmth coursing through her. Sooner than she would have liked, he dropped his hand to his side and turned toward the path again.

They strolled comfortably, wrapped in the peacefulness of the evening, quiet except for the crickets in full chorus. With each step, the years seemed to fall away.

I have to know. Katie summoned every bit of her courage. "So, no romantic interests?"

"No, I've been holding out hope for you."

She laughed, but Justin didn't. When she shot him a sideways look, he only smiled down at her, leaving her to guess whether he was joking. Several steps passed without explanation.

"Seriously, there must have been someone special. You've travelled the world, for heaven's sake."

"Not really. A few dates here and there, but the right person never came along." Justin stopped and faced her. "Rachael told me what happened with Aiden. That must have been so hard."

Katie nodded, trying to deflect the sadness that, over the past year, had often snuck up on her unannounced. She didn't want to go there. Not tonight. Not when she had finally begun to feel like her mourning was in a manageable place. And not when she was caught up in such a magical evening. "It was."

"Is it difficult being back in town?"

"Not as much this time. It's actually been helpful in showing me how much healing has taken place."

It warmed her when she thought of how unselfish he was being, freeing her to talk about Aiden. The sadness she had so grown accustomed to living with whenever she reflected on the loss wasn't nearly as overwhelming as it had been in the past. "It was a painful journey, but it taught me a lot about myself."

"Oh, yeah? Like what?"

"Well, for one thing, it changed the way I think about God. I guess I expected that, since it seemed God was the one to bring Aiden back into my life, that everything was going to work out. But God's plan didn't match mine. The only peace I found in the whole thing was knowing Aiden accepted Christ during the time I spent with him in the hospital."

He could understand that now, even celebrate the significance of it. Should she tell him Aiden had proposed to her? No, she would keep that tucked away in a pocket of her heart as a time she had known a forever kind of love. "I was angry at God for taking Aiden. It took a lot to accept it when I couldn't figure out a reason why. For a long time, it seemed so cruel. Now I think I'm at the point where I can finally accept that I may never know why, this side of heaven."

"That's pretty big stuff."

"It was and still is. But good stuff too, I guess. At least I know, without a doubt, that God is faithful."

They walked in silence for a while, enjoying the cool air of late August. The moon shone between the trees, casting dull, dappled shadows on the trail, and from time to time, glimpses of its subdued light could be seen glinting off the river's rippling flow. Was she really walking this trail with Justin? How different they both were, yet at the same time so much unaltered, despite all that had changed in their lives. The way he had allowed her to talk about Aiden spoke volumes about his strong yet gentle character.

"Katie?" Justin broke the quietness they'd shared. "I know it sounds a little forward, but can I bring you back to my place? I have something I want to show you."

She hesitated.

"Trust me. I can't tell you what it is, because it's a little surprise."

"Of course I trust you." As if there was ever a question.

––––––––––

As soon as Justin turned the key in the lock, a howling started up on the other side of the door. Justin went in first to manage Jerome's excitement.

"We're still working on the door thing," Justin explained, grabbing hold of Jerome's collar as the pup welcomed him with small leaps. It didn't take long to settle him and then Justin released his hold so Jerome could meet Katie. She held out her hand to let Jerome smell her, but he was much too friendly for that and licked it instead. She patted him around his thick neck.

"Nice to meet you, Jerome." She bent closer to his face. He licked that, too.

"Wow, he has such amazing eyes." She admired their sky-blue colour, offset by black and white fur.

"Lie down." Justin pointed to a dog bed beside the couch in the living room. Jerome instantly obeyed.

"I'll be right back." Justin waved a hand toward the living room. "Make yourself at home."

Katie meandered into the living room as he disappeared upstairs. *What is he up to?* The loft space was thoughtfully decorated, the light grey walls displaying a few black and white photographs. She wandered around the room, taking a closer look at the captivating pictures. Her eyes came to rest on the one above the fireplace, an enchanting close-up of a little girl peering out of the picture with dark eyes that drew Katie into her world.

No wonder Justin had become so successful. He could truly make a picture worth a thousand words. The stairs creaked and she backed away from the fireplace.

"Close your eyes," he called as he walked toward her. "Don't open them until I tell you."

She covered her eyes with her hands. "You always were big on surprises."

"And if I remember correctly, you never did like them, did you?" He didn't wait for an answer. "Okay, go ahead and open your eyes."

Justin stood in front of her holding a small fish bowl. Inside, a fat, orange fish swam in a lazy circle, occasionally surfacing to suck at the top of the water.

"Nice fish. Where did you get him?" Was this why he had dragged her here, to see a goldfish?

"From you."

Her forehead wrinkled. "Me?"

"It's Dumpling, Katie." He smiled, his chest puffed out slightly.

Her mouth dropped open. "You're kidding me. Dumpling? My fish from university?"

"The very same."

"How on earth did he survive all this time?" She giggled as she peered into the bowl.

"I've read they can live up to fifteen years."

"Wow, I can't believe it." She held out her hands and he handed her the bowl.

"He doesn't live in this anymore. I have a bigger tank upstairs."

"Incredible." She held the bowl up and spoke through the glass. "I never expected to see you again."

"He's thrilled to see you too, I can tell."

Katie studied the fish. He swam the tank in the same slow circles as before and she giggled. "How did you end up with him?"

"Rachael made me take him when she left school. He kind of grew on me. My neighbour comes to feed him when I'm gone."

"I guess I should say thanks for taking such good care of him."

"My pleasure."

She handed him back the bowl, and Justin placed it on a side table. "I can take you home now."

"I don't have to leave right away."

Justin shifted his weight from one foot to the other. "Actually, you do." He adjusted his jacket over her shoulders. "I'll be honest with you. You said you trust me, so let me take you back. A few more minutes with you here, and I won't trust myself."

Her stomach flip-flopped. Was he feeling the same way she was? Katie smiled and forced her feet to turn toward the door. "We could go and get a hot chocolate somewhere..."

His smile warmed her in a way hot chocolate never could.

"With whipped cream?" they said at the same time.

He reached for her hand and squeezed it as he led her to the door. Katie felt closer to him in one day than in all the days they had spent together years earlier. A connection had formed between them that she had never felt back then—a bond she knew was the result of their shared belief in God.

He held the door for her to pass through. Katie paused on the threshold. "I forgot to thank you for dinner."

"No need. It was my pleasure."

She stayed where she was, her face tipped upward to soak in the warmth of his eyes for just a moment more. He lowered his head. The feel of his lips pressed to hers was intoxicating, and she reciprocated, taking as much as he offered. Too soon, he pulled away.

"We have some hot chocolate to get," he whispered huskily.

But neither moved, and in the breaths between them, he cupped her face with his warm hands. Then he pulled her in, exploring her lips with his, kissing her fully, longingly, just the way she wanted him to.

———————

Justin sank onto the black leather chair beside his fireplace, where only a few hours before, Katie had stood. He dropped his head back to rest on the cool leather and exhaled, raking his fingers through his hair. Jerome had already found a place at his feet and plunked his head down on his paws.

"Unbelievable, God!" Jerome lifted his head. In the silence that followed, Justin attempted to sort through the wonder of what had transpired that day.

He'd worked so hard to put Katie out of his mind, and suddenly there she was. At that moment, she had seemed like an apparition that might disappear in a breath. But she hadn't. Instead, he'd spent an evening out with her, precious time that, over the years, he could only ever have imagined.

When she had spoken of Aiden, all he had wanted to do was take her in his arms and hold her until any last residue of pain had drained from her. He couldn't imagine how she had suffered. Rachael had told him that Aiden proposed before he died. What must it have felt like to find him suddenly gone? As she spoke, he ached for her, worse than when he'd first found out. Back then, he had considered sending a card but decided against it. After all, she was just an old friend he had once hoped would be more, someone who had possibly forgotten all about him. But she had remembered. That was clear enough on the trail.

After so long, she still made him feel the same way she had in university. She was the most attractive woman he had ever met and not just because of her looks. Now he understood that the beautiful light that emanated from her eyes, the kindness of her actions, the discipline she had so fiercely held to, were the result of God's Spirit in her. Her vehement decision not to date him back then was the inception of his own journey to God.

Was she still in love with Aiden? He had wanted to ask but wasn't sure he could handle hearing the truth. How long had she said she was staying? A week? And she had already been here three days. He didn't have a lot of time.

God, I'm not sure what you're doing, but whatever it is, please help me do the right thing here. I don't think I can lose her again.

CHAPTER
Thirty-Six

KATIE STUFFED THE LAST SHOE DOWN THE SIDE OF HER suitcase and pulled the zipper closed. She checked her phone and tucked it in her back pocket, disappointed that there were no messages. Her thoughts were still full of Justin. She had hoped he might send her a last-minute text. After four incredible days together, she had said a difficult goodbye to him the night before.

Lord, I've fallen for him, and now I'm leaving. Not to complain, but it seems the story of my life.

She wrestled her case to the landing. As amazing as their time together had been, she struggled with the fear that, if she told Justin how she really felt, he would suddenly be ripped out of her life, like Aiden had been. It was better to leave their relationship where it was—a beautiful memory of an intoxicating few days—than to go down that path again. She didn't think she had it in her to endure that kind of pain again. Maybe it was irrational, but it was a lot less painful to say goodbye now.

And yet, even as she thought it, she couldn't shake the feeling of loss. That somehow she was walking away from a chance to love again. An opportunity to finally have happiness overtake the sorrow of the past. It was ridiculous, though. Who told someone they loved them after four days? She hadn't said it, although her actions might have betrayed her. And now she was leaving, and he hadn't tried to stop her.

She swallowed back the tears. Rachael was due to arrive in fifteen minutes to take her to the airport, and she didn't want her friend to find her a blubbering mess.

The knock came as she struggled to manoeuvre her case down the last few steps. Startled, she loosened her grip on the bag. It bumped down the remaining steps before landing with a thud at the bottom.

"Are you okay?" Justin stood on the other side of the screen door.

Katie impulsively ran a hand through her hair, attempting to gather her composure. Beads of sweat formed on her forehead. *From carrying my suitcase, not from seeing him.* "I'm fine, just my suitcase taking a little trip of its own." She went down the last few steps and righted the case.

"Can I come in?"

"Sure. I was just getting ready to go. Rachael will be here any sec." It took everything she had to sound casual, unaffected by his presence.

He bent over to pick up something outside the door before stepping in looking adorably sheepish, his brown eyes peering up at her through a single curl that had found a place above his left eye. He opened the top of the box. "I brought Dumpling over to say goodbye. He has something to say to you."

Katie looked at him, eyebrows raised. "Really?"

"Really. But you have to get close enough to hear." He lifted the bowl from the box and held it out to her. His hands were trembling. *What is that about?* She took the bowl from him and held it up at eye level.

"Can you see his mouth moving?"

Katie laughed. "You're crazy."

"Yes, I am, crazy about you."

At that moment, Katie saw the ring, reflecting light and sparkling through the water. Suddenly, he knelt on one knee on her hall mat.

"Will you marry me, Katie?" He peered up at her with an expression full of hope and love.

He took the fish bowl from her, and she clapped her hand over her mouth as he retrieved the dripping diamond ring from the water and held it up.

"I've wanted to marry you from the first time I saw you. Isn't it time you became my wife, Katie Banks?"

This time she didn't want to run from love. Nothing held her back, and she couldn't think of a single reason to say no. In that moment, all her fears melted away as she tumbled into love's embrace.

Half delirious, she could only nod. Justin took her shaking hand in his. He slid the wet ring onto her finger and kissed her outstretched hand. And, although it was a perfect fit and modestly beautiful, it wasn't the ring Katie admired—it was the face of the man she knew God had handpicked for her to spend her life with.

Epilogue

JUSTIN FOUND KATIE IN THE SIDE GARDEN, HER EASEL propped up near the purple foxgloves that ran alongside the shady stucco wall of the thatched cottage. Their three-year-old daughter Hope painted alongside her, a miniature easel holding her own little masterpiece.

"Daddy!" Hope shouted, dropping her brush and running to Justin.

"Hi, sweetie." He gathered her in his arms for a twirling hug. "How's my little poppet today?"

"Great. Look what I did." She wriggled out of his embrace and dragged him by the hand to show off her painting.

"Well done." He winked at Katie.

"Look at Mummy's. It's beautifuler."

"I'm sure it is." Justin moved to Katie, wrapped his arms around her swelling waist, and kissed her. "Hi, honey." Little Hope giggled, her black corn braids springing up and down. She was their only child, so far—a beautiful gift from God whom they had adopted from Hope Orphanage in Zambia two years earlier.

"How are you feeling?" He rubbed Katie's nose where a smudge of paint had dried.

"Much better now the morning sickness is easing off."

"I'm glad." He kissed her cheek and glanced over her shoulder at the canvas. "It's very beautiful." He spoke the words to Hope and she smiled, moving closer to hug Justin's leg. He reached down to tousle her hair.

"How did it go?" Katie swivelled on her stool to face him. He had just returned from visiting the site for the new youth centre for underprivileged children he and Katie were spearheading.

"It went well. All set for groundbreaking next month."

They were about to launch their third centre. The first was attached to their home church, the second operated out of the local middle school. This one was different in that they had embarked on a building project to place a centre in the middle of the community.

Twice a week, she and Justin worked side by side at the centres, ministering to the youth. The only exception was one month in the spring and fall when they travelled to Zambia as a family to help out at Hope Orphanage. They led a simple life, and living off Justin's photography and her paintings allowed them the time and flexibility to travel. God had blessed them with more than they could have asked for or imagined. They had each other, and now little Hope who added to their joy, along with the expectation of another child. Propelled by their mutual passion to help others, they were thankful they had more than enough to be able to serve.

"There's a package for you inside."

"There is?" She held up her hands and he grasped them and tugged her to her feet. The three of them made their way into the house, where Justin picked up a large, flat parcel wrapped in brown packing paper off the dining room table.

Katie examined it. "What could it be?"

"Open it, Mummy! Open it!" cried Hope, jumping up and down.

Katie tore off the paper and pulled away the bubble wrap to reveal a painting. She recognized it instantly.

"Wow, that's beautiful." Justin touched the frame with his finger. "Who sent it?"

"I don't know."

She checked for a return address then pulled the rest of the paper away. An envelope addressed to Katherine Jane Burke fell out. Under the curious scrutiny of her family, Katie tore open the envelope and pulled out a letter and an official-looking document. She scanned the words, her heart pounding.

Dear Mrs. Burke,

In the last will and testament of Mr. Adam Stephen Banks of Paris, France, he hereby wills Mrs. Katherine Jane Burke, his biological daughter, his sole possession, the original painting named "Luminous Horses"...

Katie scanned the rest of the letter then shifted her gaze to the painting she had completed fourteen years prior. She swayed on her feet, and Justin grasped her elbow to steady her. For reasons she would never know now, he hadn't been able to be part of her life. But he hadn't forgotten her. He'd come to her exhibit. And he'd bought her painting.

"Who's it from, Mummy? Why are you crying?"

Katie smiled at her daughter through blurred vision. "It's from your grandfather."

One More Tomorrow

MELANIE STEVENSON

If I had one more tomorrow,
I'd find a way to hear you say
you'd love me, you'd never leave me,
you'd hold me in your heart forever.

One more tomorrow
to see you smile and linger a while,
to smell your skin, and we'd begin
to step into this life forever.

One more tomorrow
to trace your face, stand in your place,
to take the call so you'd not fall
without me forever.

One more tomorrow
to not regret, nor ever forget
our promises made. I would have stayed
with you forever.

One more tomorrow
to be with you, our love made true.
But we reached the end and could not mend
our forever.

One more tomorrow
to watch the stars and point out ours.
I'd look in your eyes and breathe my goodbye
to you forever.

One more tomorrow
to count the years and outrun fears.
Your lips on mine just one more time—
I'll hold you in my heart forever.

ABOUT THE AUTHOR

BORN IN ENGLAND, MELANIE LIVES IN SOUTHERN ONTARIO with her husband, four children, and a house full of pets. She entered the University of Waterloo as an English major and graduated with a Bachelor of Fine Arts. She has written and directed several stage plays and teaches acting classes to young people and adults. However, she has devoted the majority of her time to homeschooling her children, attending more dance competitions than is healthy, and stealing time—between being a shuttle service—to write, garden, and paint. *One More Tomorrow* is her first book.

You can find Melanie online at melaniestevenson.com and on Instagram, @melaniestevensonauthor. Melanie is a supporter of Faith's Orphans Fund. Find out more at FaithsOrphansFund.org.

MELANIE STEVENSON

SOULFOCUS
31 day devotional journal

TRIALS

DAILY ENCOURAGEMENTS FOR
OVERCOMING LIFE'S STRUGGLES

Coming Soon

ISBN: 978-1-4866-1539-1

Insightful and thought-provoking, *Soul Focus* offers daily, life-giving encouragement as you face hardship or struggle to make sense of trials in their aftermath. Journaling pages are included for your own inspirations and reflections.